An Old-Fashioned Arrangement

Susie Vereker

W F HOWES LTD

This large print edition published in 2007 by
W F Howes Ltd
Unit 4, Rearsby Business Park, Gaddesby Lane,
Rearsby, Leicester LE7 4YH

1 3 5 7 9 10 8 6 4 2

First published in the United Kingdom in 2006
by Transita

A CIP catalogue record for this book is available
from the British Library

ISBN 978 1 40740 136 2

Typeset by Palimpsest Book Production Limited,
Grangemouth, Stirlingshire
Printed and bound in Great Britain
by Antony Rowe Ltd, Chippenham, Wilts.

For my family

CHAPTER 1

Eight o'clock in the morning seemed early for a social call, even in Geneva. Fortunately Kim was already dressed when the gate bell rang. In the hope that she might later be inspired to weed the borders before winter arrived, she'd put on her gardening clothes, jeans and an old M & S shirt. She had a free day and intended to spend it at home, virtuously catching up on domesticity. She had even started to make a list. Lists didn't normally feature much in her life so that made her feel good.

Then she heard the bell.

It rang again, unnaturally loud in the quiet house. Her heart thumping, she ran downstairs to the entry phone and was not reassured to hear the voice of one of her husband's colleagues. She watched from the window as Madame Frank, the voluptuous beauty from Personnel, came teetering across the damp courtyard with Hoffer close at her heels like an amorous little terrier.

Kim opened the door. Impressively chic in black with a silk scarf draped around her broad shoulders, Madame Frank shook her hand solemnly.

1

Hoffer did the same, baring his teeth in a brief contorted smile, and then he, too, assumed a more sombre expression. After numerous repetitions of '*bonjour, madame*' they enquired after her health, and as the conversation proceeded in this polite Swiss fashion Kim began to relax a little. Perhaps nothing was wrong after all.

It was not until her guests were seated side by side on the sofa that she heard the words 'bad news'.

Her stomach turned in sudden sick panic. 'The school bus, nothing happened to the bus, did it? My son—'

'Oh no, not your son. Nothing to do with your son, Mrs Ellis,' said Madame Frank, leaning forward.

Kim breathed out slowly. Thank God, thank God.

'Rather it is *à propos* your husband, madame. When did you last see him?' asked Hoffer.

'Oh it must be over five weeks ago,' she said carefully. 'He's on a trip to South East Asia, as you know.'

'And when did he last telephone to you?'

'Not since he left.'

'Ah,' sighed Hoffer.

The tone of his voice was disturbing. 'But it's not so unusual. He doesn't often call when he is abroad.'

'But you see, madame, he's required to be in constant contact with us at the office and we also have not received a telephone call or email since four weeks. We have no absolute confirmation but we regret, we much regret, that he was very likely a passenger on a small private aeroplane that's missing in Indonesia.'

Hoffer's words sounded unreal, incredible. Kim heard what he said but she could not seem to grasp the meaning. A horrible chilly calm enveloped her. During the eighteen years of their marriage, Richard had a tendency to disappear now and then, usually because of a small misunderstanding with his employers. This misunderstanding often ended with his enforced resignation from the firm concerned. But then he would contact her after a week or so, and they would all move to yet another country where Richard, handsome and plausible, would find yet another job – selling anything from luxury hotels to pharmaceutical products.

These moves were not ideal for the family, he'd say, but he was doing his best to find his niche in the right sort of country. It had appeared that Switzerland was the right sort of country. Despite the fact that Richard travelled a great deal, or perhaps because of it, they were settled and happy here.

Until today.

'How long has the plane been missing?' Her voice, hollow and peculiar, seemed to come from far away.

'Four days, we are told.'

Four days?

Hoffer went on, 'Reports speak of it disappearing somewhere over Borneo, but we have few details. According to our agent in Jakarta, your husband took a flight with a somewhat informal airline based on one of the remote Indonesian islands. The authorities have obtained a flight plan, and unfortunately your husband's name is on the passenger list. No wreckage has yet been discovered – such a small plane missing in a jungle area, it may never be discovered.'

There was a long pause. Finally Kim heard herself say, 'But there could still be survivors, if nothing's been found.'

Madame Frank spoke. 'Our deepest condolences, Mrs Ellis. From the rumours that have reached them from tribesmen, the authorities suspect a mid-air explosion.'

'I thought you said they weren't sure what happened.'

'It seems they are reasonably sure.'

Kim stood up and walked to the window. She looked down through the trees and across the rooftops to the lake below. The early autumn mists had dispersed and she could see a yacht on the quiet grey water. Then the yacht became blurred.

'May I call your doctor? Perhaps a *calmante*?' suggested Madame Frank.

'I'm all right, thank you,' muttered Kim, holding on to the back of the armchair. They were clearly expecting her to break down, but shock and conflicting emotions paralysed her.

4

Madame Frank said, 'A friend then. I will contact a friend for you, if you wish.'

'Thank you. Perhaps later. I mean . . . I mean I'll phone someone myself.' She stared out of the window again. 'At the moment I think I'd rather be alone, if you don't mind.' It was what she wanted to say and yet she felt as if someone else was speaking, a stranger, oddly calm and controlled.

'Of course, we shall leave you then,' said Madame Frank, rising to her feet.

Hoffer intervened. 'But before parting, we need to check your husband's dossiers, files, here at home as certain papers are missing from the office.'

'No,' said Kim sharply.

'But madame, it is necessary.'

'No, it can't be, not today. Anyway Richard keeps – kept no office papers at home. And he took his laptop with him.'

'But we need to be sure of that, urgently.'

She took a deep uneven breath. 'I'll, I'll check the desk and if there are any company papers, I'll bring them to the office later.'

Madame Frank shook her head. 'It would be so much less painful for you, Mrs Ellis, if you'd allow Monsieur Hoffer to do the work for you. He would only take about half an hour.'

She stared at him. It was still hard to understand what they were talking about. 'Half an hour! No, I'm sorry, I want to be alone in my house now please.'

Hoffer's expression changed. 'You forget, madame, that it is not, in fact, *your* house. The rent for this charming villa in this exclusive suburb is paid by the company. So it is the company who holds the tenancy agreement with your landlord, not you, and now we require the property for another employee.'

The enormity of what had happened began to penetrate the blankness of her mind and Kim sank down into a chair. Then the practical automaton took over again. 'And exactly when does the company require the house?' she asked shakily.

'The terms of your husband's contract of employment state that if for any reason he ceased to work for the company, you must leave the house within one month. Now, Mr Ellis has been out of contact for over a month. That is, even before the crash he failed to keep in touch. As he appears to have committed certain other procedural irregularities, and therefore has not fulfilled his obligations, so you could be required to leave immediately.' He waved his hand. 'But the chairman does not want to put you to such inconveniences.'

'But—'

He waved his hand again and continued, 'Yes, he has kindly agreed, because of the tragic circumstances, that you and your son may stay for a further month from today and your husband's successor will be placed in temporary accommodation.'

She stared at him in astonishment. 'Richard's successor has already been appointed?'

'Yes,' said Hoffer calmly. 'Meanwhile, because the company is permitting you to remain in the house for this extended period, you will be expected to assist us with our investigations.'

Another shiver passed over her.

'We are not satisfied with your husband's accounts and records,' he continued.

'Of course, we're not suggesting anything grave. Just small oversights probably,' put in Madame Frank.

Hoffer glared as if to silence her. 'We are a company that sets high standards and it appears that Mr Ellis may have used confidential client information to his own advantage. In other words, we suspect that he became involved in a private deal, in breach of company rules. Therefore we must regret to inform you that no further salary or final gratuity can be paid to your husband's bank. Here is a letter to that effect.'

Bewildered, Kim took the letter without reading it. 'No, I don't suppose people would pay a salary to a dead man,' she said slowly.

'As I said, we believe he is actually deceased but there is, madame, as yet no legal proof of death. In any case, there were no widow's pension terms under your husband's contract. I dare say he had his own pension plan and life assurance.'

'I don't know. I hadn't thought. You don't think of these things.'

Madame Frank intervened. 'Poor Mrs Ellis, we must leave her to herself. She cannot consider all this now. We will return another day.'

'No, let him go on,' said Kim with an effort. 'It sounds as if I need to understand my situation. You're saying that, though tomorrow is the first day of October, no money will be paid into our account but that I may stay here rent-free until the end of the month.'

'Exactly,' said Madame Frank, her eyes brimming with sympathy.

'But we do expect you to cooperate in the matter of the missing records,' said Hoffer. He began to edge towards the study door as if he intended to proceed with his search regardless of her wishes.

Kim rose to her feet, blocking his way. 'Let me show you out now, monsieur. If you come back tomorrow, I'll give you any files I find that belong to the office. I don't think Richard would have deliberately broken company rules.'

She led them to the front door. They shook hands and, with further expressions of condolence, departed.

Unlocking the French windows and leaving them wide open, Kim went out onto the lawn which, she noticed abstractedly, was still soaked with early morning dew. After pacing around for a while she sat down on the low wall between the pots of red and pink geraniums. Then, examining the plants in a glazed manner, she began to pinch out the older blossom heads, dropping them on the terrace until she was surrounded by a small heap of bare stems and faded petals.

For many years to come the sharp distinctive smell of geranium leaves would remind her of Richard.

'How sad, *la pauvre* Madame Ellis, so brave, the British *sangfroid*, the shock,' said Vivienne Frank tearfully. Stopping only to repin her Hermès scarf into a yet more becoming style, she installed herself behind the wheel of the Mercedes. This operation was much enjoyed by her passenger, Hoffer, since it afforded a glimpse of majestic thigh. Vivienne was a large woman devoted to small skirts.

As she drove through the quiet streets of Cologny, he forgot his irritation with Mme Ellis and ventured to lay his hand on Vivienne's right knee which pumped gently up and down as she applied the accelerator.

To distract her attention from his advances, he agreed, 'Yes, the poor lady.'

'So young to be widowed,' said Vivienne.

'I have been checking the file. She's forty-five and the son is eleven.'

'But she looks younger, and so lovely too.'

'She may be attractive to some, but not to me,' lied Hoffer tactfully. 'In my view, all that dark hair, it is too long for a woman of her age. And those jeans . . .'

'True, she has no chic.'

'No chic at all,' agreed Hoffer, though he had enjoyed the curves which the jeans revealed. He advanced his hand a little more. 'And the skin with those freckles.'

Vivienne drove more slowly but pursued her train of thought. 'I like freckles as long as they are pale, like hers. Not too gamine. And without doubt her eyes are fine. I suppose she may marry again, but it appears she is not to be a rich widow. And no career either. Or did you say that she teaches English?'

'I believe she has a few pupils, but it is hardly a high-income job,' he said, squeezing an enjoyably plump thigh.

Vivienne slapped his hand away. 'Imbecile, I am not made of wood.'

Hoffer leered. 'That's true, that's true.'

'Keep your hands to yourself, *chéri*. I cannot concentrate. Do you want me to crash the company car? In such a case, Mrs Ellis would not be the only person without a career.'

They were silent for a while as they reached the neat promenade by the lake.

'Do you really not consider her a desirable woman?' asked Vivienne, clearly obsessed by the subject.

In his view, Vivienne had allowed herself to become too much involved in this whole case. She seemed unnecessarily upset when the news of the crash came through, overemotional and anxious. Could be due to her age. It had occurred to him lately that she might be approaching the menopause years. Sometimes he even dreamt of finding someone a little younger.

'Madame Ellis? In some ways she may be

attractive, perhaps,' he replied cautiously, 'but her temperament seems somewhat unfeminine. I have often found her over-opinionated.' It was true, he thought. He really preferred a more acquiescent, traditional woman like his former wife. Though outside office hours one noticed Vivienne's perfumed flesh rather than her personality, she, too, could be as obstructive as Madame Ellis.

Vivienne was still talking about her. 'Let's hope she'll find a nice new husband to take care of her.'

'But, my love, how old-fashioned you are. These days I thought it was correct for ladies to take care of themselves.'

Spurred on by a strange unnatural energy, Kim hurried down the tree-lined road towards the village centre. It had proved impossible to stay at home staring at Richard's endless neat files full of old bills and unimportant letters. She needed to walk, to be outdoors, to do something domestic and mindless like shopping, buying food for James's dinner. She must focus on James. Oh God, he must be protected at all costs. Everything must be kept as normal and stable as possible. How on earth would she tell him? She began to rehearse, to try and think of the right things to say, but couldn't imagine how she would begin.

An Alsatian guard dog barked and snarled as she passed the tall gates of its domain. Another took up the chorus until all the dogs in the street were barking at her. Hardly aware of them or of a workman sweeping up the early autumn leaves, Kim rushed on.

When she reached the elegant little supermarket, she took a wire basket and began to fill it with treats for James: fillet steak, crisps, Coca Cola, chocolate ice cream, nothing healthy today.

'*Bonjour, madame*,' said the familiar check-out girl, with a well-trained smile.

'*Bonjour, madame*,' echoed Kim. She handed over her credit card.

The girl swiped the card through the machine. There was a long pause. Sighing loudly, a fat woman in the queue behind began to shuffle her feet impatiently. The cashier passed the card through the machine again. Eventually, almost as embarrassed as Kim, she whispered that the card had not been accepted. It must have been damaged – or the machine was playing up. That was often the case, regretfully.

Scarlet in the face, Kim searched through her purse for some cash. She could hardly see the coins for the irrational tears trickling down her face. No, there wasn't enough money. She scrabbled through her handbag again and, to her relief, found a fifty franc note. She paid the bill and, jamming her purchases into two plastic bags, fled outside.

Home. Must get home. She was halfway there before she managed to control herself. Sinking down on a bench, she sat staring at the traffic for a while and then a squirrel climbing up the ivy of a grey stone house opposite caught her eye. Hypnotised, she was afraid it would fall. When finally it reached the safety of the roof, she felt temporarily released, able to move again. Summoning up all her strength, she put on her sunglasses to hide her red eyes and hurried back towards the village.

In the small branch of the Union de Banques Suisses, she inserted her card into the cash dispenser and tapped in her code. There was another long unnerving pause and a great deal of clicking, and then instead of spewing out cash the machine advised her it was retaining the card.

Panic mounting again, she approached the disapproving young clerk. With much opening and closing of security doors, he showed her through to the inner office.

The manager, a pale young man with thick spectacles, appeared to have been expecting her and offered his deepest condolences with polite embarrassment. Kim felt momentarily sorry for him as he struggled to convey the correct amount of professional grief.

When she was able to raise the problem of the credit card, he said, 'Regretfully, madame, your account is closed. It is in the name of your husband and the Personnel Officer of his employers has reported him as being deceased.'

'But there's still a chance, a small chance that he may be alive. There's no proof as yet. You see, there's my son . . . we need money for bills, to eat.'

She kept her dark glasses on and her shaky hands clenched.

The manager made a rapid telephone call. 'I am very sorry, madame, but, as I said, everything is in the name of your husband. We profoundly apologise if we have been premature to treat him as being deceased but, for a variety of delicate reasons, his account must remain frozen. In the circumstances, the bank is unable to allow overdrafts on accounts that have no incoming funds due.'

'I see. I didn't realise it was overdrawn.'

'Only a little, madame, but the Bank is unable to allow the deficit to augment.'

Determined not to become emotional again, she stared down at the carpet, focusing on a small black stain. She was trying to calculate how much cash there was hidden in her cupboard, when she realised that the manager was speaking. He seemed to be asking her about her resources.

'The shoe box,' she muttered idiotically.

He stared at her.

She cleared her throat, 'I mean, there's a joint deposit account in England.'

Brightening, he suggested she should open an account of her own, transfer some money from this one in England. He would explain the procedure. Once the funds had cleared the new account would function and her new credit card would arrive within two weeks, maybe less. He then produced an application form five pages long and handed her a ballpoint pen decorated with the bank's logo.

With a shaky hand, she managed to write her address and date of birth but then her mind glazed over again when she saw all the details required. Richard's birthplace? Her paternal grandmother's maiden name? Such odd questions. Most difficult of all was the one that ought to be easy: there was a box requiring an answer on her marital status. After a pause, she wrote 'widow' and stared at the strange word.

Unable to complete the form in full, she was advised to return with all the necessary information – plus a copy of her passport, her residence permit, her driving licence – as soon as possible so that everything could be arranged.

Obediently she hurried home but when she reached the sanctuary of her kitchen, she realised she had left her groceries at the bank. Probably by now the ice cream was dripping more stains on to the red carpet.

She sat down at the table and wept at last for Richard, and for the slow and unrecognised death of her marriage a long time ago.

CHAPTER 2

Polly had telephoned by chance and insisted on coming round straight away when she heard the news. A neat compact woman with sandy hair and a pointed nose, she marched around Kim's untidy kitchen, stopping occasionally to wash a cup or straighten out a pile of newspapers.

If asked whether she minded not being able to work as a nurse here in Geneva, Swiss regulations being what they were, Polly would reply that she was perfectly happy as a full-time mother and general busybody. Having no charges these days, apart from a docile American husband and two less obedient but well-managed sons, she devoted her surplus maternal energy towards charity work and looking after her friends. Kim was in particular need of her support, in Polly's view. She certainly wasn't going to get much help from anyone else.

Typical of Richard, she thought. As usual, he'd left one big God-damned bloody awful mess for Kim.

Aloud she said, 'I can't help feeling that, well, I

16

know I shouldn't say this but maybe your life will be easier without him. Oh, I'm sorry. I mean I really am, poor Richard, of course.'

'He wasn't that bad,' said Kim quietly. 'I know I used to moan about him quite often. I feel so guilty now.'

Polly tossed her sleek head. 'You had every right to complain.'

'You're a good friend, but no one could call you oversensitive, Pol,' said Kim, with a wan smile. She took a gulp of Gamay. Polly had brought a bottle and poured them both a large glass.

'Joe says I'm not tact-oriented but I've never subscribed to the theory that one mustn't speak ill of the dead. Don't tell me you're going to turn him into some kind of saint.'

'No, not that.'

Polly wiped the kitchen worktop again. 'I've said this before, but—'

Kim winced. 'Please, not today. I haven't the strength. Richard, he meant well, mostly. I realise he wasn't the best husband.'

Polly was tempted to remark that, whether he meant well or not, he was the most self-centred, vain, stupid and unreliable bastard she'd ever met, but in a moment of uncharacteristic restraint, she held back. She patted Kim's arm. 'Why aren't you eating that sandwich I made you? Must eat.'

Kim pushed the plate away. 'Sorry, not hungry.'

Polly wrapped the sandwich in clingfilm and put it in the refrigerator. Then she put the plate in the dishwasher. 'I know you're not the hysterical type, but you need someone here. Have you got any relations?'

'No, I told you. My parents died in a car crash when I was at university,' said Kim, still sounding as if she were in some kind of trance.

'Yes, I know. I'm sorry. I meant other relations.'

'Like I said, I was an only child of two only children. I haven't got any other relations.'

'What about Richard?'

'His mother died ages ago. It was something we had in common,' she said bleakly.

'Oh dear,' said Polly, who now remembered having heard this before.

'And his father disappeared before he was born. Poor Richard, he was brought up by a series of grim old cousins. He does have a sister, but they weren't close.' She sighed. 'I have to ring her. I really must tell her.'

Bursting with suppressed efficiency, Polly took out her note pad. 'You'd better think what you're going to say first. You must decide on the wording if there's going to be an announcement in the *Times* and *Telegraph*.'

'Oh well, no, because I can't put anything in the papers. Just in case he might not be dead. I can't really believe he is. Though it's almost definite.'

Polly stared at her. 'So what happens? This uncertainty, it must make things even worse.'

Kim put her head in her hands, her hair hiding her face. 'I'll just wait, I suppose.' She paused.

'It's odd . . . You know most of the time I feel detached, like an observer, as if this is happening to someone else, not me, not Richard.'

'It's the shock.' Polly patted her arm. 'But how long are you going to wait? If you can't stay in this house, will you go home?'

'No, we don't have anywhere in England. Richard always said property was too much of a liability. We've been abroad all our married life, you see.'

'What about his sister? Could you go to her?'

'No,' said Kim, suddenly emphatic.

There was a pause while Polly took another sip of wine. 'Pretty damn ruthless, these international companies, aren't they? Especially if you're on a short-term contract. Makes you realise how precarious life is for wives,' she said thoughtfully. 'We're only here on sufferance.'

Kim didn't reply.

After another moment's silence, Polly smiled brightly. 'I've had an idea. We could move the boys in together and you and James could stay with us a while.'

'You're very kind, but we couldn't. I mean, it wouldn't work. Pol, I have to stay here . . . I need, I need to get things together, for James.'

'Does he know?'

'No, not yet,' said Kim, head in hands again.

Full of compassion, Polly stared helplessly at her. It was going to be hard enough telling her own children that James's dad had gone. She paced around the kitchen again and then decided to return to the easier subject of money.

'Well, if the bank took your card – these Swiss banks, everything being in the man's name. Ridiculous. When something goes wrong, it's like you're a non-person. Let me lend you some money.'

'No, really. I've got some cash somewhere, I know. And some savings. Don't worry. I'll be OK.'

'Let me take that pile of ironing then.'

'No, I'll do it later. It helps, doing something ordinary. I'm all right, really.'

Polly shook her head. 'Don't you think you're acting just a bit too calm? It's not good to bottle things up.'

Kim looked down. 'Better this way, only way I can cope,' she muttered.

Despite her brave words, as soon as she was alone Kim found herself pacing around the house in panicky confusion. There seemed to be a tight metal band around her chest, so tight she could hardly breathe.

She replayed the conversations in her head over and over again: Hoffer's words, Madame Frank's, Polly's. Why did Polly want to analyse everything all the time, even today? Kim didn't want to examine the nature of her grief, and she certainly didn't want to talk about it.

How could she explain her feelings when they were too mixed, too raw to explain? She couldn't say aloud that, yes, she was devastated, shocked and upset about Richard, that she couldn't bear the thought of him dying alone in a strange country and she hoped he hadn't suffered.

But that also, buried deep underneath, she felt a dark and shameful sense of relief.

Eventually, after more blank-eyed pacing she managed to regain some kind of composure. In the study she stood by the desk for a while. Then she sat down and began to sift through the piles of papers. She found no office files of any sort, so Hoffer would be disappointed.

She looked for the bank folders. The blue one containing details of the National Westminster joint saving account was not in its allocated drawer, which was unusual. Richard was obsessively tidy, so much so that he achieved little else but tidiness. In the end she found the latest Natwest statement underneath some old telephone bills. It showed a balance of £23. Twenty-three pounds? She stared at the sheet. £16,000, their entire savings, had been withdrawn in August. By Richard, and he hadn't told her.

She swayed on her feet. Oh God. He promised faithfully after the last fiasco, after the deposit on the non-existent land in Arizona, that he would never again dip into their joint money without consulting her.

She raced upstairs to her bedroom. At the back of the cupboard was a Ferragamo box. She never went to dances these days but she kept the plum-coloured shoes just in case. Underneath the shoes was a cloth bag containing money she had set aside from her earnings, teaching English to three elderly ladies.

She kept her money hidden for a personal rainy day, though she raided it from time to time for presents for Richard and James, or sometimes, more rarely, a treat for herself. If only she hadn't bought that expensive dress in the July sales. With trembling hands she opened the bag. The money was still there. She counted it. A little under four hundred Swiss francs, just about enough to pay the supermarket bills for two or three weeks.

She fetched a chair from the dressing table and stood on it to reach the top shelf of her wardrobe. There, under some old sweaters, was her other secret, her personal bank savings book. She knew what it would say and she was right. £1,238.

She gazed at the statement for a while, but the sum of money remained the same, not enough to last very long in Geneva.

James found his mother by the door. He flung his school bag down on the floor and gave her a hug. 'Hi, Mum. Bloody hot on the bus.'

'Don't say bloody,' she said, but not very crossly.

'Sorry, I mean it was dead hot.' He kicked off his shoes which landed halfway up the stairs.

'D'you want a drink, darling?' she asked. When he thought about it afterwards, he remembered she did sound a bit peculiar.

'No thanks, I'm going round next door. You know Mr Marechal said I could go for a swim. Got to use the pool before winter sets in, he says. And then we're going to have tea and play chess. Told you, Mum. Well, p'raps I'll just have a biscuit and then go.'

'But I've got to talk to you.'

Something about his mother's voice made James stare at her. 'If it's about homework, I'll do it, really. It's only French today, and some maths. Not too much. I'll do it as soon as I get back. But I have to go swimming while it's still daytime, you see,' he explained patiently.

'We'll go together in a minute, but I have to tell you something first.'

'Oh,' he said. He really preferred to go and see Mr Marechal alone, because when his mother was there they would talk together about adult things and leave him to play with the dog. On his own Mr Marechal was more fun. He'd tell James stories about his son who used to be a ski racer, and then they'd talk about other sports. Mr Marechal knew all about sport, even English games like rugby. And sometimes he'd take him sailing on the lake, or play golf or tennis. Even though he was quite old with grey hair, he was better than Daddy in that way. Dad didn't have time to play with him much.

'Well, can I change first?' he asked.

'No,' she said. This time she really did sound a bit odd, so he sat down and she told him about

Daddy being lost in a plane crash and that he might not come back. He didn't know what to feel. He hadn't seen his father much lately. And when he was home, he shut himself up in his study a lot and couldn't be interrupted and sometimes they quarrelled, he and Mum. And he shouted and Mum shouted back and then she cried which was awful. All these things went round in James's head and he didn't know what to say.

Finally he stuttered, 'But Dad often goes away – then he comes back.'

'Yes, but this time they say he probably won't.'

'So what are we going to do?'

His mother took a deep breath. 'We're going to wait here and see what happens.'

'That's all right then, as long as we stay here,' he said more calmly.

Kim's landlord, Henri Marechal, sat by his immaculate pool beside his large white villa with the green roof and green shutters. He was reading Flaubert and progressing slowly. He had been too busy making money to read novels in his youth, so now he was trying to catch up. Occasionally he looked across his well-tended lawns towards the gate which led to the adjacent property down the hill.

Henri, like many Genevois, was seriously rich, but like many Genevois he lived in a quiet and unostentatious manner. He owned other houses elsewhere, but he had chosen Geneva as his home.

He liked the mix of provincial and international, the sedate sophisticated atmosphere of the small well-groomed city, and, of course, he liked the harmonious buildings and the idyllic views of the lake and the mountains. Half-Swiss, he never felt constricted by the Helvetic passion for rules and regulations. The tidy law-abiding nature of the citizens made Geneva a comfortable place to live. Public services worked, the famous trains were on time, post was regularly delivered and garbage always collected, provided it was properly sorted for recycling. All the inhabitants minded their own business and led their sober prosperous lives without bothering anyone else. Henri liked that too.

He had retired early from the international business world because he wanted to taste some more of life before the restrictions of old age set in. Usually he felt much younger than his contemporaries, for though growing solid around the waist he considered himself exceptionally fit and healthy for a man of sixty-four. But over a year ago he found that he no longer wanted to make love to Danielle, his long-term mistress. They were still friends as Henri always remained on good terms with his women, with the possible exception of his ex-wife from whom he had parted company several years ago.

Now he and the golden Labrador lived alone in masculine harmony.

Caspar pricked his ears and then dashed towards

the gate in a frenzy of welcome, ecstatic to see both James and his mother. Henri stood up and smoothed down his thick grey hair. More slowly, he followed down the lawn.

'So you see, Henri,' said Kim, coming to the end of her story, 'We won't be your tenants for very much longer.' Behind the sunglasses, she'd managed to remain calm.

Henri touch her arm. 'I am so sorry. You're far too young for all this sadness and worry, far too young.' He looked towards the pool where James was splashing about, throwing water at Caspar who was barking playfully. 'What hope is there that Richard will return?'

'None really, according to Hoffer. There was a mid-air explosion.'

'I'm very sorry,' he repeated. 'Poor Richard.'

'Thank you,' said Kim. She found it difficult to cope with sympathy. Sympathy undermined her. She dug her nails into the palms of her hands in an attempt to retain her self-control.

'How is James feeling?'

'Seems OK, but I don't think he's taken it in yet. Nor have I really.'

'Poor Kim.'

There was a silence. Then Henri said, 'They're sharks, those people Richard worked for. But there is one thing I can do. I can terminate the lease within two months, perhaps less. I don't want anyone else from that company in the house – you may stay there until your affairs are more in order. It's the right place for you and the boy.'

If only we could, she thought, as a small glimmer of hope flickered and then died. Aloud she said, 'But we have to move, I'm sorry.'

'Ah, of course, the rent the company paid was very high. I am sure I can reduce it quite substantially for you as an individual.'

'No, I didn't mean to sound pathetic. You can't, really. Not to the sort of level we . . .' Her voice trailed off. She had not explained the seriousness of her financial predicament to Henri and did not intend to. 'We have to move house.'

'But where else will you go? What about James? He's happy here, I know. And you said it was convenient for his school.'

Oh God, the school fees, thought Kim, more agitated than ever. 'Yes, yes, he loves it,' she said aloud. 'But I expect we can find somewhere else nearby. Maybe, d'you know anyone who has a small cheap flat to let, even temporarily, someone who's going away and needs a caretaker for their animals? And also I need a job, a more serious one than teaching English to old ladies.'

He smiled at her. 'You charge them so little, from what I hear.'

'Well, I don't like to ask them for too much. They're not very well-off mostly, and we've become friends. I sometimes think they need company more than lessons really. I can hardly ask them for a raise.' She shrugged her shoulders and smiled. 'One of them's a bit dotty and some-times forgets to pay me at all.'

'Then you should remind her.'

'I don't like to – in case it's a problem.'

'What a ridiculously unbusinesslike attitude. I shall try to find you some serious rich pupils, and you must send them proper bills. And as regards accommodation, you can stay on in the house, as I said.'

'No, you must understand, we couldn't accept such a—'

He looked at her thoughtfully. 'The company has already paid for one month. Please, for my sake, because I enjoy seeing you and the boy, stay for at least another month after that, as my guest.'

She started to refuse again but he interrupted her. 'Think about it for a while and you will see that it's the best thing for James, for you both. You are not calm enough to make decisions about your future now.' He smiled. 'Remember we have been neighbours for two years now and a friend in need is a friend indeed. I learnt that from my own English teacher – she was fond of proverbs.'

James cried that night for a long time. Her heart breaking for him, Kim stayed with him until he went to sleep. Then she retreated to her own quiet empty room where she lay awake in a turmoil of grief, worry and guilt – horrible sick guilt because, deep inside her, there was still a sense of relief that she would not now have to make a decision about leaving Richard.

She remembered Polly's question on a summer evening last year when they'd both had too much wine.

'Apart from the fact that you're an over-conscientious mother, why *do* you stay with that husband of yours?'

Kim had tried to be flippant. 'Why does anyone stay with anyone once the romantic stage is over? Mutual dependence? Habit? Or I s'pose a few people still cling on to traditional values like loyalty and duty. Or is it really fear of the unknown?'

'Can't believe you mean that. Sounds too bleak and cynical, even for me. There have to be loads of better reasons like affection and devotion and stuff.'

Not wanting to hear about all these wonderful happy better reasons, Kim had interrupted. 'I prefer to stick with the devil I know. And Richard loves me, sort of. Anyway he needs me. Must be plenty of women hanging in there just because they feel needed.'

Now he didn't need her any more.

When finally she closed her eyes she dreamt of him. He was floating in the lake and calling to her. She tried to reach him but he had sunk out of sight and she couldn't find him in the water.

CHAPTER 3

Next day Kim forced herself to concentrate once more on survival, her own and her child's.

Her first telephone call was to James's headmistress.

'Yes,' said Patricia, enunciating every word in her overcareful manner, 'your school fees have been paid until Christmas, and then I think we could squeeze next term's fees out of your husband's company on the grounds that they haven't given sufficient notice. But in the summer the money must come from you, if you're staying in Switzerland. We'd be sorry to lose James, and I fear it would be most unwise to move him at this difficult and unsettling stage.'

Kim took a deep breath. 'Patricia, there aren't any jobs going at the school, are there?'

'Do you have any teacher-training, any qualifications?'

'No, but plenty of practical experience of English as a foreign language. I mean, I've taught it for years, everywhere we've lived. Perhaps some of your foreign pupils need extra English tuition?'

'I am very sorry. I'd like to help, but at the British-Swiss Foundation the Governors insist we have properly qualified teachers.'

'No,' said Lionel, her solicitor in England, his pompous voice unusually sympathetic. 'I have checked your file and there is no life insurance and no personal pension plan that I'm aware of, though you should search through Richard's own papers. Such funds would not be payable in any case until your husband is proved dead. Some insurance companies may pay out a year after disappearance, but in Switzerland it could take up to five years. Meanwhile, of course, you could return to England, but, as you have spent so little time in this country recently, maybe you would be better off trying to make your own living abroad where you have contacts.'

But when she approached the Geneva language schools, they said they had no vacancy for a teacher without qualifications.

Polly put her hands on her hips. 'I know only too well how damn hard it is for an ex-pat wife to sustain a career as such, impossible really, but with such an unreliable husband, for God's sake, why didn't you get qualified as a teacher? What about before Richard? Did you say you did good works in Africa or something?'

Kim sighed. 'Kind of, not exactly. You see, when my parents died I lost the plot and dropped out of uni. There wasn't any money anyway but—'

'Oh dear, I know, you told me. Forgive me, sorry.'

'Water under the bridge. I was just about old enough to cope. Came to terms with it, as you have to. Anyway, after that, I went through a youthful idealist phase.' She smiled a little. 'Must have been thoroughly tiresome. What happened was, originally I had a lowly job in publishing, but then I fell in love with a worthy overseas-aid worker.'

'Handsome, was he?'

'Handsome and heroic, or so I thought. I followed him out to Zimbabwe and just sort of got involved in the country, moving around doing odd jobs, a bit of writing and a bit of language teaching. He didn't want to get married, not being that worthy, it turned out, so we split up. Then I moved to Kenya where I met Richard.'

'So you never had a serious job even before you became a trailing spouse?'

Kim winced. She was ashamed of her lack of a proper career and her pretty feeble-sounding CV. 'No, afraid not, Polly dear. Well, some of my various jobs were serious but not impressive. Actually I did earn quite a bit before we came to Switzerland. I used to be the bread-winner, or the rice-winner, in between Richard's bouts of employment. In developing countries they're so keen to learn English from a real Englishwoman that they don't worry about details like paper qualifications. And then I never wanted to leave James alone with Richard and the servants. I'd have had to come back to England to do a diploma course.'

'It always comes down to James. You're obsessed with that kid.'

'He's all I have,' said Kim simply. 'And it took me years and years to get pregnant.'

'But it's not healthy, this child-centred life you lead.'

Kim felt too weary to be indignant. 'I'm not child-centred, at least not abnormally so.'

'There's friends and family as well, you know.'
'Yes, but we moved so often I was always leaving friends behind. So was James. And Richard was never around. So we, James and I, sort of depend on each other.'

Polly took another sip of coffee. 'But here in Geneva you do have friends, like me and Joe, and the mums at school and good old Henri, so you could afford to lighten up on that child. You could have left him with me while you did a course.'

'I know, you're an angel, but as Richard was earning a good salary for a change, I took a break and tried to do some writing. Haven't said much about it because it wasn't a wild success.'

'Hey, I remember, you gave me copies of your travel stuff. It was great. I thought you sold some of your articles.'

'I did, but it took so much time I probably would've earned more baby-sitting.'

By and by Kim's old ladies found other friends who wanted English lessons, but, though they paid a little more, her funds were dwindling.

Then she received a letter from Richard's sister, Monica. After stilted condolences she wrote, 'You're probably stony-broke, knowing my late brother.' Monica went on to invite her to live with them for a few months. The house was very small, wasn't it, so James would have to share with Damien and they could just squeeze another bed into Tilly's room for her. Cupboard space might be a problem but they'd cope. She hoped Kim would understand but, as George's business was not doing well these days, they would have to charge her rent as a lodger. All in all, it would be tricky but a help to have her around what with Monica's chest problems and George's leg.

'Yuck,' said James. 'I hate Aunt Monica and horrible Damien and stupid Tilly.'

Kim suppressed a smile. 'Really, James, mustn't be unkind about your cousins.'

James pulled a face. 'They smell.'

'Nonsense.'

'Well, their house does. Aunt Monica smokes all the time and Uncle George always has cans of beer everywhere. Anyway, you don't like Aunt Monica either. I heard you say to Polly that she was a stingy old bat.'

Kim smiled again. 'Well, that was very rude of me because Monica isn't all that old and it was kind of her to ask us.' It was hard to imagine a worse fate than being her tenant, George's awful jokes and Monica's critical sniffs, Damian's deafening metal music and Tilly's whines, all day and every day. What a thought . . .

James shook her arm. 'I hope you're only teasing about going to live with them. We're not really going to, are we? You promised we could stay here. You promised.'

Kim looked through the offers of employment in the daily *Tribune de Genève* but no suitable jobs appeared of any kind. So she concentrated on her old ladies and on James, and on tidying the house and garden for the new tenants that Henri would eventually have to find.

There was a worrying silence from Hoffer. He did not ring with any more details about the air crash, nor did he arrive to search the house or try to evict her. Every time the telephone rang she jumped, expecting, irrationally, to hear Richard's voice.

There were reminders of him all over the house, photographs on the bookcase, coats in the cupboard. Occasionally she would open his wardrobe and sit on the bed staring at all his clothes, so many of them, hanging so neatly. What should she do with them? She couldn't actually believe he would never wear them again. In fact, she could not entirely accept that he was dead. She didn't feel like a real widow, able to mourn as a widow should, whether or not she loved her husband.

Someone somewhere must know what happened to Richard. She needed to find out something concrete, one way or the other, but she'd heard nothing from the company and had no desire to contact Hoffer or Vivienne Frank. Wondering if it was the right thing to do, she'd written to the Foreign Office in London and received a brief acknowledgement to her letter: they would look into the case.

Several days passed, days of waiting and long dark sleepless nights when she paced about thinking and worrying.

Then Henri telephoned and asked her to come over and see him. She was certain he wanted to tell her he had found a new tenant. Feeling increasingly depressed, she walked slowly around to his house. It was a fine autumn day with a chilly breeze and as she passed under the shade of the cedar she shivered in her thin cotton jersey.

Henri was sitting on the terrace waiting for her. With his usual gallantry, he ushered her into the house and offered her a glass of wine.

She smiled. 'Better not drink at lunch time or I might lose concentration with my pupils this after-noon.'

'How prim you British are at times! This is a delicious Mont-sur-Rolle from one of my own vineyards. It's very light. Just have a little sip. I'd welcome your opinion of it.'

'Well, OK, thank you very much. You're so persuasive. How can I refuse?'

She noticed that as he was pouring the wine his hand shook a little. She wondered if he were unwell. His lined face was tanned dark brown after a summer's sailing. He certainly looked fit enough, and, today, almost handsome in a cream linen jacket that disguised his solid waistline.

He smiled at her with his bright admiring gaze. He looked at all women of all ages like that. She'd seen both sulky teenagers and cross old grandmothers purr with delight in his company. There was always a mischievous, flirtatious undertone to his conversation that must have been a great success in his day.

'So how is your search for another job or new accommodation going?' he asked.

Oh dear. She tried to smile. 'Very badly. Not sure what we're going to do, but something will turn up, I dare say. I expect you want to know because of the house. Maybe we should fix a definite day for moving out.'

'Sit down, Kim. Relax.'

Perching on the edge of the elegant brocade sofa, she began to sip the pale gold wine rather fast. She looked around at the dark portrait of Henri's grandfather, the clockmaker, and at the heavy-framed Alpine landscapes and the chandeliers that were a little too large for the height of the ceiling.

Why had they come inside? Usually Henri preferred to sit on the terrace until winter finally arrived.

'Where's Caspar?' she asked, missing the bouncy welcome. She'd always wanted a dog of her own but their wandering life made it too difficult. Caspar was the next best thing.

'He's in the kitchen. I don't want him interrupting,' said Henri, pacing about the room amid the ornate French furniture. He turned and said suddenly, 'I would like to make you a proposition.' His voice was unusually solemn.

She looked up.

'You are reluctant to accept my hospitality,' he went on, 'because you say you can offer no payment, nothing in return.'

'Well, you speak perfect English. You have a gardener and a housekeeper. You cook rather better than I do and, unless you've written your life story or something – I used to do a bit of editing in one of my jobs.'

'No, I have not as yet begun my memoirs, but there is one other suggestion. Please understand that I am putting it in this businesslike manner because we have little time – I fear you may disappear at any moment. And then there is the age difference between us. If you were nearer my age I would take a more traditional approach.' He smiled but seemed marginally less well at ease than normal. 'I should like you and James to stay in the house for at least one year. I will pay all your living expenses, including the school fees. As you know, I am a rich man.'

'That's so kind but—'

'Please, I haven't finished. This is not a kind or honourable proposition, but then I am not entirely an honourable man. What I ask in return is that every Thursday evening you should dine with me here, after which I should like to make love to you.' He spoke slowly and seriously. 'You would be home by midnight,' he added.

Kim blushed scarlet. She found nothing to say. He's mad, she thought, excruciatingly embarrassed.

He smiled gently. 'You're shocked or repelled by the idea? Or extremely offended?'

'I, er . . .'

'Of course, the arrangement would cease immediately should your husband return.' His expression became more mischievous. 'Have you ever been unfaithful to him?'

'No.'

'So as a chaste woman you are very shocked by this suggestion?' His questions seemed serious rather than playful.

She blushed again. 'No, um, not shocked or offended, of course not, but very surprised. I . . .'

'You hadn't thought of taking such an old man as a lover.'

'It's not that. I mean to say, I don't think of you as old, but—'

'You didn't think of me as a lover?'

'Well, I don't, er, don't have lovers.'

'Why not? It's a most amusing pastime. Is it a religious thing with you? It cannot be that you loved your husband too much. It often seemed to me that your marriage was not happy. Oh, forgive me if I am putting salt on wounds.'

'No, you're not but . . . Well, I'm not especially religious, but perhaps I never had a love affair because I don't know if that sort of behaviour is a good idea, for me anyway. That sounds prim.' She rushed on. 'Anyway our marriage wouldn't have stood the strain. If I'd fallen in love with someone else, I'd have wanted to leave.' She paused and then she said, 'It isn't so extraordinary not to have lovers, is it? I know lots of faithful women.'

'How interesting. And I have known many unfaithful ones. But now you are, we assume, a widow, a single woman, and so you can lead a less restricted life. It seems to me you have been doing the right thing for far too long. Of course, one admires a serious woman but so much good, responsible behaviour must be rather depressing. You would find an affair excellent for the morale, even with an old man like me. I should be most honoured if you could consider me for the job of your first lover and protector.'

She continued to stare at the floor. 'You've always been a good friend, and I like you, we all do, especially James, of course, but . . .' She looked up at him and gave another uncertain smile. 'Perhaps you are teasing me. I'm not sure how serious you are about all this.'

'I am perfectly serious. You speak of James. There will be many advantages for him because all your other wild schemes would involve further disruption to his life at this difficult moment. This way, you can stay here for as long as you like if the arrangement is a success. I should add that I don't require absolute fidelity for I am aware that other younger men will desire you, and you may eventually meet someone more suitable than myself.' He looked quizzically at her. 'Perhaps there is already some young admirer dying of unrequited love for you?'

She shook her head firmly. 'No, there isn't.'

'But if you do take a younger lover, I would not want to know. I don't consider honesty in these matters a good idea.' His voice grew softer. 'In my case, it's highly likely, however, that I would be faithful to you, Kim, because you are the woman I have been thinking of for a long time, ever since you arrived in Geneva, in fact, although it took me a while to realise it.'

She gulped.

Henri continued, 'I dare say you're worried about what people might think about your becoming the mistress of a rich old man as soon as your husband is gone, but no one need know. We would keep it a secret from everyone, especially James. This is why I would suggest restricting our rendezvous to Thursdays only.' He lowered his voice and spoke even more confidentially. 'I shall tell my housekeeper that I would prefer her to come in on Saturdays rather than Fridays, so I could each Friday deal with any evidence there may have been of your presence upstairs. You could tell James and your babysitter that you are editing my book and that we meet together each Thursday to work on it.'

Despite herself, she smiled. 'I thought you said you hadn't written anything.'

He shrugged his shoulders. 'As it happens, I do have the manuscript of a novel you could glance at occasionally. And by the way, I would suggest you employ that young teenager as a babysitter, the Australian girl who stays the night. She would suspect nothing.'

She raised her eyebrows. 'You seem to have thought the whole matter through extremely thoroughly.'

'Of course. But then I have been making optimistic plans for many days now.'

Help, she thought. 'I had no idea.'

'You will probably need a little time to decide. Or perhaps you would prefer a probationary evening? Or a trial period of one month perhaps, in case the first time is not a success. There is such a thing as first night nerves and love tends to get better as one goes along. If you are not entirely satisfied, the contract can be cancelled. In my case, I am certain of satisfaction.'

The whole idea was so extraordinary that she began to laugh. 'You're crazy.'

'Such arrangements used to be commonplace in France.' He smiled mischievously.

'Yes, but it all sounds so old-fashioned.' She searched for something polite to say. The whole idea was totally out of the question. 'I'm flattered, very flattered really. I mean, it's very kind of you, but . . .'

'On the contrary, I'm not kind. As you say, I am old-fashioned, and I am also selfish. You're in a difficult situation and I am taking advantage of it. Of course, if you find the proposition totally unacceptable and wish to reject it, you may still live in your house until you find somewhere else. I would never throw you out on to the streets. But I am sure James would prefer to stay here.'

'Yes, but—'

'You see how I am playing the James card – a very strong one. A mother always wants what is best for her child.' He stood up. 'And now would you like some more wine or would you prefer to go away and consider the matter?'

'Yes, I do need some time to think.'

'How encouraging,' he said gravely.

CHAPTER 4

Hoffer was looking forward to his new confrontation in Cologny. He had decided not to bring Vivienne this time as she was inclined to take a soft-hearted approach. She had even persuaded the Director to continue paying health insurance for the family of the stupid and greedy Richard Ellis, whose whereabouts, alive or dead, he had still not ascertained, but whose in-expert attempts at trading on the side he had easily uncovered. It was now hardly necessary to search the house, though he intended to give Madame Ellis the impression that he might still insist on doing so.

On arrival he handed her the cardboard box filled with Ellis's office debris, a couple of pens, a spare razor, a photograph of the family.

She examined the contents. 'Have you heard any more about the plane crash. Is there any new hope of survivors?' she asked.

Her face was pale and her voice unsteady. He thought for a moment that her self-control would desert her and that he, Hoffer, would be able to provide comfort. But she remained quiet, gazing at the small heap of her husband's possessions.

As he was telling her about the lack of any further news from South East Asia, Hoffer studied her. She was better dressed this time, in a blue skirt, rather short, providing an opportunity to study her long legs. He imagined them in erotic positions and found it a pleasant vision. Looking up from his musing, he said, 'Of course, we are continuing with our enquiries and will let you know immediately of any news. But meantime if I can be of any assistance at all here in Geneva . . .' He gave an obsequious smile and stretched out his hands.

She stared at a point somewhere above his head. 'No, thank you,' she said coldly.

Arrogant bitch. He decided to put her in her place. 'Regretfully, madame, though your landlord has terminated his lease with the company, you will still be unable to stay in this house, or in Switzerland at all for that matter. It is a question of your residence permit. Your own permit depends on your husband's being an employee of the company, and now, sadly, that is no longer the case. We shall therefore be obliged to inform the Bureau of Immigration of the situation, and your residence permit will no doubt be withdrawn.'

'What, straight away?'

She looked most upset. Hoffer was pleased to have again penetrated her frosty calm. 'If not immediately, then soon, I imagine. Of course it is possible that I may be able to delay my letter to the Immigration authorities.'

She stared at him, then returned to her former haughty manner. 'You must do the right thing, Mr Hoffer. No doubt the company always prefers to stick to the letter of the law. I'll tell my advisers what you have said.'

'So have you come to tell me you have made a decision?' asked Henri.

Kim smiled momentarily. 'No, I haven't.'

'That smile makes me hopeful,' he said.

'I can't help smiling at you sometimes, though I don't much feel like it at the moment,' she said seriously. 'But there's another problem.' She told him about Hoffer and the residence permit. 'So regardless of your, er, kind offer, it looks as if we shall have to leave.'

'Ah, but because of your new job in my publishing company you can obtain a new permit of your own.'

She shook her head, smiling again despite her reservations. 'What job, what publishers?' Have to give him full marks for persistence.

'Well, because various established firms have failed to appreciate the quality of my writing, some time ago I decided to set up a small publishing company of my own. So far it is a company in name only. I am the director but there are no offices, no employees. But now I can offer you the job as its chief editor. As you only have one book to edit in as much time as you want, you should not find the work too burdensome. This way I could pay you a salary. Such an arrangement would be more discreet than merely paying you an allowance for reasons unspecified.'

She laughed. 'I'm overwhelmed. You seem to have an answer to everything.'

'So does that give you the information you need to come to a decision? Not that I would wish to put you under any pressure.'

'I'm under a great deal of pressure, not least from you,' she said gently.

His face was contrite. 'I'm sorry. You've been recently widowed and I am far too importunate. It is because I long for you to accept my proposition. I've thought of little else recently.'

He smiled his twinkling I-adore-you smile and she saw again how persuasive he must have been as a young man. 'Tell me, Henri, have you had many lovers? Or maybe you are more comfortable with the term mistress – have you had many mistresses?'

He shrugged. 'Not so many.'

'Five? Ten? Twenty?'

'No, no, not twenty. I am a faithful man. It always lasts for several years.'

She grinned. 'Tell me about them. Who was your first love?'

'My wife, Heidi, of course. I was a virgin, well, almost a virgin, unusual though it may seem today.'

She decided it would be unwise to ask how one could be almost a virgin. 'A good Swiss name, Heidi,' she said aloud, trying not to giggle. 'So who came after?'

'Do you really want to know all this?'

'Yes, yes, I do. When did you first stray down the primrose path or whatever?'

Henri needed no further prompting. 'Alas, after ten faithful years I was tempted by Katia, most alluring. She led me astray – I was such an innocent, with a very romantic nature.'

Kim raised her eyebrows.

'You don't believe me. Things were so different then. You see, I fell in love with Katia. She was a business contact, and when she invited me to stay the night, I was unprepared, unused to such flattery. As a red-blooded man, one could not resist. Indeed I have always thought it bad manners to refuse a lady.'

'That can't have made Heidi very happy, if she found out.'

He sighed. 'She did discover the affair, and that made me feel such guilt.'

'So you left Katia?'

He sighed again, a deep sad sigh. 'Yes, eventually.'

'And then?'

'And then, let me see, ah yes – Sabine, a charming French woman, very sophisticated. So slim, so chic, a wonderful sense of style.'

'You were in love with her too?'

'Yes, she was the one I loved for more than six years, but sadly she went away to join her husband in Indo-China. I was broken hearted.'

She was amused by his woebegone face. 'What did Heidi think of all this?'

'Poor Heidi, she doesn't have a tolerant nature. Perhaps if she had been more understanding we should still have been together. Unfortunately she visited some female relation in America who raised her consciousness, or some such expression. And then, worse still, she undertook Personal Development Training. Quite wrong for a Swiss woman who, like the Germans, are most suited to *Kinder, Kirche, Küche*. Or so we Neolithic men believe.'

'So before her consciousness-raising did Heidi only want children, church and kitchen?'

'*Mais non*, she had other interests of an artistic nature such as découpage – very traditional here – and she also collected canes, walking sticks.'

Kim was again trying not to giggle. 'Découpage is very pretty but . . .' She had a vision of Henri's poor wife chasing him down the street brandishing her precious walking sticks.

'Women should always collect some form of art or artefact,' pronounced Henri. 'It gives them an occupation. For instance, Sabine collected perfume bottles. She had over one hundred, I remember.'

'And what did she do with them, all those bottles?'

'Displayed them, of course, in a cabinet. She was most gifted with selecting antiques and all forms of design. You see that corner over there, with my German silver collection – Sabine helped me with the lighting. I have not made any alterations to that arrangement after all these years.'

She was tired of Sabine so she changed the subject. 'Who was your next lover?'

He paused, deep in thought. 'Ah, Rosa, I believe, but she was more or less on the rebound from Sabine and did not last. She did not come from the right background. Too independent, and too adventurous.'

Wise woman, thought Kim with an inward smile.

'Then finally Danielle came into my life,' he continued in full swing, 'a most intelligent, well-read person. I think you met Danielle when you first came here at a cocktail party I gave to welcome you.'

'And is she still around? I don't think I've seen her lately, have I?' Not that she was a great loss, in Kim's view. She'd never warmed to the well-groomed, overpoweringly vivacious Danielle.

'We are still friends, but no longer lovers.' He sighed. 'For a long time now I have been dreaming about you and you alone. There's no fool like an old fool,' he added with a smile.

Kim was still thinking about Henri when the head-mistress rang again. 'I am afraid there's going to be a problem about next term's fees. Though your husband's company has paid for James until Christmas, I can't hold them to an additional term after that because they have just enrolled a new child. You see, we're a small school and we can't afford to offend people. But I'll keep James's place open if you can guarantee the fees for the Spring term. I don't want to put you under any pressure but, as you know, we do have a waiting list.'

'All right, yes, he must stay. I'll be organised by then,' said Kim wildly.

'Are you sure? I know you don't want to disrupt his education, but have you thought of the local Swiss school?'

'I know, I know, but he's rather unsettled at the moment, and he'd have to change language and friends and environment.'

Patricia sighed. 'Yes, that's difficult, and I'm afraid he hasn't been his usual cheerful self lately.'

'He needs stability, you see. He's had to change schools about six times already. And you know I met someone whose child was ostracised and bullied at the local school because he was foreign and different. I can't put James through all that. I just can't uproot him again, not at his age.'

'We'd like to help but—'

'Don't worry, Patricia. I'll find the money.'

Kim spent that night, as she had many previous nights, tossing and turning and searching her conscience. It would be quite wrong to go along with Henri's plans. She just couldn't do it.

Yet it would be greatly to James's advantage if she were to take the easy way out of her problems.

Still wide awake after an hour she got out of bed and went downstairs to find a biscuit to eat. Sometimes this helped to send her to sleep and sometimes it didn't. Then, even more sinfully, she took the whole packet back to bed with her, placing it carefully on the bedside table between the alarm clock and the telephone. Lately she'd taken to sleeping on Richard's side of the bed for some reason.

Richard was always a good sleeper. It used to drive her mad that he snored away all night while she lay awake.

If only she knew what had happened to him. He wandered constantly around her mind like a restless reproachful ghost.

Lying there, she tried to recall the better days, the happy time when they first met in Kenya where Richard was attached to the British High Commission. He had a youthful vigorous swagger and she'd been flattered, bowled over, that such a good-looking army officer had singled her out for attention. He'd looked fantastic in his uniform, tall and fair and quite irresistible. Her girlfriends were impressed, too. 'What a gorgeous man,' they said.

And she'd been loved in return. He told her she was the light of his life. Heady stuff. One evening he'd recounted the story of his awful bleak unsettled childhood and she vowed to herself that she would make it up to him. They'd have lots of children and be a proper family, for ever and ever.

But then in the early years she came to realise she'd attached herself to an invisible man, a will o' the wisp. Military life had given him discipline and order which vanished once he left the army. She'd known he was sometimes erratic and unreliable, but then young men often were. She hoped she could become the new rock, the centre of his life.

She was too dependable, in fact. Everything became her responsibility. 'Yes, darling, of course I'll do it,' he'd say. But he didn't. 'No, darling, sorry I forgot to take the car to the garage. Too busy. You'll have time, won't you?' Stupid unimportant things, but the stuff of endless marital quarrels.

They quarrelled about money too. She was too careful with it. She was a burden, tying him down with worries about cash for housekeeping and the cost of James's shoes.

Richard's own shoes had to come from Lobb's, of course, or the best quality local hand-made equivalent he could find. He liked to aim for the lifestyle and accoutrements of an English country gentleman. If they had been rich, she wouldn't have minded his sartorial ambitions – she understood they sprang from insecurity rather than snobbery – but soon his extravagance became a major source of conflict. The general lack of money didn't bother her but she hated the constant rows about how money should be spent. It was hard to maintain Richard's upwardly mobile tastes on a downwardly mobile income.

Had they remained in love none of this would have mattered, but the emotional instability was even more worrying than their fluctuating finances. In recent years he'd still claimed to adore her, especially after a few glasses of whisky, but these declarations were spasmodic, and often at variance with his actual behaviour.

And she'd come to prefer the times when he was away, either in mind or in body, to the times when he was the caring, attentive husband.

Now she'd been told she had no husband. She was a free woman. A strange thought. But Henri was suggesting she should immediately enter into a contract with him. It would solve all her problems.

According to Henri.

A few days later, pretending to herself that it was just a harmless shopping trip, Kim went to the Lingerie Department of Grand Passage, Geneva's biggest department store, where prices were less exorbitant than in the little boutiques in the rue du Rhône. She wandered among the frothy displays and marvelled at the fact that so much could be paid for so little. Under the watchful eye of a grey-suited dragon lady, she picked a handful of bras and asked to try them on, a task she hated, particularly when the assistant would not leave her in peace. Miraculously, one fitted. With unaccustomed extravagance, almost as if the act were involuntary, she chose the creamy coffee lace version along with the ridiculously expensive matching knickers. Before she had time to change her mind, she paid for them in cash from her remaining Swiss francs.

Then, to give herself time to think, she went for a long walk, window-shopping along the street, staring at the luxurious displays of shoes and handbags. She walked up to the Old Town and along the cobbled streets, where the boutiques and houses grew ever more exclusive. She stood staring at the blue-green spire of the cathedral de St Pierre and remembered the afternoon when she had climbed the hundred and fifty giddy steps to the top with James and Richard.

That had been one of the good days when they'd first arrived in Geneva. Richard was full of optimism about the wonderful new job in a beautiful new city and she'd almost begun to believe that they would at last find some kind of stability.

But now the world had turned upside down again.

Walking down the hill back to the car along the quiet streets, Kim was still deep in thought when she saw an old woman sitting slumped on a roadside bench. She stopped when she recognised Eliane, one of her former pupils who had only attended two or three English lessons and then disappeared. She hadn't seen her for over a year. Eliane was reputed to have fallen on hard times and moved away from all her erstwhile friends. As they chatted Kim noticed how frail the woman had become, her skin grey-white and puffy around the eyes. Although the weather was chilly, she was curiously dressed in two ragged cardigans, a thin cotton skirt and winter boots.

After a few minutes' conversation Eliane announced she must go home. She stood up and began to totter along the road. Her steps were so uncertain that Kim felt compelled to offer her a lift.

'Where do you live?' she asked when they finally reached the car.

Eliane eased herself slowly into the passenger seat and then replied, 'Le Lignon. I expect it is en route for you. You are lucky. I wish I could afford a car. The bus is slow, very slow.' A faint odour of alcohol and second-hand clothes filled the air.

Kim knew Le Lignon was the opposite end of town. She smiled ruefully. The long drive through heavy traffic would be her penance for buying exotic underwear with what could only be sinful intent.

Eliane seemed to be asleep as they drove across the city. After a few wrong turns, Kim found herself in what appeared to be a derelict factory area in a reclaimed swamp by the river. She woke Eliane, who indicated that a bleak high-rise complex was her home. Kim stared in dismay at the crumbling concrete towers, the graffiti, the broken windows. She had never seen this other Geneva before.

Eliane shook her head. 'I apologise for not being able to show you my apartment,' she croaked. 'I have to meet a friend. But if you are looking for cheap accommodations, this is a reasonable area for respectable ladies of limited means.' Forgetting to say thank you, she stumbled off towards the sign saying Tabac et Bar.

On the way back the car started to make a strange thumping sound. Oh no, please, begged Kim. As if in answer to her prayer the noise stopped as suddenly as it had begun. The same thing had happened last week, but she had ignored it. The car was due a major service, but she had ignored that fact too, unable to face the idea of a mammoth garage bill to add to all the others on her kitchen windowsill. The thumping sound was obviously a warning of worse to come.

When she finally parked in her driveway, she lifted the bonnet but there was nothing to see – there never was if you didn't have a clue what to look for. But she mustn't procrastinate a moment longer. To forestall further disasters she rushed inside and telephoned the garage. She could bring it in next week, conceded the receptionist, as if doing her a huge favour.

Putting the hateful difficulties of dealing with the garage to the back of her mind and enormously relieved to find herself safely home, Kim went upstairs, unpacked her purchases and spread them out on the bed. As she paced around the room, she acknowledged that she had almost made up her mind. She was willing to do anything to keep her promise to James that they should stay here, anything to avoid uprooting him yet again and taking him to live in a place like Le Lignon. She could no longer afford the luxury of prim, ladylike scruples. The security that Henri offered her seemed irresistible.

Besides, as she'd been telling herself during the past weeks, fulfilling her side of the bargain couldn't be that difficult, could it? Even if she didn't love or desire him, he was a nice man, wasn't he? Women all over the world had sex with men they didn't want, just as she had dutifully slept with Richard.

Nevertheless, she couldn't really, actually go through with it. Could she?

She paced about for another half hour. Then suddenly she picked up the telephone and dialled Henri's number.

'*Allo?*'

She gulped. 'It's Kim. I was wondering if you would like me to come and have dinner with you on Thursday,' she said in a rush.

'Kim? You spoke so fast. What did you say?'

'I said I'd have dinner . . . at your house . . . on Thursday.'

There was a long sigh. 'I think that would be a most excellent idea,' he said. 'You cannot begin to know how happy that suggestion makes me.'

As soon as she had put down the receiver she wanted to reverse her decision. She sank down on the bed. Her hand stretched towards the telephone to redial and say no, no, not ever. But she did nothing, remaining there staring blankly, shocked, ice-cold and almost unable to breathe.

James was surprised and delighted that his mother had hired a *Harry Potter* DVD for Thursday night. He almost forgot to ask where she was going.

'Just popping round to have dinner with Henri – to help him with his book,' she said in what sounded to her like an over-casual voice.

Once Alison, the babysitter, had arrived Kim served the spaghetti bolognese, James's favourite dish, and went upstairs. Neither James nor Alison seemed to notice anything unusual about the way she looked or behaved.

She ran her bath, tipping in half a bottle of bubbles, but she felt too nervous to soak for long. She dried herself carefully and, hoping it wouldn't clash with her scent, an elderly bottle of Miss Dior, she anointed her legs and arms with the body lotion James had given her for Christmas.

She donned her new underwear and, holding in her stomach, studied the effect. Oh dear, she thought, what the hell are you doing, Kim? She opened her wardrobe. What would be a suitable garment to wear? Nothing too virginal, nothing too tarty. Selecting an old favourite, a dark red tight-waisted longish dress with buttons down the front, she stared at her reflection in the mirror again. Oh no. A fat frump. She looked like a dark-haired version of Doris Day – Doris-on-a-very-bad-day. The dress appeared to have shrunk and her bust was bursting out all over. Hands shaking, she tore off the dress and substituted a silk shirt and straight black skirt, which also seemed too tight and over-voluptuous, but would have to do.

Then she remembered her old but still smart black jacket which lent her an air of efficient respectability. In fact she now looked so severe he would probably change his mind about taking her to bed.

Not that she was a brilliant lover anyway.

Ignoring the mess in her room, she crept downstairs. 'Goodnight. Have a nice evening,' she said to James and Alison, but they were both preoccupied with the television and hardly noticed her leaving.

As it was dark, she walked around the front way rather than through the garden and every step she took seemed to require an effort of will.

Her heart thumping with dread, she rang Henri's doorbell. He opened it almost immediately and Caspar rushed to meet her, jumping up and down, his tail wagging furiously. With a high false laugh she pushed past the dog and then realised she had failed to greet Henri.

She went to him and held up her face.

'*Bonsoir, ma chère* Kim,' he said, kissing her on the cheek three times in the polite Genevois manner, just as if it were a normal occasion.

He opened a bottle of champagne and poured her a glass. She drank it quickly, playing with the dog and making constrained conversation without looking at Henri. Quite soon he hurried her into dinner.

He had laid the table in his dark dining room with shining silver and cut glass. With great ceremony, he produced the first course – thin pale slices of salmon marinated in lemon juice and peppercorns. It was light and delicious. She managed to eat half of it, washed down with copious amounts of wine. Then he disappeared to the kitchen leaving her staring at the white linen table cloth for what seemed like half an hour, but was probably no more than five minutes.

'*Escalope de veau*,' he announced proudly.

She sat pushing the veal around her plate for a while and then gave up.

'You don't like veal? The sauce is too strong? Too much?' he asked.

'It's delicious, really, but I'm not hungry.'

He smiled tenderly at her. 'You must relax.'

'Sorry . . . but I'm terrified,' she said in a small voice.

'You have nothing to fear. I shall not ask you to tie me to the bed and beat me with a whip, dressed in a G-string and black leather boots.'

She laughed nervously. 'I didn't even think of anything like that. I'm far too conventional.'

'I myself have always found conventional methods extremely satisfactory. Whatever is right for you.'

She managed another weak smile, wanting more than ever to escape. 'All this talk is making me even more petrified.'

'In that case, shall we skip the dessert and the coffee?'

'Yes, I couldn't eat another thing, I . . .'

'Would you like a liqueur to give you courage?'

He went to the sideboard and took out a dusty bottle. She took the small glass he offered and sipped it. It tasted of apricots, sweet, sharp and strong.

'Have one of these,' he said, producing a huge box of gold-wrapped chocolates.

She tried to make the drink last, but suddenly found she had finished. Matters could not be delayed any longer.

He held out his hand. His palm was damp and it came to her that he, the sophisticated Henri, was nervous.

As he led her up the stairs, she found herself swaying and stopped, clutching the banister. Gently but firmly, Henri pulled her on. Finally they arrived at his bedroom where one blue Chinese lamp illuminated the large double bed. They stood looking at each other. He seemed like a stranger rather than the neighbour she had known for so long.

When he drew her towards him, he was less tall than she remembered, not much above her own height. She put her arms around his waist and found it a long stretch. Richard was, had been, tall and slim and young. Now this man, who was none of these things, was going to kiss her. She steeled herself not to turn away.

He tasted of brandy and chocolate. A smell of masculinity and expensive aftershave enveloped her. It was all right. She found she could respond a little. He drew back and unwrapped her slowly and carefully, like a long-awaited but fragile present. All the while with gentle fingers he touched and admired.

She watched him, as if from a great distance, as if she were an observer at the scene or an actress playing a part. Soon she was standing shivering and naked in the middle of the room and, conscious of this alarming fact, she ran to the bed and hid beneath the covers.

While he undressed she kept her eyes closed, not wanting to see him. He was beside her in a very short time.

She held her breath.

'My lovely, lovely Kim,' he murmured.

With numerous subtle detours, he began to make skilful unhurried progress, exploring and approving and exploring again. Relaxing a little, eyes still closed, she found herself responding to the tenderness in his voice and the finesse of his slow sensual approach. Gradually his touch became more and more intimate, more and more arousing. Now and then he stopped, tantalisingly, and she waited, half-dreading, half-longing for his next advance.

Finally she whispered, dazed but insistent, that she couldn't wait any longer, that she wanted him now.

And when he took her at last there was for a moment a strangeness, a sense of violation. Then, quite soon, it seemed that making love with Henri was the most natural thing in the world.

Afterwards he held her in his arms, kissing and caressing her, repeating again and again that she was an adorable wonderful creature.

'I'm not used to it – being cherished like this, I mean,' she said, warm in the glow of their mutual gratitude.

He looked down at her. 'I hope to cherish you again before you go home, and for a little longer,' he said smiling. He touched her face. 'You don't know how happy you have made me, my beautiful love.'

'I'm glad. And I'm happy too,' she said truthfully.

On her way home she laughed inwardly with a mixture of guilty relief and jubilation. It was an appalling way to behave, but Thursdays were going to be all right. She was now a kind of high-class tart, a rich man's mistress, and it had turned out a great deal better than she deserved.

CHAPTER 5

Neat and wholesome in a tweed skirt, Polly settled herself down in the kitchen and accepted a cup of coffee. 'Well? Tell me all. Must say, this is more interesting than a soap opera. With you around, one hardly misses English telly at all. So go on, how was it?'

Kim tried to hide an annoying blush. 'Quite OK, actually. But that's enough about that.' She smiled brightly. 'How was your committee meeting yesterday? I bet you were a very efficient chairman.'

'Chairperson, please. The International Spouses Club is strictly PC, but don't try and distract me. I want to hear all about last night, every detail. Well, perhaps not every detail would be suitable for my delicate ears.'

'Maybe it's not your business, Polly dear.'

Polly grinned. 'You made it my business by telling me your problems. And I *am* your closest friend.'

'I only told you about Henri because you would've been suspicious and wondered why I wasn't broke any more. It's a secret, remember? You swore you wouldn't tell a soul, even Joe.'

'Of course. My lips are sealed. Anyway, I only ever tell my husband what he needs to know and he certainly doesn't need to know about this. But just reassure me about your night of passion. I was pretty worried about the whole deal. I mean, taking a lover for financial reasons is not exactly normal behaviour for a lady like you.'

'We all change when needs must,' said Kim, reddening again. 'Besides, last time we discussed it you urged me to go ahead. Seem to remember you thought a sugar daddy was an ace idea, in view of my limited qualifications for any other kind of employment.'

'I was joking, sort of. I knew you were desperate and Henri is still reasonably attractive in a crumpled sort of way, apart from being a tad fat and too old.'

'So you said. Several times. Anyway, he's not fat. Just rather solid.'

'Well, you would know all about that, wouldn't you?' Polly grinned. 'Sorry. Actually when I arrived I thought you looked very pretty and glowing, and a bit smug, so I guess it must have been OK. Or did you just lie back and think of England?'

Kim laughed. 'All right, you can stop worrying. I may've crossed the line that separates ladies from the rest, but it was fine – rather fun, if you must know – but never, ever ask me about it again.'

Polly gave a low whistle. 'Well, well, well, good for Henri. Obviously life in the old dog yet.'

'Please, Pol, no more remarks of that nature.

The discussion stops here. I made my decision for my own reasons, and luckily it turned out OK, much nicer than I deserve, I admit.'

'Right, I'll change the subject then. See what a good friend I am – I've found you a job, only part-time, not well paid enough to save you from a fate worse than death but better than nothing. I don't think you've met Beverly-Jane, the health freak? No? Well, she's an enterprising American gal who's got herself a grant from some Swiss-International foundation to produce a book on alternative medicine, and she needs someone to write it with her. So I suggested you. I said you were a good writer and would be extremely interested in her work.'

'But I don't go in for all that weirdo stuff. Anyway why should she choose me? There are loads of more experienced journalists in Geneva. What about . . .'

'Why are you always putting yourself down? You'll never get anywhere unless you have confidence in your own abilities. That's what Joe says and he's right.'

'Yes, Polly,' said Kim with mock humility.

'Anyway, back to Beverly-Jane – she needs a Brit because the book has to be in British English according to the rules of her grant. Apparently it was set up according to the will of an eccentric English lady, widow of some old Swiss banker. I showed BJ your travel articles and she thought they were great. And another factor is that her husband works for Joe and so she wants to please me. She's the ambitious type. But when I gave her the impression you were into alternative health too, that clinched it.'

Kim grinned. 'Don't you think she may notice my ignorance on the subject?'

'You can mug it up in a couple of days. Anyway old BJ is far to busy rabbiting on to listen to what anyone else says – or doesn't say.'

From the outside Beverly-Jane's apartment looked conventional enough, but inside Kim felt as if she had walked into a market garden. Vegetation covered every shelf, not house plants but tray upon tray of bean sprouts, bowls of cress, young wheat and other seedlings she didn't recognise. The rest of the decor tended towards the ornate oriental with two black Buddhas, large china elephants and wooden Thai temple dogs. The walls were hung with Japanese prints and bamboo screens stood in place of curtains and doors.

A trim youthful middle-aged blonde, Beverly-Jane – 'Call me BJ', she insisted – shimmered about the room in tight black trousers and a flowing multi-coloured shirt. She looked like a dancer dressed in butterfly costume, Kim thought.

'This is going to be just great. I knew as soon as I met you that we were going to get along together. Polly told me about your problems and I knew I had to help. That we would help each other. Polly is a lovely gracious person, isn't she? I just adore her, don't you?'

'Oh yes,' said Kim. Polly, *gracious*? She took out her notebook. 'So where do we start?'

'Maybe we should find out a little more about each other first. Lock into each other's biorhythms. How old are you, Kim? Forty-five? You look a little older. Did you ever try Omega 3?'

'No,' said Kim grimly. She was more used to being told she looked young for her age. All this tension must be taking its toll.

'Well, maybe it's something you British don't know about. You probably worry about fat in the diet as we all do, but Omega 3 is a good lipid – kind of super polyunsaturated – we get it from wild game and grass-fed animals and particularly fatty fish.'

'Oh, you mean cod liver oil?'

'Right, very good, Kim, and every cell of our body needs this fat and we can't manufacture it ourselves.'

'Not sure I want to manufacture any more fat.'

'Right, I know, but I'm sure I can help you with your little figure problem. As we get older, we need to eat fewer calories and take more exercise. I used to be a little overweight myself. I wonder if you're doing the right kind of exercise programme, Kim. I'll show you my routine. Don't worry, it's low-impact and I'll start you off at the beginner level.'

'Very kind, but maybe another day . . . Uh, BJ, don't you think we should talk about the book? Should we outline some kind of plan? What structure do you have in mind?'

'I appreciate your serious attitude. Now where to start? I have so much I need to share. My life has been transformed by some of the discoveries I've made, but everything is kind of diffuse, inter-related yet individual.'

'Then how about structuring it like a medical book – on parts of the body, like the skin or the bones?'

'No, no, I'm interested in the whole person, not the parts. That's where conventional doctors go wrong.'

Kim thought and then she said, 'Well, I know it's a cliché but perhaps something simple like A to Z then?'

BJ smiled happily. 'Great idea – we'll start with Aromatherapy and go all the way down to Zones. A to Zee, New Health for You'n'Me. I just love it, Kim.'

'Zones?'

'Yeah, Zone therapy, facial massage. I guess rubbing the forehead is known to be relaxing but did you know that pressure just under the mouth can help with constipation? And rotating around the skin on the jaw bone stimulates the sex glands and can cure impotence.'

Kim managed to avoid raising her eyebrows. 'How fascinating. But shouldn't we be getting back to the alphabet plan? What comes after Aromatherapy?'

'Well, we can have Bache Flower Remedies, then Colonic Irrigation. Maybe we should put that under I for Irrigation because there's Crystals too. And then we have Colour Therapy. Oh dear, that's too much for C.'

'Remind me about Colour Therapy.'

'You know, the colours of the rainbow are part of the electromagnetic spectrum. Using radiation through colour we re-establish our balances – emotional and physical – and restore our aura. We always have to think about the balance between the aura and the chakras. Colour can help us with this. Of course, we can combine aromatherapy with colour therapy.'

'Uh, yes, of course. Well, what about D?'

BJ stared at the ceiling. 'I can't think of D right now. Or E.' She rubbed her hands together again.

'Vitamin E perhaps?' suggested Kim.

'No, we should save vitamins for V. E? E?'

'Why don't we just jot down everything you want to write about and we'll talk about the alphabet next time. Maybe it's better to concentrate on aromatherapy today. Have you got any research notes I can write up?'

'Yes, I do, but even better I have the essential oils. I'll give you some.' She shimmered away to the kitchen and returned brandishing a small red box full of minute bottles. 'Read the notes carefully. It is important to use the right oil for the right purpose. Don't you just love the avocado? Rub some on that dry patch of skin on your elbows. Take them all, take them all. You look like you could use them.'

'Thanks,' said Kim shortly. The oils were expensive, she knew. It was a generous present. All the same she had a strong desire to punch BJ on the nose. 'So what time do you want me here tomorrow?'

'Oh any time, any time. Just give me a call when you're ready to come along. Any Tuesday, any Wednesday. They're my right-brain creative days when I don't believe in watching the clock too much. You just fit me in when you can. Let it all hang loose, Kim. I sure do.'

Back at home, slurping around in her almond oil bath Kim decided, rather to her annoyance, that she did feel rejuvenated. Maybe there could be certain advantages in working with BJ. Thoughtfully she rubbed the appropriate zone of her forehead in the hope of bringing the promised peace and tranquillity to her nervous system.

Her conscience was far from clear, but leaving aside the moral aspects – not easy – her situation had improved since those awful days after Richard's disappearance. She had found a temporary way to survive: apart from teaching English, she now had two additional part-time jobs, editor and kept woman. As the first two were not well paid, Henri was her true means of support. And James's, of course. She had done it for James but, really, that was a pretty weak excuse for bad, if expedient, behaviour. Then she smiled to herself, thinking of Thursday evening.

Today she had blushed with shame – and relief – when she'd opened her bank statement to find that Henri's generous payments had arrived in her account. But quite apart from this, many new aspects of the situation worried her. She remembered the way his eyes lit up whenever he saw her. What would happen if Henri's current light-hearted crush on her developed into something more serious? Maybe she was being irresponsible towards him. But he was a sophisticated man, he would know it had to be a temporary arrangement.

After her bath she stood naked in front of the mirror. Despite BJ's rude remarks, she thought she looked a little thinner, but there was something else. Something Polly had noticed. A new self-confidence, a new awareness perhaps. Richard had made her feel dull and unwanted. Henri made her shine.

She grinned at her reflection again and reminded herself she was not in fact Kim the youthful sex goddess but good old Kim, the housewife and mother. Quickly she dressed and went downstairs to cook supper.

As she peeled and chopped and rattled pans, her mood darkened. She kept looking at a faded holiday photograph of herself and Richard that James had pinned on the kitchen notice board. Richard looked more handsome than ever, thin, tanned and fit, like a film star playing one of those second world war heroes. He had his arm around her. The perfect husband. The flaws didn't show in a photograph.

Funny how in every photo he looked the same, forever young. Now he always would be.

She brooded about her appointment with the British Consul next day. Having heard nothing further from the Foreign Office in London, despite all her letters, she'd decided to make an approach locally. She desperately needed some information, anything, about the plane crash. Even if they never found his body, it was wrong not to know more about where and how he had died. Once she knew that, she could bury him, mentally, with the right amount of mourning. Then maybe she'd feel shriven, absolved, and maybe one small part of her large burden of guilt would slip away.

Walking up rue de Vermont dressed in her best suit, Kim expected a building appropriate to the British Consulate-General and was surprised to find it housed in a small and undistinguished modern office block. She entered the lobby and, studying the signs, discovered that the Consulate did not even occupy the whole building. The United Kingdom had offices on the fifth and sixth floors.

A man of her own age came out of the lift and eyed her up and down. She smiled back at him because, tall in his grey suit and striped shirt, he was so obviously British.

'If you want the Consulate,' he said in English, 'you have to take the other lift.'

She thanked him, faintly annoyed that he, in turn, had immediately recognised her nationality. When she reached the sixth floor, she found a mammoth queue of variegated people. She waited her turn with increasing anxiety and impatience, but was finally informed that the Consul was ill and, as her appointment was not an emergency, it should be rescheduled.

Having steeled herself to discuss Richard's case, she felt a devastating sense of anti-climax but there was no point in making a scene. There were plenty of foreigners around doing just that. Upset and discouraged, she took the lift back to the lobby where she again saw the same Englishman pacing about by the plate-glass entrance.

'Hello,' he said. 'That was quick. Distressed British Subjects, as we call 'em in the trade, have been known to spend days up there.'

'I'm sure I must've been at least half an hour. What a waste of time. Though I'm not as cross as some of the other customers.'

He smiled in a friendly way. 'Actually, I thought as you came out of the lift you did look rather fed up. I've been waiting here for ages myself, and personally I'm extremely distressed about it. I seem to have been stood up.'

'Oh dear. Well, if you'll excuse me . . .'

He took a step or two after her. 'D'you know the way all right? All the roads around here look the same.'

'Oh yes. I'm not a tourist. I live in Geneva.'

To her surprise, he began to accompany her down the street. He had a determined manner appropriate to his broad-shouldered Empire-building good looks. She was about to say something repressive when it occurred to her that he might be able to help. 'You don't work in the Consulate yourself, do you?' she asked.

'No, on the other floor. I'm a diplomat in the UK Mission to the United Nations.'

'Mission?'

'Yes, a diplomatic mission, of course. Not a religious one. Some people get confused.'

She smiled politely, disguising the fact she had been momentarily confused herself.

'So if you live here you must have been to the UN, have you?' he asked, waving his hand in the general direction of the Palais des Nations.

'No, I'm ashamed to say.'

'But you should go on a tour. It's a truly amazing place. It's hard to imagine what all those thousands of bureaucrats from all those countries do there all day.'

She stood still. 'Do the Indonesians have people here?'

'Yes, of course. Why?'

'Oh, just wondered. Well, look, I'm nearly at my car. Nice to talk to you. Goodbye.'

He stopped beside her. 'I suppose you wouldn't help me out, would you?' he asked in a rush.

'Help you out?' She tried to sound as discouraging as possible. She tended to distrust handsome men on principle and this one was altogether too forward, however polite his manner. Well, perhaps he wasn't exactly handsome. His hair was an ordinary sort of brown and his eyes were a medium sort of blue – bright, intelligent, humorous eyes, though. His face was weather-beaten and well-used, but the whole effect was quite attractive, some might say very attractive.

'You see,' he said, 'I was supposed to be taking a visiting diplomat out to a business lunch at the Perle du Lac and he hasn't shown up. And as the table is booked, I wonder if you would care to join me? Unless you go there every week and are bored rigid by it.'

She smiled at the thought of such luxury. 'Hardly every week, no. It's a very generous invitation but I couldn't possibly—'

'And then you could tell me about your interest in Indonesia.'

She hesitated. He really might be a useful contact, she told herself. 'But we haven't been introduced,' she said with a smile.

'How remiss of me. My name is Mark Fitzpatrick. Nationality British, age forty-nine, solvent, marital status semi-detached and my hobbies are skiing and tennis. My ambitions are to promote world peace, save the environment and, most important, take you out to lunch.' He held out his hand.

She shook it. Then she said as gravely as possible, 'Kim Ellis, forty-five, not very solvent, so my ambition is to make some money. Marital status uncertain . . . but I'm not free,' she added hastily.

'But you would be free just to come to lunch today, wouldn't you? It would be a great pleasure and it would also save my face with the head waiter of the Perle.'

'Well, all right, thank you very much,' she said, ignoring the warning bells ringing at the back of her mind. It's OK, she told herself, I can handle this. I'll explain things to him so he isn't under any illusion. Anyway, men and women have business lunches all the time. It's normal.

Mark studied her as they walked down towards the lake. It was her magnificent thick dark hair that had first attracted him. Then he had noticed the eyes, not startlingly large but light navy blue with curling lashes. Her long jacket disguised her figure, but she could be a little plump. A fault on the right side. Mark had gone off skinny women, women like his soon-to-be ex-wife, Bella.

The fact that this woman had confessed to an uncertain marital status was intriguing. He would find out the rest at lunch. It was his profession to glean information, and he wanted to know everything there was to know about Kim. Her suit was smart but not excessively fashionable and she described herself as an impoverished expatriate – normally a contradiction in terms. She wore a wedding ring but perhaps her husband had left her. Or was that wishful thinking? He must refrain from too many questions at first.

'I never get tired of the views here,' she said as they reached the lake. Her sudden smile was so lovely that he only narrowly avoided walking into one of the ubiquitous plane trees lining the pavement.

She seemed at home in the grand restaurant and tactfully selected the set lunch menu – rather to his relief as A La Carte at the Perle was serious money. He noticed she had a good appetite. Bella had always picked at her food, much to his annoyance.

When Kim had polished off her *salade tiède* and her *filet de turbotin*, she began to tell him without much prompting about her husband's plane crash and how she wanted to find out what had happened. She told her story calmly but her voice grew increasingly strained and she kept drawing invisible patterns on the tablecloth with her fingernail. Mark longed to take her in his arms there and then. He found himself promising to dig up all the Indonesian contacts he knew, though he advised her to persist with the proper channels at the Consulate.

He was impressed to discover she lived in Cologny, a fact that suggested she could not be all that impoverished. When he asked her about her money-making ambitions, she said she'd been joking. She wasn't really broke. She had several jobs. She became more cheerful when he encouraged her to talk about teaching English to absent-minded old ladies and editing a crazy alternative health book. She was even more expansive about her son.

Her manner was open and natural, but not in any way flirtatious or responsive to flirtation. In view of her recent bereavement, Mark decided he would have to take things extremely slowly.

Kim smiled at him. 'When you gave me your instant beauty-queen-style CV you said you were semi-detached. What does that mean?'

'It means my wife and I have separated, with divorce proceedings under way. We haven't been living together for a while.'

'Oh, I'm sorry.'

'So am I, in a way, but it was never a great success even at the beginning.'

'I know what you mean,' she replied, and then looked down. 'But what about children? Do you have any?'

'No, there was a time when we thought of starting a family, but it didn't happen. Fortunately, as it now turns out.'

'Yes, just as well,' said Kim awkwardly. As if by mutual agreement, the conversation turned to general matters.

Later, as he walked her back to the car, she said, 'I seem to have been doing all the talking, but it's your fault. You asked me so many questions.' Her wonderful smile flashed again.

He grinned. 'Next time we meet I'll tell you the story of my life in minute detail.' He looked at her and then he said impulsively, 'When will you come and have dinner with me? How about Thursday?'

Flushing, she looked down again. 'I'm busy on Thursdays.'

'Oh well, what day could you come then?'

'I don't know. There's my son, you see.'

'Are babysitters that hard to find in Geneva?'

She continued to stare at the pavement. 'No, but he's rather unsettled at the moment, about his father.'

'Of course, how stupid of me. Perhaps later on. But while he's at school, you could have lunch with me again soon, couldn't you? Next week?'

'I don't know. I don't really eat lunch usually.'

'If you make an exception, I can introduce you to my Indonesian colleague.'

She smiled at last. 'Thank you, that would be very helpful.' Then she took a deep breath and said seriously. 'I do want to meet the Indonesian, but I just want to say, the thing is, Mark, look, if I come out to lunch again, it won't be a date with a capital D, will it? Because I can't go in for that sort of thing.'

'I understand. Forgive me. You're newly widowed. But if you need advice or a friendly shoulder to cry on . . .'

'Sorry if I sounded presumptuous or hopelessly unsophisticated,' she stuttered. 'I meant, I'm not sure how . . . I just want to be absolutely clear that I don't consider myself free.'

'Because there's a faint chance your husband is still alive?'

She hesitated. 'There isn't much hope but . . .'

Mark said gently, 'I'm sorry.'

'No, no. In different circumstances . . .' Her voice trailed off. 'Sorry, but thank you for a very nice lunch. It was such a treat. Made me feel a lot better.'

'Then you'll have lunch again. Here's my card – with the official crest so you can see how extremely respectable I am.'

CHAPTER 6

James was sitting on his mother's bed watching her make up her face. 'Why are you going out again, Mummy? You have dinner with Mr Marechal every week and you don't take me. And now you're going out to another different party.'

'As I told you, I go to Mr Marechal's on Thursdays to help him with his book.' Though she could hardly explain the true nature of her evenings with Henri, she felt uncomfortable deceiving her child.

'Anyway,' she added with a smile, 'you often go round to see him on your own, and you play golf leaving me behind, and there's all the other sports you do without taking me.'

'Yes, but that's not at night,' said James plaintively. 'What time will you be back?'

'After you're asleep. It's a dinner party.'

'Where?'

'Over in Petit Sacconnex.'

'Whose house?'

'No one you know.'

James studied her again. 'Why are you putting all that stuff on your eyes? You don't usually. You didn't when you went to Henri's.'

'I have to be smarter tonight. It's a formal kind of evening. D'you like my dress? I haven't worn it for ages.'

He looked her up and down. 'Yes, I think you look very pretty, all blue and shiny. And you smell nice . . . Mummy, why were you singing to yourself just now?'

'I often sing.'

'No, you don't. You never used to sing at all.'

Kim sang a little more as she drove to Petit Sacconnex where Mark Fitzpatrick lived, according to the invitation in her handbag. It was a stiff white card formally engraved to the effect that the Counsellor (Economic Affairs) of the United Kingdom Mission to the United Nations requested the pleasure of her company. Someone with neat handwriting, perhaps his secretary, had filled in her name and the time and date of the party. It was an extremely elegant invitation of the type that Kim hadn't received for years and she couldn't resist accepting it, even though she had no intention of encouraging Mr Mark Fitzpatrick, however respectable he might be.

She found the grand block of flats more easily than she expected and decided to wait a while in the car park in order to avoid arriving early. Then after a few minutes she began to feel conspicuous, so she entered the lobby and found Mark's name on the list of residents. Waiting for the lift, she passed the time by reading a huge notice detailing the many rules of good behaviour required of the tenants: no noise, no showers or flushing of lavatories after 10 pm, no washing of cars anywhere any time, proper supervision of children and dogs, and strict instructions about using the communal laundry room only during the times allocated to each apartment. She smiled, remembering anecdotes about Swiss neighbours and their somewhat officious nature. Every Swiss wants to be a policeman, according to Henri.

Finally on the sixth floor, she stood outside Mark's flat and wondered why she hesitated to ring the bell. A waiter in a white jacket answered the door and ushered her into a large room decorated like a display in Harrods's furnishing department, with seas of beige carpeting, mahogany reproduction tables and plump chintz sofas.

To her embarrassment, she was the first to arrive. Mark greeted her effusively. 'You look wonderful,' he said, gazing at her.

She smiled back and then turned away, admiring the apartment, all his books, his traditional watercolours, the view over the city at night and anything else she could think of in a voice which annoyed her by its breathlessness. Stop gushing, you fool, she said to herself.

'Only the pictures and books are mine. The rest, the furniture, belongs to Her Majesty,' he said.

'Kind of her to provide you with such a nice flat.' Waving her hands towards a set of prints, she asked, 'Is that Winchester Cathedral? Such a lovely town.'

'Yes, I was at school there.'

'Really?' Why was she sounding like a half-wit?

'So glad you came,' he said after a pause. 'I was afraid you might not.'

'But you sent me a formal invitation and I accepted.'

There was another silence between them and then the door bell rang. Mark touched her hand and went to greet several guests who had arrived at the same time. Though she was introduced to them all, Kim forgot their names immediately. While she was making small talk to a grey-haired Swiss couple, out of the corner of her eye she could see Mark pinned into a corner by a buxom young blonde who batted her eyelashes in the swooping style of Marilyn Monroe.

Kim found herself at the opposite end of the long dining table from her host. Seating was 'according to protocol' he explained quietly as he showed her to her chair. The blonde, who turned out to be married to a senior official from Brussels, was sitting on Mark's right-hand side and the other place next to him was occupied by an older woman with a severe grey face, no doubt also the wife of a VIP.

Kim tried to show an interest in the conversation about the World Trade Organisation. Her neighbours at the table were a plump monosyllabic Finn and handsome but deadly serious

Swedish professor of statistics, and she sought in vain for common ground. Judging by Marilyn Monroe's tinkling laughter, the talk was a great deal more amusing down the other end of the table, but whenever Kim looked in his direction, Mark caught her eye and smiled.

His manner was urbane and sophisticated, but there was something about his macho, healthy appearance that didn't fit with her idea of a typical stuffy Foreign Office type or pale intellectual Wykehamist. He looked as if he should be on the rugby pitch, no, striding across the grouse moor or sailing a yacht over ten-foot waves.

'What are your views on the Swiss education system?' asked the professor, interrupting her reverie. She gathered together her scattered opinions and conveyed them as best she could.

Though the food was rich and delicious, and efficiently served by the waiter and an immaculate maid in black, it was a disappointingly dull evening. An Indonesian diplomat had been invited but apparently was unable to come. Mark himself seemed too preoccupied with his duties as host to pay her much attention and she wondered why she had been asked.

Some time after eleven o'clock the party broke up and she put on her coat in the hall along with the other guests. She was about to leave with the Swiss couple when Mark detained her. 'Don't go for a minute. I need to talk to you,' he murmured.

No way. No way. 'I should be going. Could I phone you?'

'No, not really.' He smiled at the Swiss couple. 'Goodnight again, madame, monsieur,' he said firmly. 'I promised to lend Mrs Ellis a book and I quite forgot.' He bundled them into the lift and then frog-marched Kim back into the sitting room.

'What book?' she asked, annoyed that she had so easily been persuaded to stay.

'Take your coat off again. Let me get you a drink.'

'No thanks, I'm driving.'

'Some coffee. No? Mineral water then.' He removed her coat and poured her a glass of Perrier. Then he sat beside her, whisky in hand. 'Phew. Thank God that's over. Rather a stuffy party, sorry. Hope you weren't too bored.' He leant towards her. 'But I do need to ask you some questions. Firstly, how did you get on with Helen?'

She took a deep breath. 'Helen? Oh, yes, the Consul. She was very kind. But my second visit wasn't much more fruitful than the first. She promised to make some follow-up enquiries through the Foreign Office. She seemed to think I needed some sort of letter from the Indonesians about, well, about the crash and a copy of the passenger list which would sort of prove that Richard . . . But I haven't heard anything from her,' she added, as calmly as she could.

'Poor Kim.'

There was a silence.

Eventually he asked, 'What was your husband's job exactly?'

'Thought I told you. He was a kind of salesman. His company deals in machinery. They're middlemen. They help people in one country export it to another. It seemed to involve Richard travelling all around the world.'

'What sort of machinery?'

'I don't know. Industrial, I think.'

'Was Richard an engineer?'

'No, no, he started off in the Army and then left early and became a glorified salesman of anything he could sell. For instance he worked for one of those big pharmaceutical companies in one country and then he sold tractors and things, big farm machinery, somewhere else.'

'Hm,' said Mark again.

'So where's all this leading?'

'It's leading to the fact that my Indonesian colleague has heard of him and about the plane crash.'

Suddenly cold, she asked, 'And what did he say?' Her fingers dug hard into her palms.

'He's making more enquiries.'

She stood up. 'Is that all? Is that all? Everyone says that. Endless enquiries and we never get anywhere.' Then, before she could stop herself, she burst into tears.

Mark took her in his arms, rocking her gently. 'I'm so sorry, so sorry. I didn't mean to upset you. I know it isn't much to go on.'

She pulled away from him, trying desperately to control herself.

'It must be dreadful losing someone you love and not knowing what happened,' he said.

'But I didn't love him, that's the awful thing,' she burst out, beginning to cry more stormily.

He took her in his arms again, stroking her hair. He said nothing until the sobs subsided. 'I've been in the same boat so I know. Do you want to talk about it?'

'No,' she said abruptly. 'Sorry. I'd better go.'

'You can't go yet. Your eyes are all red and swollen.'

She smiled weakly and pushed back her hair.

'That's better,' he said. 'You don't look good when you cry.'

'Bloody rude and insensitive . . . and not very diplomatic,' she said, managing another feeble smile.

'Are you sure you don't want to talk about your marriage?'

'No,' she said flatly, 'you talk. I don't want to get all weepy again.'

'I don't mind. Be as emotional as you like.'

She shook her head. 'I find it easier to cope if I try and bottle things up a bit, whatever people say. I'm afraid if I let go, then I may lose it completely.'

'Whatever you want. Perhaps you're right. Come to think of it, it's only the current generation who think one should let it all hang out – the current generation of Westerners, that is. People like the Thais still admire restraint, disapprove of emotion.'

'Like us, the so-called British stiff upper lip, no drama permitted.'

Richard, a major dramatist, had disliked 'fussing' in other people, though his own fusses were another matter, she remembered.

She looked up and realised that Mark was waiting for her to speak. 'But anyway,' she said, 'I'd much rather hear about you, your marriage.'

He raised his eyebrows. 'So you want me to tell you about my personal problems, but not discuss your own?'

'Yes, if you don't mind. It may help my sense of proportion. As long as it's not too painful for you.'

'No. More banal than painful really.' He smiled. 'I'll have to bore you into a calmer state of mind then.'

'I won't be bored,' she said. 'But tell me quickly because it's late.'

'It's not a quick story. In any case, the very least you can do after weeping all over my new suit is to let me confess all in as much detail as I want.'

She looked at her watch. 'OK, I leave at midnight. That gives you ten minutes.'

'You're a hard woman,' he said. 'Go and wash your face and I'll start.'

In the shiny bathroom she splashed some cold water on her eyes and combed her hair. Her mascara had run so she looked like a drunk racoon. What a mess, she said to herself, rubbing her eyes with a tissue and making them redder still. Past caring, she returned to the sofa to sit beside him. 'OK, tell me the whole story. How did it begin?' she asked.

He paused, staring into his whisky. She watched him. He looked older when he didn't smile.

'It began twenty years ago, when we met,' he said, 'and when you're young, as you know, you often fall in love with the image of a person. It's a very common phenomenon. I'd just come back from Thailand and Bella seemed to me the epitome of English womanhood, blonde, pretty and athletic. I was bowled over, mad about her. When I got to know her better, I vaguely realised that she didn't have many interests outside looking good and being sporty, but I thought I'd be able to broaden her outlook.'

She smiled. How typically male.

As if she had spoken aloud, Mark went on, 'Yes, I suppose I was rather arrogant as a young man, and over-ambitious too. Bella wasn't ambitious at all. She worked at the General Trading Company selling equipment for the upper classes like picnic baskets at five hundred pounds a throw, nice quality guaranteed, she would say.'

'I see. A sort of jolly Sloane.'

'Yes, quite jolly in those days, and I thought it was an advantage she didn't have a serious job. You see, lots of diplomats' wives hate moving abroad because it means disrupting their careers and most of them complain ad nauseam about trailing around the world as appendages to their husbands. But Bella said she wouldn't mind being just a wife.' He paused.

'And?'

'What I didn't realise is that girls like her don't flourish abroad any better than career women. She's just too English to adapt. Mind you, for any woman, any person, it's a difficult gypsy existence . . . well, you understand.'

'Yes,' she said. 'I know all about travelling, fitting in everywhere and nowhere.'

He looked at her. 'Not even in England?'

'Not really, not these days. I feel odd, different.'

'But you cope.'

'More or less,' she said thoughtfully. 'You learn to grow a tough shell and carry it along. And I used to try to stand back and be self-sufficient. That way, it's easier to move on. I mean, sometimes you feel it's not worth getting to know people properly and making friends because you'll be going soon.'

'Yes,' he said. 'I know.'

'When I was young, though, I used to enjoy the life, wandering around the world.'

He smiled, searching her face. 'You're not so very old.'

'I know, but . . . In the early days I really used to like the excitement and the challenge, but we moved so often.'

'How often?'

'Well, almost every year.'

'My God, why?'

'Richard, he changed jobs a lot.'

'Poor Kim, what a nightmare. And it must've been hard work too, always having to find somewhere new to live and dealing with tricky foreign landlords, and the new school and so forth.'

She smiled. 'Yes, all the boring details that men tend to assign to women. But I survived. Had to.'

He asked her about the most difficult place she'd ever lived and she told him about Lagos, the constant power cuts, the burglaries and the general terrifying insecurity. He listened attentively to everything she said. He was a good listener, she thought, when he went to fetch another drink. Unless it was a line, part of his seduction technique . . . It struck her that seduction by Mark wouldn't be out of the question. If it weren't for Henri. Hastily she looked down to avoid communicating her thoughts.

Mark was talking about Asian plumbing and how it made you appreciate somewhere like Geneva even more.

'Yes, this is a wonderfully well-organised place,' she said.

'And do you have a good landlord here?'

She flushed. 'He's very nice – but we're talking about you now. Go on about your wife.'

His smile vanished. 'Oh, well, you see,' he said with a sigh, 'even at the beginning Bella never liked living abroad, just couldn't manage without all the social things that made her tick.'

'You mean Sloane Square and the parents' house in Hampshire?'

'Gloucestershire, actually.'

'So this Joan Hunter-Dunn missed the cool Cotswold sun?'

He laughed. 'Exactly. She might have been OK somewhere like Colonial India, but of course that sort of society doesn't exist any more. She didn't like diplomatic parties, found them impossibly dull and stuffy.' He waved his arm towards the dining table.

Rather nice hands. Large capable hands for a large capable man. 'Um, maybe Bella could have a point,' she said.

'Oh dear. Were you bored stiff tonight? As I said, protocol demands where people sit, but I thought you'd like the handsome prof. Seemed a nice fellow, only met him once before.'

'I don't think I locked into his esoteric wavelength, though Marilyn Monroe seemed to have no trouble surfing in on yours.'

He smiled. 'How very disrespectful you are about my guests and my party as a whole. I shan't ask you again.'

She was contrite. 'Sorry, I didn't mean to be rude. It must be a strange life for you too, being official all the time and entertaining strangers in your official flat with Government furniture and everything.'

'One gets used to it, fitting into a shell, as you put it, except mine is a ready-made Foreign Office shell. Actually it lessens the culture shock if you have the same furniture everywhere you go. And moving around is made slightly easier for us: there are embassy staff who help with housing and so on. In fact, as one gets more senior, the main problem in diplomatic life is to avoid becoming pompous. Or turning into an over-polite automaton.'

'You don't seem too hopelessly pompous yet. Nor are you exactly over-polite.'

He smiled at her, a long steady smile, his eyes bright, and she was again aware of the strong current of sexual tension underlying this friendly sympathetic conversation. 'But you keep changing the subject,' she said hastily. 'Go on about Bella. So did she stop going abroad with you?'

'Yes, gradually. She began to spend more and more time in our house in Richmond supervising endless renovations. Then she got a job with an interior decorator friend and became a kind of career woman after all. Now she wants to marry one of her clients who has a large country house – sort of chap she should have married in the first place, I suppose.'

He spoke calmly enough, but there was an edge to his voice which made her want to comfort him in turn. She began to stretch out her hand but then restrained herself. 'Oh dear, poor Mark,' she said.

'I don't mind. In reality, it ended a long time before we began divorce proceedings, but for one reason or another we drifted along in our parallel worlds without officially separating until now.'

'You sound very tolerant about it all; sanguine is the word I'm searching for.'

He sighed again and took a large sip of his whisky. 'Yes, I suppose I passed through the furious, resentful stage a while ago.'

A question had been on her mind for some time. After a pause she asked casually, 'So do you have anyone, a girlfriend, I mean?'

He leant back. 'No, but in the past I admit there was usually someone wherever I was posted, nothing serious though.'

'Why not?'

'I don't know. Once bitten, twice shy, I suppose. I was afraid of another mistake.'

She shook her head. 'So all over the world there are broken-hearted women weeping because you have loved them and left.'

'No, no.' He looked a little guilty.

'I bet it's yes, yes,' she said, standing up.

He rose to his feet. 'Where are you going?' he asked softly.

'Home, of course.'

'Stay a little longer, please.' He touched her arm.

Suppressing a sudden frisson, she said quickly, 'No, there's the babysitter. She's only a teenager. I can't keep her up any longer.' A lie. The babysitter was spending the night as usual.

Before she could avoid him, Mark took her face in his hands, gazing down at her intently. 'When shall I see you again?'

Feeling as gauche as a schoolgirl, she broke away. 'I don't know,' she called over her shoulder as she hurried into the hall. 'Thank you very much for the party. I'll get my coat. Is this where you put it? Oh dear, no. Seems to be the broom cupboard.'

'Calm down. Here's your coat. Let me hold it for you. Take your time. I'm not going to attack you, not this evening, anyway.'

She smiled and buttoned up her velvet collar.

He bent down to her. 'Now kiss me goodnight – on the cheek will do for now – and then we can part friends.'

She did as she was told. He was so tall that it was difficult to kiss him without leaning against him, but she managed.

'You see how trustworthy I am,' he said, keeping his hands behind his back.

'Yes, but—'

'You're going to tell me yet again that our friendship has to be platonic for now. It's OK. I accept that.'

'But I mean it,' she said seriously. 'I'm not being coy. You must understand, I'm not free, and won't be in the future.'

He opened the door for her. 'I know, you have to stay inside your shell for the time being. But you must come out some time. I'm a patient man. Goodnight, Kim.'

When she reached her car, she sat for a while without moving. Then she drove slowly back to Cologny. Despite his words, somehow she thought it unlikely he was strong on patience.

CHAPTER 7

James arrived back from a visit to Henri pink with delight. 'Mr Marechal wants to take me to the Escalade. Is that all right? Please can I go?'

'Yes, how kind of him. Of course you can.' Kim felt guilty that she had never taken James to see this December pageant.

Guilt, major and minor, seemed to be a permanent emotion these days. A major worry was that she'd been unable to spur on the insufferably slow pace of the enquiries into the air crash. Could she have done more? Had Richard been lying injured and dying in the jungle while she'd been wringing her hands in Geneva, and then falling into Henri's arms?

She was now almost accustomed to guilt about having chosen to become a rich man's mistress instead of trying to support herself like a proper modern woman, but she worried that Henri, whom she had supposed to be immune to deep feelings, might be falling seriously in love with her. And then there was the minor problem of Mark, who seemed to be under the false impression that she was, or soon would be, available and fancy free. She did not have the courage to tell him about her affair with Henri and why she owed him her loyalty.

James was still talking about the Escalade. Henri was fantastic with him, even more so than before.

'Mr Marechal says we must dress up very warm. Are you coming with us too, Mum? It's next week. Tell me about it. What happens?'

She pondered. 'A long time ago, almost four hundred years ago actually,' she began, 'the Dukes of Savoy attacked Geneva and the townspeople beat them off. So they still celebrate the victory every year and parade about on horseback in old uniforms with pikestaffs and muskets.'

'Mr Marechal says he's going to give me the biggest chocolate *marmite* I ever saw. Tell me again about the *marmites* too. I forgot the story when I was trying to explain it to a new boy at school. He kept thinking I meant the stuff you spread on your bread in England. He couldn't understand the difference between Mar-might and mar-meet.'

She smiled, as she always did, at James's perfect French pronunciation. 'At Escalade time children usually get *marmites*. You remember those mini – or not so mini – chocolate pots full of marzipan vegetables? It's in memory of the great Geneva heroine, Mère Royaume, who threw her soup kettle on to the enemy soldiers as they stormed the ramparts.'

'Oh yes, I remember. So will you buy me one too, as well as Mr Marechal?'

'We'll see. They're pretty expensive, and if Henri has promised you a large one that'll be more than enough chocolate. I'll ring him to say you'd love to go to the parade, but I don't think I can. I've got too much work on at the moment, for Beverly-Jane.'

That was only half the truth. In fact the idea of appearing in public with Henri made her feel uncomfortable.

'Why don't we ever go out together? Are you ashamed of me?' complained Henri gently, holding her in his arms late one Thursday night.

Kim hugged him, sleepy and contented. After they had made love, she always felt a heady satiated peace which blotted out all her guilt and worries, temporarily at least. 'Of course not, but, I don't know, I'm happy the way things are. I prefer it to be a secret still, don't you?'

'If that's what you want, but we could still dine together now and then. It would be quite normal for you to go out with your landlord.'

'OK,' she said. 'But not to a restaurant. We could go for a walk or something, with James and Caspar. That would be nice.'

He stroked her arm. 'No, not merely a walk with James. Why not a restaurant one evening, just the two of us?'

She smiled. 'Because of the way you gaze at me.'

'How do I look at you?'

She kissed his cheek. 'You're doing it now. All starry-eyed and soppy.'

Henri chuckled and pinned her down by her shoulders. 'Soppy? Soppy? You are extremely impolite sometimes. If I didn't like you so much, I would . . . I would throw you out.'

She smiled up at him, then, wriggling away, she sat up. 'Don't laugh, but I've had an idea. You can come with me to the United Nations Fair tomorrow. There's so much to see you won't want to stare at me.'

'What is this fair?'

'You know, it's like a Christmas bazaar, a *kermesse*, in aid of charity. All the countries have a stall – the UN wives organise it. But maybe, on second thoughts, you'd find it boring, a bit too female.'

'But no, I adore female occasions. All those dusky ladies buying and selling their wares, it sounds most erotic.'

She laughed. 'One thing it won't be is erotic. Except I can guarantee you one pretty woman. I'm going with Beverly-Jane who you're always wanting to meet.'

'Ah this Bee-Jay, yes indeed. How I long to see this strange person after all your descriptions.'

'She's rather attractive, as I said, though of a certain age. Just right for you really.'

Smiling, he caressed her more intimately. 'One passionate woman at a time is enough for an old man like me.'

'Oh, I don't know,' she murmured, her eyes closing, 'you do pretty well if I may say so . . . and if you don't stop doing that, you'll have to make love to me again and then I'll never get home. Mm, Henri, please, I . . .'

Next day, pulling Henri behind her, Kim fought her way through the multi-coloured crowds at the Fair in the lofty halls of the Palais des Nations. Henri kept wanting to stop at the Indian jewellery or look at the Japanese paintings, but she was determined to find some precious English Christmas crackers.

In charge of the British stall she found a flustered girl who was trying to explain in halting French to a bemused Swiss what crackers were for.

'No, not biscuits, not to eat. *Pour la table de Noël*, to decorate to make pretty, *joli. Pour les enfants*, the children. *Cadeaux* inside, little presents, hats.'

The Swiss looked increasingly puzzled 'Hats?'

'Funny paper hats, *en papier*, you know,' said the girl, her ringing Home Counties accent becoming desperate.

Kim was startled to hear a familiar deep voice in her ear.

'That's what diplomatic life is all about,' said Mark. 'Explaining obscure British customs in strange languages to confused foreigners.'

'Oh, er, Mark, hello,' said Kim, suddenly even more flustered than the girl behind the counter.

She hadn't expected to see him at such an occasion and she was unprepared for the thump of excitement his appearance caused. Waving her arm, she said, 'This is Henri, my landlord. He came to buy Stilton but there isn't any.'

A head taller than everyone else, Mark shook hands and, with the hearty young stallholder, began a conversation about the best place to buy English produce in Geneva. The two men seemed to be getting on very well, thought Kim anxiously. Too well. She was horrified to hear Mark suggest they should all have lunch together at the Bazaar.

'I don't think we can stay,' she said quickly. 'I promised to meet a friend and I haven't found her, and the food isn't really very substantial here and—'

'An early lunch here would be delightful,' interrupted Henri. 'It would be pleasant to sit down. This place is too crowded with busy ladies, charming though they look in all their national costumes. United Nations food is no doubt highly original too. Why don't you find your BJ friend and we can all eat together?'

Both Henri and Mark appeared very taken with Beverly-Jane, who was sporting a black catsuit with yet another of her multi-coloured transparent shirts, an ensemble which displayed her excellent figure to its best advantage. She talked non-stop on the way to and all during the cafeteria-style lunch, where they were obliged to perch on uncomfortable folding chairs and eat luke-warm curry from plastic plates.

'Isn't this just wonderful?' cooed BJ, tossing her biscuit-coloured curls. Kim noted cattily that her roots needed doing.

BJ waved her chopsticks in the air. 'I do love to eat ethnic. And all for charity. And I just love the rice in the little bowls. I'm a bowl person myself.'

'Aren't you worried about all that cholesterol in the coconut sauce?' asked Kim mischievously.

BJ put her bowl down suddenly. 'You're right. I should be more careful. And, Henri, I don't think a man of your age should be eating this.'

Henri smiled at her, bemused. 'Are you an expert in nutrition then, madame?'

'I certainly am. You and I should go over to the American stall because they have a new health food section this year with a whole lot of great books that will really help you, Henri. You need to stop eating that unhealthy stuff right now.'

To Kim's astonishment, Henri did as he was told and allowed himself to be led away.

'Very polite man, your landlord,' said Mark, his eyes twinkling. 'Can I get you something else to eat?'

'No thanks, it may disturb my aura or my chakra,' said Kim.

'What's that?'

'I have no idea, but it's something you have to balance, according to BJ.'

He grinned. 'And how is your general balance these days? You look as marvellous as ever.'

'And you're as diplomatic as ever. By the way, who was that poor girl selling the crackers?'

'Just one of the wives.'

'Just one of the wives,' she echoed. 'How dismissive you sound.'

'Sorry, I take it all back. That was Rachel, nice girl, mother of two, spouse of Charles, a First Secretary.'

'Still a bit dismissive, but at least you've given her a name.'

'She's not as much fun as your friend Beverly-Jane. Will Henri be safe with her?'

'Oh, I think so. She does have a husband.'

He smiled. 'What a nice woman you are. In my experience, the possession of a husband doesn't necessarily hamper a femme fatale.'

She flushed but he didn't appear to notice. Looking around, he lowered his voice. 'But seriously,' he said, 'talking of husbands, I did have some news of yours yesterday. I rang you this morning but you were out. I guessed you might be here so I came to try and find you.'

Her stomach knotting, she stood up suddenly. 'I can hardly hear you. Can we go somewhere more private?'

Eventually after walking around the edge of the noisy hall, Mark opened a door and found an unpopulated corridor.

'Well?' she asked, putting the bag of crackers down on the floor.

He put his hand on her arm. 'Kim, according

to my contact, there's a report that your husband may have left Indonesia just before the crash and gone to Maising.'

Her head swam and she leant back against the wall for support. 'You mean . . . he may be alive?'

'Unfortunately, there's no confirmation either way as to whether the man who went to Maising was your husband – names often get confused – or whether he was on the plane that crashed. The latter is much more likely, I'm sorry to say.' He hesitated. 'But there's also information that before he disappeared the Indonesian authorities were interested in talking to him.'

Hardly aware of what he was saying, she gulped and then asked shakily, 'But is he still alive . . . or isn't he?'

'They don't know. I'm sorry. This must be very difficult for you.'

She stared at the floor. Wild questions raced around in her head. Picking one at random, she stammered, 'Why did the Indonesians want to talk to him?'

'They told me it was confidential.'

'Look, I must know. I have a right to.'

'Yes, I'm sorry,' he said. 'I believe you do. Well, apparently they suspect he may have been trying to supply small arms to separatists in that part of the world.'

'*What?* D'you mean gun running, smuggling to terrorists?'

'Whether you call them terrorists, freedom fighters or separatists depends on your viewpoint. But, in any case, a subsidiary of the company Richard worked for is involved in the arms trade, more or less legitimately. They're self-proclaimed security advisers or something of that nature, as he may have told you.'

She stared at him. 'No, he didn't. I didn't know, or I wouldn't have encouraged him to work for them. Oh God, this is awful.'

'He could, of course, have had some perfectly innocent purpose in visiting these remote parts, but the Indonesians would have liked to ask him what it was.'

She dug her nails into her hands, still barely able to take in what he said. 'But you think there's a chance he may have gone to Maising – I can't even remember where that is.'

'It's a tiny state made up of several small islands in the South China Sea between Indonesia and Malaysia.'

'And why would he have gone there?'

'I don't know. There are no reports of anti-government factions, but then there's always a criminal market for arms.'

She flushed. 'Richard definitely wouldn't have sold guns to criminals,' she said hotly. 'He may not have been the brightest person in the world, but he wouldn't do that.'

'Look, I'm sorry. I've made matters worse. Perhaps I should have kept the whole thing to myself until I found out something concrete. We still have to face the fact that most likely he was on that plane.'

Shocked and bewildered, she turned away without speaking.

'Can I drive you home?' he offered.

'No, my car's here. I must find Beverly-Jane and Henri. I'm all right. It's just . . . the uncertainty of it all.' She turned back towards him. 'I'm glad you found out all that stuff. I didn't want you to keep anything back. However bad the news is, I need to know.'

'All right, I'll see if I can get hold of any information from the Maising end,' he said. 'You look very pale. Can I get you a glass of water or something?'

'No thank you. I just want to be on my own for a bit.'

'I understand. Look, there's a chair over there. Why don't you sit down?'

'I'm OK, really.'

'If you ever need to talk about it, I'm here.'

'Yes,' she said, on the edge of tears.

'Perhaps you would come out to dinner with me next week then?'

She looked down. 'No, sorry, I can't.'

'How about the week after?'

'No, it's too difficult. I really can't—'

He touched her shoulder again. 'I understand. Well, I'll phone next week to see how you are. Goodbye then, Kim. If I hear anything further I'll let you know.' He turned and strode away down the long marble corridor.

But I don't want Richard to reappear. I want him to stay dead and gone. She tried to push this terrible thought away, but it hung at the back of her mind like a dark dense cloud.

CHAPTER 8

'I've got something to tell you,' said Kim next day.

'Yes, who was that hunk you were lurking about with on the edge of the Bazaar?' asked Polly, examining a dying plant on Kim's window sill.

'I didn't see you. You said you weren't going to make it this year.'

'Well, in the end I did get there,' said Polly. 'My committee meeting was cancelled luckily. I wanted to buy some New Zealand cheese. You get tired of all this French and Swiss stuff. Sometimes you long for good old mousetrap, don't you? And it was a terrific bargain.'

'Uh.'

Polly smiled. 'You're not paying attention to my earth-shattering discourse on cheeses. So who was he? And where did you disappear to?'

'Who?'

'You know damn well who. The chap in the suit, tall, dark and distinguished.'

'Oh, you mean Mark? He's just someone from the Foreign Office here, the Embassy, Mission or whatever, who's been trying to help me find out what happened to Richard. Listen, Polly, I—'

'Really? Across a crowded room I thought I sensed a *Brief Encounter*, pulses racing, hearts throbbing, all that. Does Henri know about him?'

'No racing pulses. Just a product of your over-active imagination. And Henri has met him, yes. You see—'

'So did he find out anything, this FO chap?'

Kim took a deep breath. 'That's what I've been trying to tell you. He said it's just possible Richard went to some obscure island instead of taking the plane that crashed.'

Polly stared and then sat down suddenly on the kitchen chair. 'He wasn't on the plane? So he isn't dead?'

'I don't know. No one does. Nothing's definite. I'll just have to wait for hard information from someone somewhere. And you see—' Then she decided not to mention the arms dealing. It could just be a wild rumour that would be contradicted next week.

'I'm sorry, really I am . . . I wish I could help.'

Kim tried to keep her voice steady. 'Everyone wants to help but no one can. Not unless they know if he's alive and where he is.'

'That's not true. Henri has helped you, in his own way.'

Kim gave a wan smile. 'Yes, he has and so have you. Sorry, Polly, I'm all churned up again . . . I had sort of come to terms with things and now I just want to be sure about Richard, one way or the other. I mean, of course I'm glad if there's a glimmer of hope, I really am, but then I feel guilty in case . . .'

In case I don't want him back, she thought.

'I know,' said Polly gently, as if she had spoken aloud.

'That UN Bazaar was the greatest,' said Beverly-Jane a few days later. 'Did you see those cute little Chinese ornaments I bought?'

'Yes, lovely,' said Kim, without looking up.

'I got a load of Christmas presents. I'll show you later. And there were some wonderful whole-food ideas – we need to incorporate them in the book. You are what you eat, I always say. Maybe we should have a kind of double *A to Zee. New Food for You and Me.* What d'you think? A for, er, aubergines, B for beansprouts and C . . . C for?'

'Aubergines aren't exactly new. Anyway I think we should finish the first book the way we planned it, and then you can do health food for your second.'

'You are just such a sensible, sensitive person, Kim. I really appreciate your input. But you've been acting kind of quiet lately. Did you buy the new all-star exercise video like I recommended? It should help you with your thigh problem.'

Kim was too preoccupied with worry about Richard, and everything else, to be irritated.

'No, I didn't,' she said absently. 'I don't seem to be in the shopping frame of mind at the moment.'

'Mood is so important. If you're short on energy, you should take a multi-vitamin supplement, especially if you're dieting. And maybe some Evening Primrose.'

'Yes, OK, I'll get some,' said Kim. It was easier just to agree rather than confess she hadn't started the diet BJ had drawn up for her, though she seemed to have lost some weight anyway.

'I told your landlord he needs to take vitamins. What cute guys, those two at the Bazaar. The tall handsome British one – he reminds me of a young Harrison Ford, with a touch of Hugh Grant.'

'He's nothing like either of them,' said Kim crossly.

'Well, he has that quiet English charm and sense of humour like Hugh, but more macho and craggy. And I just adored your landlord too.'

Kim raised her eyebrows. 'So who does he remind you of?'

'No one special. He's different, kind of sexy for his age. Nice dark bedroom eyes.'

Turning away to hide the expression on her face, Kim said casually, 'Glad you like him. He's a nice man.'

'Very nice, very nice. I'm going to visit with him next week. He's interested in aromatherapy.'

'Is he indeed?'

'Yeah, and I told him about my friend who does Shiatsu. All these relaxation massages are excellent for people with a health problem like Henri.'

Startled Kim stared at her. 'Health problem? Henri? I didn't know that.'

'Oh well, I guess I shouldn't discuss what my patients tell me. This is strictly confidential information, Kim, and I am only telling you because you're his neighbour.'

'It isn't serious, is it?'

BJ waved her arms. 'Oh no, just high cholesterol, but he should be on a strict diet, from what he tells me. All this cheese he eats – very bad. He sure needs my advice.'

Kim breathed a sigh of relief. 'But lots of people have high cholesterol, it isn't necessarily dangerous. And I didn't know Henri was what you call a patient, in fact I didn't know you were qualified in any medical way.'

'Well, no, I'm not exactly medical, of course, but I do have a masters degree in Alternative Health studies. And I believe that by opening people's minds to the variety of therapies available I can really help them.'

'And so now you're going to help Henri,' said Kim dryly.

'Why yes. Like, he's never even heard of the healing power of crystals.'

Kim telephoned Henri immediately she reached home. He said he hadn't told her about his minuscule problem because there was nothing to worry about. He had regular check-ups, he took pills and the doctor was more than satisfied with him.

Kim was reassured. BJ had been exaggerating as usual.

Nevertheless the incident had made her realise how much she'd come to care for Henri.

She shouldn't even be thinking about another man. She would now, today, tell Mark about him. Mark would then stop pursuing her and she'd then stop, well, being aware of him. This awareness was quite mild, of course, probably just a normal healthy female reaction to a good-looking man – Polly and BJ had both commented on his charms, after all – but the frisson she felt in his presence made her feel disloyal to Henri and complicated her already complicated life.

But she liked Mark, she needed him as a friend, needed his help as regards Richard. That's why she must tell him now, before it was too late, before he became emotionally involved.

She stared for a long time at the telephone. Then she picked up the Geneva directory and looked up the number of the British Mission to the United Nations. After further hesitations and wanderings around the house doing little chores in a half-hearted manner, she dialled the number and was put through to Mark's secretary only to find that he was out. When the girl invited her to leave a message, Kim declined. What could she say? Two hours later she rang again but he was still out. This time she left a message saying she had called.

At last at 9.30 that evening he telephoned.

'I'm sorry,' she said, aware that she seemed to be constantly apologising.

'Sorry about what?'

'For not really saying thank you for all your efforts trying to find out what happened to Richard. It was all a bit of a shock and—'

'Of course it was, I know. Good God, I didn't expect any thanks. I'm just sorry the information about the man in Maising was so nebulous. I'm still making enquiries, of course. I'll let you know if I hear anything.'

'So there's no further news?'

'No, afraid not. I'm sorry to be pessimistic but—'

'You think the most likely thing was that Richard was on the plane?'

'I do.'

Her first emotion was sadness followed by a kind of relief which made her feel bitterly ashamed. Then she felt yet more guilt about the fact she had been blocking out her thoughts about Richard, pushing him to the back of her mind again. The uncertainties about his death were so difficult to live with that she had tried to stop thinking about it.

'Are you all right, Kim?'

'Yes.'

There was a pause.

'Was there any other reason you rang?' he asked eventually.

Pulling herself together, she said, 'Yes, there was. I would like to invite you out.'

'*You* invite *me*?' His voice was suddenly full of happy enthusiasm. 'So are you asking me round to your house?'

'No, I thought a restaurant, I mean nothing grand, but—'

'Pity. If I come to you it would save a babysitter. You're always so worried about babysitters.'

She smiled to herself. 'Yes, but I'd rather go out.'

'Why don't I get something ready-cooked from the *traiteur* so we could eat at your house together? It'd be more relaxing.'

'It's never very relaxing with James around. He doesn't go to bed very early.'

'Well, you could come here then,' he said.

'But it was me who invited you.'

'I go to restaurants all the time,' he said. 'It would be lovely if you could come to my place.'

'But—'

'You'd be quite safe. I never jump on women unless invited to do so.'

She laughed. 'OK then. Thank you. I'll come.'

When she put down the telephone, she caught sight of herself in the mirror and smiled. 'Oh my God, what an idiot you are, Kim Ellis,' she muttered aloud.

She spent a great deal of time deciding what she should wear for her last evening with Mark. First she chose a longish black straight skirt and then remembered it had a split which tended to reveal too much thigh if she sat in a careless manner.

A mini would be too provocative and her calf-length tartan too dowdy. So she decided on black trousers and a white silk shirt with a black suede waistcoat – a smart but androgynous outfit. Anyway, she was pleased she could now get into the trousers.

As she drove towards his house she became increasingly nervous, rehearsing again and again what she would say to him. She had been rehearsing for several days already. Should she speak after dinner or before? If she waited until after dinner, she might lull him into the hope that the evening was going to turn cosy, or he might be so charming and luscious that she would forget why she had come and then she would have to run away at the last minute and could be accused of prick teasing. A horrible phrase but it was the one that sprang to mind. No, she would have to say her piece straight away – well, after she'd had a drink, even if it meant that the evening would end there and then. As it was bound to.

'Hello,' said Mark, gazing at her with flattering attention. 'You look wonderful. I'm glad you've arrived. I was afraid you wouldn't come.' Before she could turn away, he had kissed her quickly on the lips.

Kim smiled up at him. All her resolve was beginning to melt already. 'Hello,' she said in that breathless girlish voice that annoyingly surfaced in his presence.

'Come and sit down.' His voice sounded strange too, and his eyes were shining, fixed on her face.

On the mahogany coffee table was a bucket containing a bottle of champagne. Seducer's equipment. Oh dear. She accepted a glass which she drank far too quickly. Aware that his gaze seemed ever more intense and that she was becoming stupidly flirtatious in response, she rose to her feet and said, 'Sorry, but I—'

He stood up too and before she could continue, he took her in his arms and kissed her. Leaning against him, head reeling, she couldn't help kissing him back.

He pulled her down on to the sofa and began to kiss her even more thoroughly. Holding on to the last thread of her self-control and prompted by a sharp jab from her conscience, she pushed him away.

'No,' she said in a loud whisper. 'No, please we have to talk.'

His eyes twinkled. 'Must we? I'm not really in the mood for a chat.'

'I know but I have to make a confession.' Seeing he was about to ignore her words and kiss her again, she blurted out, 'I already have a lover and I don't want another one.' This was not the tactful way she had planned to tell him.

He stood up immediately and paced towards the door.

'Oh hell, I'm sorry,' she said, scarlet in the face. 'I didn't mean to kiss you – it was just impossible not to. I'm sorry. I did try to tell you in the beginning that I couldn't, wasn't free. I do like you but . . . sorry, really. I shouldn't have come here. I'll go now.' And she managed to get past him without looking at him.

Once in the hall, she again opened the wrong cupboard for her coat. Gulping for breath, she finally found it.

Then she felt a hand on her shoulder. 'I think I'd like a little more explanation than that, if you have a moment,' he said quietly.

Holding her coat in her arms, she sat down on a chair in the hall.

'Come back into the sitting room,' he ordered.

'No, I'd rather stay here.'

'As you wish.' He gazed down at her. 'On reflection, perhaps I don't have a right to ask, but I would like to know. Yes, I suppose you did try to tell me in the beginning, but I thought you meant I should keep my distance because you were a grieving widow. Seems I was wrong.'

She flushed again. 'I did grieve, I do grieve, in spite of the fact that I didn't love Richard.'

'Sorry, I didn't mean . . . that was unforgivable of me,' he said more gently.

They were both silent for a while and then he asked, 'So have you been consoling yourself with this lover for a long time?'

She stared at the floor. 'I don't have to tell you a thing. It's not really your business.'

'But I thought we . . . But you kissed me just now in a pretty responsive manner. Unless perhaps that's par for the course as far as you're concerned?'

Suddenly furious, she stood up. 'Is that what you think?' Before he could stop her, she opened the front door and, still clutching her coat, clattered away down the stairs as fast as she could. It was a long way down and he probably could have caught up with her if he had followed, but he did not do so.

Well, you've done the right thing for a change, she told herself as she stood in the car park savagely scraping the ice off her windscreen. And you still have Henri, just remember that.

Henri was looking forward to the aromatherapy visit. He had deliberately scheduled it for a time when Kim would be out teaching and his cleaning woman, Mme Dubois, would have gone home. He did not want Beverly-Jane's exotic appearance to cause any misunderstanding.

This proved to be a wise precaution because, though BJ arrived dressed in a conservative medical-style white jacket with matching trousers, she brought with her a folding treatment-table which she set up in the middle of the salon. She then invited him to remove his shirt and recline on the table. An old woman like Mme Dubois might well have misunderstood why he had to strip half-naked in the presence of a glamorous blonde. And even Kim might have her doubts.

It was a most agreeable experience, he thought, having a beautiful woman massage fragrant oil all over his chest. Somebody had been good at massage but he couldn't remember who. Perhaps it had been Sabine, or maybe Alice (one of the mistresses he forgot to mention to Kim when he listed them all those weeks ago).

'Close your eyes, Henri, relax,' said BJ, kneading his substantial flesh with her strong fingers.

He did as he was told and then opened them again slightly because when she leant forward the unbuttoned collar of her clean white uniform afforded an excellent view of her bosom, a view made all the more attractive by the fact that she wore no bra. There was something in the air that gave him the impression she would not particularly mind if he squeezed one of her charmingly pointed little breasts, but he restrained himself, for Kim's sake.

'Turn over,' ordered BJ, and so Henri again obeyed. She massaged his back and then worked rather further down his backbone than he might have expected.

'Your lower sacral muscles are tense. Next time you should be in a towel, no pants. That wouldn't be a problem, would it?' asked BJ in a bland professional voice.

'No problem,' murmured Henri, his face on the table. 'Just as long as I am fit for the family skiing trip at Christmas.'

'You still ski? That's great. You're in excellent shape, though you could lose a few pounds.'

'There are many things I can still do,' said Henri.

'I'll bet there are,' said BJ, and her right hand

massaged its way again to the bottom of his spine and hesitated a moment. Then the hand gradually returned to his waistline.

Henri lay still, concentrating on breathing normally. He was doing his best not to laugh or grab hold of Beverly-Jane, or both. She then hammered all the way up and down his spine in a chopping movement, using both hands.

He looked around. 'That reminds me of a little Thai girl I once knew.'

She lowered her eyelashes and smiled seductively. 'And did she give you a full Thai body massage?'

'I can't remember,' said Henri, turning over and sitting up. 'Now to change the subject, what would you recommend for skiing exercises?'

As BJ was leaving she offered him a course of six aromatherapy sessions as it was much cheaper that way. With only a moment's hesitation Henri accepted this bargain. If more than massage should be offered, he was confident he could resist, since he was becoming quite virtuous in his old age.

CHAPTER 9

Henri's Range Rover bowled along the auto-route beside the cold grey lake. Checking that James was asleep in the back, headphones clamped to his ears, Kim whispered, 'Doesn't your daughter think it strange you should invite us to your chalet for Christmas?'

Henri smiled, his eyes on the road ahead. 'You asked me that before, many times, and I said no. I explained to her that you and James were friends who'd had a bad time and needed a holiday.'

'But Christmas is a family occasion. She'll probably resent us. Bound to.'

'Possibly – but Beatrice and I are not close. She's only coming to Wengen to keep an eye on her inheritance.'

'I'm sure you're being unfair. It's not like you to be so cynical, Henri.'

'Sadly, I don't get on well with my daughter. She does not approve of me – hasn't forgiven my behaviour towards her mother. But I confess I'm looking forward to seeing my grandson. I don't see as much of him as I would like.'

'How old is he? I forget.'

'Six.'

'Lovely age.' She rubbed her forehead. 'But what about your son? Have you heard from him?'

'Oh, a card and a letter. But he is still abroad, somewhere in Asia doing good deeds. He always seems more interested in saving the world than seeing his father.'

'Oh dear, does he disapprove of you too?'

Henri laughed. 'Not as much as Beatrice does.'

Glancing back at the sleeping James, Kim said, 'But you don't think she, Beatrice, will suspect anything about you and me – our relationship, I mean?'

'I don't consider it disastrous if she does.' Henri pulled out to overtake a slow-moving goods vehicle. 'But certainly she will think that you're far too young to be interested in an old grandfather like me. And I've told her you are working on my manuscript.'

'But you haven't even shown it to me yet. You really should have done. What if she asks me about it?'

'Just say I have asked you not to discuss it with anyone. However, I see no reason why she should regard our relationship as anything but platonic.'

She shook her head. 'A woman has an instinct for these things. And then she's probably aware of your not altogether squeaky-clean track record,' she added with a smile.

'Beatrice thinks of only three things: first money, second her role as la Contessa. Like many children of the bourgeoisie she is excessively keen on the aristocracy. Her mother was the same. In fact it was she who pushed Bea into a bad marriage.'

'Poor Beatrice. About the marriage, I mean. I know how she feels.'

'I very much doubt if you do,' said Henri, sounding unusually severe. 'I am sure that you married for love, however mistakenly. But Beatrice married for social position. As a little girl she wanted to be a queen and she never grew out of it. As long as she remains the Countess, I don't think she particularly minds the lack of love in her marriage.'

Maybe Beatrice was determined not to be hurt, as her mother no doubt had been, thought Kim. But she didn't say this aloud, of course.

After a pause Henri shook his head and continued in a lighter tone of voice, 'My daughter's third priority is her own appearance. She'll be far too concerned about whether her ski suit is more elegant than yours to worry about anything else.'

'My new ensemble is extremely smart and deliciously pink, but I won't tell her you gave it to me though.' She patted his arm. 'I love my early Christmas present – you're so nice to me.'

He smiled indulgently. 'It's my pleasure.'

After a pause Kim said, 'So Beatrice will be there when we arrive?'

'Yes, yes, but she's only staying three nights, as I told you. Wengen is far too dull for her. She's going on to Gstaad where she has more fashionable friends.'

'Well, when she's at the chalet you won't creep across the corridor at night, will you? I bet it's all old and wooden and creaky.'

He chuckled. 'Like me.'

'Seriously.'

'Seriously, you are worrying too much, but since even the smallest pin dropping down sounds like machine-gun fire, I won't creep across the chalet – until Beatrice has gone.'

She stared at the mountains in the distance. 'And her Italian nobleman husband won't be there?'

'No, as I said, they seldom spend time together these days.'

'Not even at Christmas?'

'No.'

'That's very sad for her, and your grandson.'

Kim thought of Richard once more. Despite his wanderlust, he had always made it back for Christmas. This was the first time they would spend the holiday without him. Though James was showing few signs of missing his father, it was lucky he would be preoccupied with skiing. As ever, she was thankful for Henri's kindness.

In the back seat James woke up half an hour later expecting to have arrived, but it seemed as though the journey would never end. He looked around at the valleys with their neat little Swiss houses. The fields and trees were white with frost but there was no sign of snow. James munched his way through a packet of biscuits to console himself. Occasionally he passed a titbit to Caspar when no one was looking. Then James felt thirsty but no one wanted to stop for a drink.

After what seemed like forever, Mr Marechal drove off the autoroute and the roads became narrower and steeper until they reached a big multi-storey car park in a village in the dark valley. Lauterbrunnen, it was called.

'Coldest car park in the world,' said Mr Marechal, rubbing his hands together. But they had to leave the Range Rover there because no cars were allowed in Wengen. It took ages to unpack the car, James thought, and there weren't any luggage trolleys so he and Mr Marechal had to go and fetch them from the floor above. *Then* they had to push all the skis and luggage along endless concrete corridors until they reached a tiny railway station where they found a small green train – the Wengernalpbahn – which Mr Marechal said was a cog-railway, not quite clockwork but looked as if it should be. James couldn't picture a clockwork railway, but Mum seemed to think it was a great joke when Mr Marechal told her that some of the points were operated by hand.

They threw their suitcases into an open wagon at the front of the train and sat down, panting with relief. James began to feel better. After a lot of announcements in funny sing-song German, the train began to moan and groan its way slowly up the steep mountain. At first all they could see were fir trees, but suddenly the train cranked round a bend.

'There's Wengen,' said Mr Marechal proudly, pointing to a sunny village on the shelf of the mountain.

At the station Mr Marechal hired an electric sledge to take them to the chalet. James stared around at all the decorative wooden buildings – hotels, shops and chalets – and the snow-covered streets of the little town. There were no cars at all, just crowds of brightly dressed skiers, and everyone seemed to be smiling. He sensed a magical happiness in the air and, catching the mood, began to feel it would be the best holiday ever.

Henri's daughter had a long nose which she looked down to great effect, despite the fact she was only about five feet tall. 'I have put your guests on the ground floor. Papa,' she said, barely acknowledging Kim's presence.

'No, no,' said Henri firmly. 'Those basement rooms are too cold in winter. Kim can have the big back bedroom and the children can share.'

'But, Papa, Eduardo won't like that, he's not used to sharing a room. And it also means we shall only have two bathrooms between five of us. I told you many times you should install a new shower at least. This chalet is really not equipped for entertaining.'

'I'm sure we can manage,' said Henri.

'Perhaps James could sleep in my room,' suggested Kim.

Beatrice gave a chilly smile and the compromise was agreed. 'This evening I've booked a table for three at the Eigerstube. Eduardo is longing to spend time with his grandfather and I should like to have a family discussion,' she announced.

Henri protested that his guests could not be left to fend for themselves on Christmas Eve, but Kim said tactfully that she was too tired to go out.

When Eduardo returned from ski school, he proved to be much more appealing than his mother. Kim was touched by the way he flung himself into his grandfather's arms. Tiny with bright black eyes and a thick mop of shiny black hair, Eduardo spoke English well, but with a curious broad Glasgow accent. Beatrice explained proudly that he had always had British nannies, but unfortunately Nanny had gone home for Christmas.

Lively and mischievous, Eduardo seemed to be missing the absent nanny's discipline. Beatrice shouted at him a great deal and constantly threatened to send him to his room. When the threat was actually carried out, he stayed outside the door for a couple of seconds, then peeked round to find himself immediately forgiven. Half an hour later he was in the dog house again for the next misdemeanour. It was not going to be a very relaxing Christmas.

'By the way, er, Kim,' said Beatrice when they

were alone in the kitchen, 'I haven't had time to get a tree. Will you go down and get one from the village? The decorations are in a cupboard in the cellar, by the door. You can decorate the tree while we're out tonight.'

Kim was a little taken aback by these commands but she smiled and said it would be fun for James.

'And order a ready-cooked turkey at the *traiteur* while you're down there, will you?'

'Anything else?' asked Kim.

'Well, we always do the catering in turn here. Guests help too. So I think it would be simpler if I put you in charge of the whole Christmas dinner. I'm afraid I haven't had time to do much grocery shopping, what with getting the house ready and skiing and fetching Eduardo from ski school. We need things for breakfast and so on for the holiday period. I've made a list. But you won't have to carry it all. They do deliver. Here, take some money.'

'No need, thanks,' said Kim, struggling to remain polite. She was beginning to feel some sympathy towards the absent Italian husband.

'Do you have a daddy?' asked Eduardo. He and James were laying the table for tea in a haphazard manner.

James straightened the knives. 'He's gone,' he said repressively. He didn't want to discuss fathers, particularly with this little kid who was always showing off and sitting on Henri's knee.

'Gone?'

'Dead.' There, I've said it again, thought James. Each time he had to tell a new person it felt odd. At school having a dead father was regarded as cool. It gave him a new status even. And the teachers were so sympathetic. He sometimes felt guilty about not being sad enough.

Now people had already almost forgotten. Some of the new children even seemed to think Henri was his father. He didn't disillusion them.

Eduardo, too, looked impressed by dead. 'So is he in heaven now, your daddy?'

James stared at him. 'Yes.' It was all he could think of to say.

'My daddy is in Rome with my Italy grandmother,' confided the child. 'I stay with him sometimes. He has a Lamborghini.'

James now remembered that Mum had told him not to mention Eduardo's dad but the kid didn't seem to mind. He was probably too young to worry.

Anyway, you get used to things. Plenty of people don't have fathers.

Henri was up early next day, but Eduardo and James were already beside the Christmas tree studying the parcels, while Kim was making breakfast.

'Can we open our presents before we go skiing?' asked Eduardo, jumping up and down.

Henri smiled and said they must wait for his mother.

'Just one, just one tiny present,' pleaded Eduardo.

'All right, you boys go and fetch some logs from the store and then you can open one present only. Put your coats and boots on, it's very cold out there.'

As soon as they had gone, Henri drew Kim into his arms. 'Happy Christmas, *mon ange*,' he said.

'Happy Christmas,' she murmured into his ear. 'I've bought you a very dull present. There didn't seem to be anything suitable for a man who has everything.'

'I'm sure it will be lovely, but you could give me a little extra something in addition.'

'What? Tell me.'

'An extra special long night of love.'

She laughed. 'OK, I see no problem with that request just as long as we wait until the coast is clear.'

Suddenly she heard the clatter of footsteps on the stairs and pushed him away.

Beatrice stood in the doorway staring at them both. She knows, thought Kim, disturbed by the malevolent expression on her hostess's face.

'*Joyeux Noël*, Papa,' said Beatrice with a grim smile.

With help from Henri, Kim managed to produce a passable Christmas meal and the following three days passed without outright hostilities, but the atmosphere continued to be chilly when

Beatrice was around. Fortunately she spent most of the day skiing with a glamorous-looking Italian girlfriend while Henri and Kim took charge of the children. In effect, this meant that Kim had to look after Eduardo as she was the weaker skier.

'Will you take me up the T-bar? Maman never wants to go with me,' he pleaded.

Kim groaned. Eduardo was too small and too light to balance an adult on the meat-hook lifts, but in the end she was persuaded to accompany him. With the bar tugging around her knees, it was difficult to steer a parallel course up the steep slope and she was sure that sooner or later they would come to grief.

They had not gone very far before Eduardo crossed his skis and, with a loud scream, fell into a nearby snow drift. She let go of the bar and edged across to drag him upright. Fortunately he was unhurt.

'That T-bar is an effing eejit,' he shouted, furiously dusting the snow off his Ralph Lauren ski suit.

She grinned. 'What interesting English your nanny taught you.'

He blushed scarlet. 'Don't tell Maman, please. She gets cross if I say bad words. She might send Nanny away.'

'No more rude words, but of course I won't tell on you. We're friends, you and I.'

⋆   ⋆   ⋆

The fact that Eduardo seemed to have suddenly developed such a crush on Kim did not endear her to his mother, and Kim was deeply relieved when Beatrice departed for Gstaad the following day. They all went down to the station to see them off.

'I'll come and see you in Geneva soon,' promised Eduardo, kissing Kim lavishly.

'Phew,' whispered James as the train departed. 'What a pair of dorks. Now we can enjoy ourselves.'

James's idea of enjoyment was to be on the mountain from dawn until dusk, skiing as many runs as possible. One day Kim decided as they emerged from a mountain restaurant after lunch that she was tired and so, leaving James with the ever-energetic Henri, she began to make her way down to Wengen. The visibility was bad and she skied the run sedately, pausing from time to time to admire the misty view of the Jungfrau which appeared from time to time through the clouds. Then, as it began to snow gently, she became aware of another skier behind her, a tall man in a blue parka, black hat and dark goggles. He was going at about the same pace as she was.

The narrow path down to the village through the fir trees wasn't crowded but her enjoyment was spoilt by the hiss of skis close behind. Glancing back she saw the same man. She slowed down so he would overtake, but he remained behind and she began to have the uneasy feeling that he was followng her. He was still there, though now further back, when she reached the open pistes just above the village. To ensure that he didn't follow her right to the chalet, she accelerated as fast as the city slopes would allow and then diverted to the track by the Café Oberland. Kicking off her skis, she dived into the hot smoky tea room.

She had just sat down when to her dismay the man appeared in the doorway. He stood there, looking around, taking off his hat and goggles. Her heart turned over and suddenly she began to laugh in relief. The tall figure looming towards her was Mark.

'What are you doing here?' she asked, flushing. She couldn't help being extremely pleased to see him.

'I was pursuing a pretty woman in a pink suit all the way down the mountain.' He ran his hands through his hair and turned to catch the waitress's eye.

She smiled. 'Why didn't you stop me, call out, say who you were? You scared me.'

'Thought you might run away again. Now I've got you cornered.'

A fat woman at the next table gave her lapdog a piece of chocolate cake and stared inquisitively as Mark squeezed himself into the seat beside Kim.

'So have you been here all over Christmas on your own?' she asked.

'Yes, I wanted to escape a hearty lunch invitation from the Ambassador's wife.' He smiled. 'But mainly I came here to see you as I said.'

'I don't believe you.'

'It's true. I've been having lunch in Kleine Scheidegg every day because I knew you'd be bound to show up there sooner or later. And today you did, so with great stealth and subtlety I shadowed you down the mountain.

She grinned. 'Apart from the fact that I didn't recognise you in your goggles, it wasn't the slightest bit subtle. But how did you know I was in Wengen?'

'Your colleague, Beverly-Jane, told me.'

'I didn't know you and she were buddies.'

'If you remember, you introduced us at the UN Bazaar and then she called me at the office to ask if I wanted an aromatherapy session. She said I looked like I could use it. I quote.'

She raised her eyebrows. 'And what did you say?'

'Naturally I agreed. I thought it would be rather fun and indeed it was. And I was able, again in a subtle manner, to ask her a great many questions about you. Luckily she is wonderfully indiscreet.'

'What BJ doesn't know, she invents,' said Kim lightly, none too pleased.

'Hm,' he said. 'Well, she knew you'd gone to Wengen for Christmas and she also knew your landlord was going to be there, so she presumed you had gone together.'

'With my son and Henri's married daughter,' she said quickly.

He looked at her. 'We need to have a chat.'

'About Richard?' she asked, immediately on edge.

'About all sorts of things. What will you have to drink?'

She became aware that the Swiss woman appeared to be listening to every word. 'Look, couldn't we discuss this elsewhere? Let's have a quick glühwein and go.'

Slithering over the patches of ice between the cowsheds, they arrived in Wengen. It was now only mid-afternoon and most skiers were still on the mountain so the village was quiet and empty.

Mark brushed the snow off his jacket. 'Will you come to my hotel for another drink? In the safety of the lounge, of course,' he added.

She smiled. 'I have a better idea. We'll go for a walk instead, with Henri's dog. He needs a run.'

He looked disappointed. 'But it's snowing.'

'So what? You ski when it's snowing, don't you? I'll just change out of my ski gear and meet you by the station in a quarter of an hour.'

'So is Henri the lover you spoke of?' he asked as they walked slowly along the deserted road towards Inner Wengen.

Oh dear. 'Yes,' said Kim.

'And how long has he been in this happy state?'

'Since just before I met you.'

'Quite soon after your husband disappeared?'

She flushed. 'Yes.'

'And were you in love with Henri for a long time before that?' He was staring straight ahead as he walked.

'No, he was just a friend.'

'And you're in love with him now?'

'I'm very fond of him,' she said quietly.

'But not in love?'

She kicked a lump of snow. 'It's really not fair to ask me these questions.'

He paused and then he said, 'BJ was of the opinion that if a woman had something going with Henri she had it made. Again, I quote.'

She frowned. 'I hate the idea of you gossiping about me with BJ.'

'It was a general point,' he said hastily. 'She was referring to any woman, not you, women in general. Don't worry. I made no comment. I just let her talk. You know how she does.'

'Yes.'

The snowflakes were becoming thicker, enveloping them in quiet whiteness. They paced along in silence for a while, past the rows of shuttered chalets towards the ghostly fir trees ahead. Caspar pricked his ears when he saw a disagreeable-looking black terrier, but the animal soon vanished into the mist.

'To change the subject entirely,' said Mark, 'what will you do if it turns out Richard is alive after all?'

Suddenly tense, she stopped. 'Have you heard something?'

'No, no. Though I'm seeing a chap from Maising in the New Year to instigate further enquiries.'

'When?'

'I don't know. He's ringing me.' After a few more steps, he said 'You didn't answer my question. What would you do if Richard did come back?'

'I'd get a divorce. I don't want to be married to an arms dealer, even an amateur one. And I don't love him. Or respect him. I used to think you couldn't just divorce someone because they were inadequate, but now I realise I don't even like him.'

'And then what?' he asked carefully. 'Would you marry Henri?'

'I wouldn't marry anyone.' She turned away from him. 'I think we'd better walk a bit faster. It's getting cold.'

After a while he said, 'I wonder how your husband financed his private arms dealing?'

'I'm sure it was with our money. He may be a fool, but he wouldn't steal from the company, whatever Hoffer implied.'

'You must be quite well off then.'

She stared at him. 'No, quite the opposite.'

'So how did he finance himself or did someone else finance him? Did he have a partner?'

'I don't know. I don't know. All I know is that all our own money disappeared.'

'Well, it's impressive you can support yourself so well then,' he said in a neutral tone of voice.

Kim said nothing.

After a long pause he went on, 'But BJ let slip she couldn't afford to pay you much, certainly not what you're worth, she said. So it occurred to me you probably need someone like Henri to keep you afloat.'

She said uncomfortably, 'Henri is a nice man and I do love him in a way that's hard to explain. He rescued me when I was in a very difficult situation, and he's very good with James.' With a great effort, she added, 'And yes, he does support us, if you must know.'

'I see.'

She rubbed her gloved hands together. 'Look, I don't want to discuss him any further. And I'd be glad if you'd keep everything I've told you to yourself.'

'Of course.'

'And my finances are not your business either. You really don't have a right to ask about these personal things the way you do.'

'No, forgive me. But I did need to know how you felt about Henri,' he said evenly. 'It appears you're committed to him then?'

'Yes.'

Despite his unemotional tone, she felt she had hurt and probably shocked him by telling him the truth about Henri, without telling him the rest. She wanted to confess that, despite Henri, she was far from immune to his own advances, that she was in fact strongly attracted to him, that she lay awake night after night imagining what it would be like to be in his arms. That when, just now, she'd seen him in the Café Oberland, her whole body had reacted with a sharp and painful longing. And that she was still trying vainly to suppress these inconvenient feelings. She had Henri and that should be enough.

Anyway now he knew about Henri, what did he think of her? Probably that she was some sort of tart, sleeping with a rich old man for money.

'Have you had other lovers?' he suddenly asked, echoing her thoughts.

She looked down. 'I was faithful to Richard, until Henri.' It was true but she wondered if he believed her.

During the ensuing silence, she suddenly realised they were a long way from the village. 'Shall we turn back?' she suggested.

Straining at his lead, Caspar began to bark furiously at a plump marmalade cat sheltering on a neat stack of logs under the eaves of a chalet. Indignant, the cat sprang up, arching its back and spitting with rage. Caspar lunged at it, pulling her suddenly forward so that she fell heavily on to the icy road. 'Stupid bloody dog, belt up,' she cursed. The cat disappeared leaving Caspar barking frustratedly.

Kim sat on the ground rubbing her knee.

Smiling, Mark held out his hand. 'Such

language! Didn't know who was the crossest, you, the cat or Caspar.' He pulled her up but did not let her go. Instead he kissed her, just as passionately as before. Taken by surprise, she found herself wanting to respond, as before. Guiltily, she tried to break away but somehow he wouldn't let her.

'Let's go to my hotel,' he murmured after a while.

Her face was burning in the cold air. 'Not a good idea.' She felt a good deal less resolute than she sounded.

He pulled her to him again. 'Mm. I think it's an excellent idea.'

With some difficulty she said, 'I can't, because of Henri.'

'You're not married to him.'

She stepped back. 'No, but I'm, we're kind of together.'

'Right.' He walked on, and then he stopped and moved towards her again. 'You won't change your mind?' he asked more gently, brushing the snow off her hair. He stared intently at her.

She looked down at the road. 'No, I can't,' she said. 'Sorry.'

'No, I'm sorry. I shouldn't push it, but somehow I—'

'You see I do like you,' she said, knowing the words were inadequate. 'It's just that—'

'OK. You don't have to repeat it all yet again.'

They walked back to the village in silence.

When they reached the bridge under the railway, he stood still. 'Look, I apologise. I got it wrong just now. I realise you'd prefer me to stop hassling you. I won't make any further moves.'

'Oh,' she said, hiding the sudden jolt of misery she felt. 'Well, you're quite right. But—'

'But what?'

'Well, I hope we can still see each other some-times. I don't have that many friends in Geneva that I can afford to lose one. Couldn't we be friends and all that?'

He winced. 'Yes, possibly. Anyway, I'll go on trying to find out about Richard, if I can.'

With an abrupt gesture, he turned. 'I'm going this way. Goodbye then, Kim. I'm not going to pressure you any further, you'll be glad to hear. But you know where I am, if you need me.'

'Goodbye,' she said, confused and unhappy.

That night was New Year's Eve. She stood with Henri in the crowded square watching a group of villagers in national costume ringing giant cowbells which they wore around their necks. Everyone was shouting and laughing, and hearty young Englishmen were leaping about brandishing champagne bottles and throwing streamers. She looked around again and again, hoping to see Mark but he wasn't there. She had already decided that her New Year's resolution would be to bury her feelings for him. Of course, she'd made the resolution a hundred times before, but this time she meant it. Heavy-hearted but determined not to admit it, even to herself, she put her arms around Henri and James and they watched the fireworks together.

CHAPTER 10

The next week, back in cold and foggy Geneva, Henri made his own New Year resolution. Plucking up his reserves of courage, he called on Kim one morning and plonked a large brown folder on her kitchen table.

'At last I have brought you my manuscript,' he began in an embarrassed rush. 'And then we must start to edit it. First, I would like you to read it through and tell me what you think.'

Before she could even pick it up, he left, calling out, 'Don't say a word until you've finished it.'

After two hours he felt like telephoning to ask what she thought, but decided she wouldn't have quite finished it yet. Then it occurred to him that he had failed to ask her how busy she was: she might not have had time even to start. He decided to take Caspar for a walk to take his mind off the matter.

But as he marched along the wintry road he thought of nothing else. It was an excellent novel, he felt. No one had read the English version, except of course the secretary who had been entrusted with the typing. Though she had pronounced it to be wonderful, Henri wasn't entirely certain of her literary judgement. The French version had been rejected, sometimes quite cruelly, by several ignorant Swiss and French publishers, but now he had translated it for the benefit of the English-speaking world, he was confident of finding a market. As he had already told Kim, he would if necessary publish it himself.

When he returned from the walk, he telephoned her but received no reply. He phoned again from time to time but declined to leave a message on the tiresome answering machine. He didn't succeed in speaking to her until seven that evening.

Kim sounded distracted. 'Oh, Henri. Yes, sorry, I was here some of the time, but up in my room. I left the answerphone on so I could concentrate on your book. I'm rather busy now this minute, cooking James's supper. The book? Yes, I've read quite a bit of it. Enjoying it, rather fun. Hard to discuss till I've finished. Can I talk to you about it on Thursday? Damn, something's boiling over. Must dash. See you soon.'

Henri heard her put down the receiver. *Merde.* Maybe she didn't like it. Why hadn't she said more? Why had she only read 'a bit'? What did she mean by 'rather fun'? It was a serious novel about the destruction of the Swiss mountains by tourism. It wasn't intended to be amusing. Perhaps she meant the graphic sex scenes were fun – she did find that sort of thing surprisingly humorous.

As Thursday drew near, his tension grew. He was hurt that she hadn't telephoned to say how much she liked it. Perhaps that meant she did not. Maybe the grand theme was above her head. She was a foreigner after all. But foreigners do care about the environment. That charming Beverly-Jane was especially concerned.

Kim arrived on Thursday carrying the manuscript under her arm. She grinned. 'For once we're doing what we're supposed to be doing on Thursdays.'

Henri took her in his arms. 'Perhaps we could start the evening by going upstairs,' he murmured, 'then I may feel a little calmer.'

He thought for a moment that he detected a reluctance but, as soon as he had undressed her, his own desires became all important and she seemed to respond with her usual happy enthusiasm. She was a beautiful woman, he thought, as he looked down at her flushed face. And he cared for her much more deeply than she realised.

After they had made love, he did not linger but hurried her downstairs to dinner. 'I have produced a simple meal of *charcuterie*, followed by *pot au feu*, so that we may concentrate on our intellectual pursuits.'

Before she could take a mouthful of the spicy salami, he asked for her opinion of the book.

She took a sip of wine and began to crumble her

bread. 'Um, I haven't quite finished it. I'm at the part where the two young farmers quarrel and scheme because they both want the new ski lift to be built on their land. I like that chapter. And the old man who disapproves of any change . . . Oh yes, and that gem about villagers not speaking to people who live on the other side of the mountain because they consider them to be foreign. That's good. Parts of it are very good.'

'Yes, yes,' he said impatiently, 'but the novel as a whole, the style, the theme, what do you think of that?'

She paused and stared at the tablecloth. 'Well, er, your written English isn't quite as fluent as your spoken. Perhaps in parts the language is a little too formal in style. And, in others, it's—'

'Well, naturally, I expect it needs a little editing from a native English speaker,' said Henri.

'I enjoyed the book, really, but shall we eat and then talk about it after?'

It was not the rapturous reception he had expected. Offended, Henri picked up his knife and fork. 'Tell me first, what did you think of the heroine?' he asked after another couple of mouthfuls.

Kim paused. 'Well, to be honest, I found it a little difficult to warm to Maria – what with her long blonde hair, the big bouncing breasts, the wasplike waist and the firm rounded buttocks. Then there was her lacy lingerie, or the lack of it – she seemed to be a nymphomaniac. I don't see how she could have had time for all that sex, what with running her restaurant, four young children and a farm.'

Henri grinned. 'She has lots of energy.'

'Yes, but we never see her at the restaurant, let alone with the children or on the farm. All she does is wander around the mountains panting with lust and ripping off her knickers every time the ecologist or any other man appears. Incidentally, I don't think it would be possible to have sex on a chairlift without falling off.'

He chuckled. 'We must experiment one day. What about the hero?'

'The scientist who's built like Arnold Schwarzenegger and behaves like James Bond?'

'Yes,' said Henri smugly. 'He's an excellent character, don't you think?'

'He's a good character for an adventure novel,' she said.

He digested this. After a pause he asked, 'Do you consider this an adventure novel? Because I do not.'

'Look, Henri, let me just edit it – it's a bit wordy in places. And then someone else can assess it. It's more of a man's book than a woman's.'

Henri stared at her. 'But I have written it for women. I love women and I was sure they would enjoy reading about a handsome very masculine hero and a beautiful heroine battling together to save our mountains from developers.'

'Yes, it's a good idea for a novel,' said Kim.

'Er, shall I go and get the casserole? Is it in the oven?'

Again he felt irritated by her insensitivity. After the *pot au feu* had been served, he asked, 'What do you mean by "wordy"?'

'Well, this may be over-critical, but you did ask for my opinion: the thing is, sometimes your sentences are a bit long and rambling, with lots of sub clauses and parentheses. In fact, apart from all the sex, it reads rather like a Victorian novel.'

Henri tried to dampen his rising anger. 'But it's a style I admire.'

'Yes, but it isn't fashionable these days. Maybe it's to do with the translation. French is probably more flowery than English. We Anglo-Saxons don't go in for very high-flown prose.'

'It seems to me entirely appropriate to use a classical style for a grand theme.'

She grinned. 'Maybe . . . but I'm not so sure about your purple passages about sex in the cowsheds.'

He pushed his plate away and stood up. 'I was inspired by *Lady Chatterley's Lover*,' he said stonily. 'That was quite lyrical.'

'Yours is a contemporary novel – styles have changed. Some of your similes are striking, but there are just too many of them. By modern standards, it's rather overwritten in parts.' She picked up the typescript and began to read aloud:

'"Like a vigorous young chamois, a young stag seeking his first doe, he sprang quickly upon the verdant ledge beside her, the life-blood pounding loudly in his ears and with his powerful muscular arms he grasped her bare creamy-white shoulders. Her lithe catlike body, which was already sweating from the exertion of the climb, became fiery and volcanic at his unfamiliar touch and she gasped hoarsely as his tiger eyes pierced deeply into hers. He pushed her roughly down on to the springy velvet grassy cushion, soft with emerging spring flowers that cloaked the mountainside, her long blonde hair spreading wildly around her like a golden spider's web. Almost immediately her long legs began to part and she moaned softly with increasing pleasure as his fingers probed her secret places which were already damp, swollen, joyous, ready to receive his powerful manhood. Gazing down he recognised in her the wild primeval spirit of the mountain, the Jungfrau, the virgin, waiting to be taken".'

Henri grinned. 'Well, of course, she isn't a virgin but she seems like one to him.'

Kim shook her head. 'I have a few other problems.'

'Such as?'

'Well, for a start I think there are too many adjectives and adverbs.'

'I like adjectives and adverbs: they bring one's work to life.'

'Yes, but in my view you have too many . . . Henri,

154

is this going to work, you and I collaborating? Perhaps we're too close. If you really want me to edit your book then I'll have to make criticisms. You don't have to accept what I say, but you should be prepared to consider it carefully.'

He paced towards the window. Then he took a deep breath and turned to her with a smile. 'You're right, Kim. Please continue. What do you think of the rape scene in general?'

She paused and then she said, 'Well, personally I don't like reading about rape. As it's in the first chapter, it may put women off reading the rest of the book. And the rape is quite a lot more graphically bodice-ripping than the scene I've just read.'

'But the rape of Maria by the engineer symbolises the rape of the mountains. Her beautiful pointed breasts are the mountains, you see, and the lush dark valley, fronded with ferns, is—'

'Quite,' said Kim. 'Look, shall I just edit one chapter and then we can talk about it? It's going to take me quite a long time.'

'But my secretary used the spell-checker, she said.'

Kim sounded impatient. 'I'm not worried about the spelling. Look, Henri, just leave it with me and I'll see what I can do.'

When Beverly-Jane arrived for her second aromatherapy visit, Henri noticed that her white jacket was unbuttoned even lower than last time. Instead of trousers, she wore a pleated navy-blue miniskirt, short as a tennis dress, and shiny black stockings with white shoes. He helped her set up the treatment couch and offered her a glass of champagne.

'Oh, Henri, how lovely! I've always been a champagne girl,' she cooed, lowering her eyelashes.

He lifted his glass to her. 'Sorry to delay matters but I have to make an international phone call. I shan't be long. If you are bored, perhaps you would care to glance at the opening pages of my novel. The manuscript is on the table.'

'Your novel? Why, Henri, what a privilege! I'd love to look at it. I didn't know you were a writer.'

'I thought you would be interested since you are a creative person yourself,' he said.

When he returned some ten minutes later, Beverly-Jane looked up from the manuscript with a sigh. 'It's just wonderful, Henri. I can hardly bear to put it down. What a gift you have.'

He smirked. 'You can take it home with you if you like. I have several copies.'

'Why, thank you. I'd just adore to,' breathed BJ, putting the manuscript beside her case. 'Now, we must start our treatment session or I'll be late for my next appointment. Naughty boy, you forgot to change. I told you, I prefer my patients to wear a towel only.'

Henri smiled and went to change. He returned downstairs wearing a short white towel around his plump waist. He heaved himself up on to her couch. 'Is this what all aromatherapists advocate?'

'I have my own methods. I combine several therapies, you know,' said BJ.

'How interesting . . . do you think I should shut the curtains? It's rather sunny today.'

'I'll do it. Good idea. It'll help with your meditative processes,' said BJ.

She ordered him to lie on his stomach and began to knead his shoulders. Henri kept his eyes open. He was not disappointed because when occasionally she bent down to search in her case for the right essential oil – the essential essential oil? – he could see the lacy tops of her hold-up stockings and even, now and then, her insubstantial black knickers.

BJ massaged lower and lower down his back. As she massaged, she made more complimentary remarks about his writing before moving on to discuss serious matters like diet and exercise. Henri grunted now and then. Gradually, breathing a little faster, she slipped the towel down towards his thighs and began to pummel his buttocks in an energetic manner. Henri found this most arousing and was afraid that his arousal would soon be conspicuous.

BJ pulled the towel up again. 'Turn over on to your back now, Henri.'

As he did so, she gave a throaty seductive laugh. 'My, oh my,' she said. 'And I hadn't even gotten around to that department.'

Henri sat up. 'So what shall we do about it?' he asked, looking her straight in the eye.

'There's quite a few things I could suggest,' murmured Beverly-Jane.

Afterwards Henri felt guilty, though in a way Kim had brought it upon herself by being somewhat less warm from time to time recently, and particularly unkind and unappreciative about his book. And it had been impossible – in fact it would have been impolite – to refuse such a charming temptation so charmingly offered by BJ. She was an understanding woman. Not only did she have a perfect body but she was also extremely athletic. He closed his eyes and began to relive some of the delicious moments of their encounter. What imagination!

And she was intelligent as well. When they were drinking a little more champagne before she left, she had explained why she identified with the heroine of his novel. She was looking forward to reading the whole manuscript and would bring it back next time.

'Ah,' said Henri, 'So there will be more aromatherapy?'

'Why yes,' she said innocently.

'In that case, there would also have to be discretion.'

She had agreed with a mischievous smile that discretion was essential. 'I am a married woman, as you know, and I take my marriage seriously, but everyone needs a little spice in their life, and sex is great for the aura.'

Henri wondered if he would be able, at his age, to satisfy two such lovely ladies. As they were both, in their contrasting ways, most alluring, he decided he was willing to try.

'Would it be possible to schedule the aromatherapy for a Monday?' he asked.

CHAPTER 11

Kim waited to hear from Mark. Now she had confirmed his suspicions about her relationship with Henri, he would obviously no longer want to pursue her romantically, but she hoped he would still be willing to continue searching for information about Richard.

After a few weeks of silence, Mark at last telephoned to say that a friend from Maising was paying a fleeting visit to Geneva and could spare her an hour in the afternoon. They agreed to meet for tea in the café of the Red Cross museum, which had been chosen as a convenient rendezvous for the visitor.

She arrived far too early and stood waiting outside, uneasily looking over her shoulder at the group of life-size stone prisoners by the entrance. Rather than remain in their eerie hooded presence, she decided she might as well tour the exhibition and so, buying a ticket from a dithering attendant, she went cautiously down the stairs.

When her eyes became accustomed to the darkness of the underground museum, she stared about, mystified by the huge screen portraits hanging all

160

around her. She recognised Florence Nightingale and was peering at the guide leaflet for an explanation of the rest when an elegant middle-aged woman sidled up to her and asked mysteriously, 'Do you want the battle of Solferino cinema?'

'I expect I do,' whispered Kim, 'but what does all this mean?'

The amateur guide then launched into a long explanation that this first section was devoted to humanitarian acts and writings before the founding of the Red Cross.

'But what is the significance of the Battle of Solferino?' asked Kim.

The woman looked shocked at her ignorance. 'It was at this battle in 1859, or rather during the dreadful aftermath, that the Genevois Henri Dunant was inspired to found the Red Cross,' she recited. 'He was visiting Solferino on business and saw thousands of soldiers dying due to lack of medical care. He returned to Geneva determined to do everything possible to organise relief for the wounded in future wars. But he devoted so much time to the Red Cross that eventually his business affairs failed and he was obliged to leave Geneva in disgrace, never to return.'

'How sad,' said Kim, genuinely moved.

'And in the middle of the museum you will see a huge white statue of Henri Dunant sitting under the only natural light in the museum, a glass pyramid. The architect who created this modern museum design was—'

'I'm rather short of time. I think I had better hurry on,' said Kim quickly, 'but thank you so much, madame.'

After the Battle of Solferino, Kim found herself among row upon row of long brown file boxes. She read a panel informing her that these contained seven million cards compiled in Geneva to identify prisoners in the 1914–18 war. She shivered and walked on, staring at the interior walls which chronicled all the wars and disasters that had taken place since 1863, year after year after year. She moved to the section devoted to World War Two, but when she saw some of the harrowing film footage, she found she couldn't stay long.

'The Red Cross and Red Crescent movement believes that its strength and influence lies in the fact that it is impartial. It makes no judgements and therefore is allowed access to prisoners of both sides in a conflict,' she read.

Then she found a life-size prison cell and a notice explaining that in an identical cell, four metres square, a present-day Red Cross delegate had found seventeen prisoners. The concrete floor of the museum cell was embedded with, and completely covered by, seventeen pairs of footprints.

Ashamed of her own trivial worries, Kim fled upstairs to the café.

Mark was waiting, glad of this excuse to see her. Her appearance caused an emotional jolt which he disguised with a hearty greeting, determined to keep his distance from now on.

He had initially found it difficult to come to terms with her confession that Henri supported her and that she had begun the affair so soon after her husband's disappearance. When he had first met her, he had admired Kim both as a chaste and grieving saint, and as a strong resilient woman, a woman who had supported her family and held them together as they travelled around the world. Now he was forced to regard her in a different, more realistic light. She was undoubtedly stoical and brave, but not quite as saintly as he'd imagined.

Of course, it wasn't unusual for a widow from an unhappy marriage to seek swift consolation. That charming old bastard – that damn rich old bastard – must have been lusting after her for years, and made his move with expert timing when she was alone and desperate. But was it more than desperation that had driven her into his arms? It seemed she did actually love Henri: she had certainly made it clear she was not much interested in his own advances.

On New Year's Eve he had stood in the darkness above the square in Wengen and, looking down, he'd suffered from an acute stab of jealousy when he'd seen her arm in arm with Henri and her child. Together they gave the impression of a small, solid family group.

His feelings towards her now? There was no

point in being in love with a woman happily attached to someone else but as soon as he saw her he knew they hadn't changed. He desired her to the point of obsession.

Today she looked more beautiful than ever in that natural, slightly untidy way he found so endearing. After listening to her vivid description of the museum, his instinct was to put his arm round her and comfort her, but he restrained himself.

Eventually she stopped talking and looked around, pushing back her dark hair, a familiar gesture he remembered.

'Don't tell me your friend isn't going to show up,' she said.

Mark smiled. 'He'll come. Don't worry.'

'Tell me again about Maising. It's not a place I know anything about.'

'It's an independent country consisting of about a hundred small islands between Indonesia and Malaysia. The capital is called Maising, as well as the country, just to make things simpler.'

She looked round at the entrance. 'And the man we're going to meet?'

'Ang Song? He's a very nice chap, I was at Cambridge with him. It's just luck he's here having a meeting at the Red Cross HQ. He's an international charities man, a world-wide do-gooder, but I thought he might know something about Richard because his brother is the Maising chief of police. It's one of those small countries where everyone important is related to each other.'

'So he's quite influential.'

'Yes, but be careful what you say. Don't ask him to take any action without discussing it with me first.'

Kim began to fiddle nervously with her cup and saucer and then slowly she tore her paper napkin into smaller and smaller shreds and made neat piles of debris in a row on the red table.

Mark watched her, studying her hands, sturdy hands with short, sensible unpainted nails. She still wore her wedding ring, he noted.

Together they watched each other.

Kim was aware of a greater distance between them. She felt that Mark was staring at her in a curiously remote, uncomfortable manner. From time to time there was an awkward silence and she was relieved when Ang Song finally arrived.

He was tiny, dapper and handsome with a smooth beige face and a thin black moustache. He was obviously delighted to see Mark. After polite preliminaries and reminiscences about their university days together, Mark broached the subject of Richard.

Apparently there were reports that a man called Eves had arrived at a commune of European neo-hippies on one of the remoter islands of the Maising group near Indonesia.

'Our name is Ellis,' she said impatiently.

'But there is a similarity. It is possible that the names have been confused, transmitted wrongly,' said Ang. 'We have to rely on simple village heads to give us information. We cannot afford to police many of the islands on a regular basis. In fact, we only send police from the capital if something goes wrong. Usually we have to work on the principle that no news is good news,' he added with a smile. 'If the hippies don't disturb us, we don't disturb them.'

She caught her breath. 'So you don't know if it's Richard or not. Why should it be him?'

'It seems rather a coincidence that a man called Ellis is lost in Western Indonesia, and then a man by the name of Eves turns up on a neighbouring Maising island,' said Ang, folding his elegant hands together.

'Do these new-age hippies have any means of communication?' she asked.

'Yes, they are not totally against the modern world, I gather.'

Shaking her head, she said vehemently, 'Then this man can't be Richard because he certainly wouldn't have let Christmas go by without getting in touch.'

'I see,' said Ang. 'Well, if I hear any further news, I will contact Mark. It is possible that we may eventually one day have to send police to the island. Some of the hippies may be involved in a separatist movement on the Lahn archipelago.'

'But why should hippies be interested in separatists?' asked Mark.

'They want to put themselves as far away from the law as possible. Sometimes even Maising's lax legal system interferes with them – now and then we confiscate a consignment of drugs just to show we haven't forgotten them.'

As soon as Ang had left for his next appointment, Kim grabbed hold of Mark's arm. 'Maybe I was wrong, perhaps this Eves man is Richard. Perhaps we should ask the Maising people to send someone to the island to see him.'

'Hm,' said Mark thoughtfully. 'If you urge them to investigate, it may end up with Richard's being arrested and languishing in a foreign jail for years on end.'

Kim turned pale as an image of the museum cell came into her mind. 'But why should he be arrested?'

'Because he may be selling weapons to these dissidents.'

She stared at him. 'So you're telling me I should do nothing?'

'You're certain that if he were alive he would have got in touch at Christmas?'

'Yes.'

'Then maybe the Indonesians were right after all. Perhaps you'll have to accept the fact that he was on the plane that crashed. I'm very sorry, Kim.'

White-faced, she stared at the table without speaking. Then she said, 'I wish I could do something.'

'I know,' said Mark. 'Look, I'll try the Consul

again, see if she'd heard anything.' He looked at his watch. 'Sorry to have to leave you like this, but I have to get back to the office.' He led her outside into the grey winter afternoon and said a polite goodbye, with a chaste kiss on her cheek.

Somehow it didn't feel like the right moment to tell her about his wife's impending visit. Bella had telephoned this morning to announce that she was coming to Geneva 'for a teeny-weenie discussion'.

CHAPTER 12

Mark showed his diplomatic card and passed through the waiting crowds into the empty baggage-claim hall. He stood by the barricade, watching the passengers queuing up at the yellow line to present their passports to the unsmiling Swiss officials. He could not see Arabella and was beginning to hope that she had changed her mind and decided not to come. But then she appeared, keeping herself a little apart from the queue. It seemed she had abandoned her former English country lady style: she was now dressed in a severe pale grey suit.

Full of misgivings, he greeted her politely, unable to avoid an airy couple of kisses. As they waited for her luggage to emerge from the black mouth of the carousel tunnel, he asked where she was staying.

She smiled brightly. 'Hotels here seem to be jolly expensive and I'm not feeling terribly rich at the moment, so I thought I'd just stay a night or two with you. You don't mind, do you, darling? We do need to have a little chat about this and that.' Her British voice rang out across the background

169

noise. Some of the passengers nearby turned and gazed admiringly at her. Tall and well-groomed, she still made a glamorous picture, he thought, but she was thinner than ever, so thin that her face had become sharp and angular.

An hour later she was standing in the middle of his apartment, taking stock. 'Darling, I'm not sure I'm mad about this room, especially the repro furniture – and the curtains, oh dear. I can't understand why you didn't choose one of those lovely villas on the lakeside. I mean, there's not much point in being in Geneva if you're not on the lake,' she said, taking off her velvet hairband and running her fingers through her long straight ash-blonde hair. She always made a point of displaying this, her best feature, to its greatest advantage.

'I didn't have any choice about accommodation. The flat goes with the job, belongs to HMG. Anyway it's fine, and very convenient for the office,' said Mark. 'By the way, I've put your baggage in the spare room.'

'Yes, that's best for the time being. Hope your maid won't think it odd if the lady of the house sleeps in a different room.'

'But, my dear Bella, you are not the lady of the house.'

'No, not really, but you never know.'

Mark raised his eyebrows. 'Would you like a drink?' he asked.

'No, I think I'll have a cup of tea. I know it's evening here but I'm still on English time. Let me get it. I'm rather good in strange kitchens, if you remember. Is it this way? Oh dear, what a tiny kitchen for such a large flat. Where's the kettle? Oh yes, this one. Didn't we get it for a wedding present?'

Mark gave a wintry smile. 'No, we didn't. As you may remember, you kept most of the wedding presents. That was our agreement.'

'Nice big fridge though,' she said with a wave of her hand.

'It belongs to the government.'

'Where are the cups? And the milk?'

'In the blue and white carton marked *"lait"*. Cups in this cupboard. Not a wedding present either. I bought them a couple of years ago.'

'You're sounding rather possessive, Mark. I haven't come here to steal your things, you know.' She took the carton of milk out of the fridge. 'D'you take sugar?'

'No, I haven't done during the last twenty years.'

'Oops, I forgot how my bad memory used to annoy you.' She smiled.

Eventually with maximum drama, she assembled the tea and placed it on one of the despised coffee tables. He avoided sharing the sofa with her. 'Tell me, Bella, to what do I owe the honour of your presence and how long are you staying? You seem to have brought two rather large suitcases.'

'Yes, isn't it a bore, had to bring fabric samples – they even had the nerve to charge excess baggage. Tell you my plans in a mo. Just better go and hang up my frocks. You're not taking me to any official parties tonight, are you? Hope your maid is good at ironing. I've bought masses,' she added.

Mark sat and waited. What the bloody hell was she up to? He poured himself a rather too dark whisky and soda. 'Well?' he asked when she returned.

'You don't seem all that pleased I'm here,' she said.

'On the contrary, I'm always happy to see you – as long as it's in small doses.'

She pursed her lips. 'I just thought it would be fun to come and stay for a few days and perhaps see if I can find some clients here. They're getting a bit thin on the ground in England, even though there's supposed to be this great economic recovery.' Her eyes darted around. 'Darling, I really do think we should change those curtains. Who could have chosen such a boring material?'

Mark ignored the aside. 'If you found clients here, you'd want to keep popping backwards and forwards, and you might find you regularly needed a bed in Geneva. And frankly, Bella, it's out of the question for you to stay here on a regular basis. Anyway I'm not even sure how long I'll be here myself.'

Unperturbed, Bella said, 'Well, yes, maybe, but

172

I wouldn't always have to inflict myself on you because clients usually offer a bed. Now, have you got any ideas who I should approach? You must have some rich Swiss friends, or are they all dreary diplomats or even more tedious UN bores?'

'My only contacts are international bureaucrats, no one who would be of the slightest interest to you,' said Mark firmly and not altogether truthfully.

'That's not very helpful. But luckily Minty Pensworth-Abbot – d'you know her, she's awfully nice – she gave me a couple of suggestions. There was one woman who's a sort of Hapsburg, I believe, and then there's someone else who knows Sally Burton – such a sweetie, have you met her? And Clarissa Talbot who lives in Verbier most of the time.'

Eventually Mark interrupted her in mid name-drop. 'What does Cosmo think about this visit? You're supposed to be engaged to him. Doesn't he disapprove of you staying with your nearly-ex husband?'

She sighed. 'Cosmo absolutely insisted on going to Scotland to stay with some ancient relations even though he knows I find them a bore.'

'But I thought you always believed in meeting people in case they become clients.'

'No way. Cosmo's cousins are anti-decorator. They just sit about drinking neat whisky under ghastly pictures of stags at bay and they use moth-eaten rugs to cover the holes in their dog-eared sofas. They actually refuse to consider decorating their so-called castle, though, God knows, they need it, both the cousins and the fearful dump they live in.'

'You can't describe a sofa as dog-eared. It usually applies to books.'

'Sometimes you're a bit pompous, dear heart. Dogchewed, dog-ridden, whatever. Dog-eared sounds best to me.'

'Reverting to Cosmo,' he said patiently, 'you're still going to marry him, aren't you?'

'Yes, I think so.'

'You think so?' Christ, wasn't she certain about it?

'Well, he's a bit overbearing sometimes.'

'Poor chap. In what way? I thought you told me he was amazingly easy-going compared with me.'

'Yes, but he's terribly opinionated sometimes. Like you but in a different way.'

'You mean he has different opinions from yours?'

'Exactly,' said Bella, as usual failing to detect the irony in his tone. 'You know, originally I did up his London flat for him and that was fine. He gave me a blank cheque and so I did what I wanted and it was absolutely perfect. Everyone says so. I found some wonderful fabrics at Colefax & Fowler at knock-down prices and had them made up by a frightfully nice little woman in Barnes. You have to know the right people, as I told him. Now I've got some fabulous ideas about his country house and he says he doesn't want to change anything. But he must see that I've got to.'

'Must he?'

'Well, yes, of course. I need a show place in the country so people can see my work, and anyway I simply can't live with the combination of his first wife's bad taste and his mother's junk, and his grandfather's Indian mementoes, or whatever ancestor it was. Admittedly some of the furniture is lovely – the genuine stuff, not like this – but the rest is indescribably shabby and desperately uncomfortable to live with. You can't even see the good pieces because of all the appalling junk.' She waved her arms dramatically. 'And he's being terribly stingy about resurfacing the tennis court. You know how important a good court is to me. Unfortunately he isn't much of a tennis player, more of a huntin', shootin', fishin' type. Those sort of sports are all so expensive. Must try and wean him off them.'

As she talked Mark studied her and wondered, as he had done so often in the past, why he had been so much in love with her. Her pale blue eyes, which had once seemed so alluring, now contained a hardness that had not been apparent in the early days. It was an unnerving thought that he, supposedly a good judge of character, had been too taken up with her youthful sex-appeal to recognise the woman she would become. But then maybe she would have become a different woman if she'd had children.

'Does Cosmo have any offspring?' he asked aloud.

'Yes, two rather nice teenage boys, but I'm not sure if they like me,' she said wistfully. 'Still, they like Fluff and she adores everyone, as you know.'

Bella's passion for dogs in general and her spaniel Fluff in particular was her redeeming feature as far as he was concerned.

'Yes, how is Fluff?'

'Not so agile these days,' said Bella sadly. 'Cosmo's looking after her for me.' Her voice softened as she talked on about Fluff. 'He says she's too old to be trained a gundog now, but anyway I'm not particularly keen on shooting. Seems a bit pointless to kill all those poor stupid beautiful pheasants. That's a bit of a snag about Cosmo, this blood sports lark. Must try to wean him off them, as I said.'

'If I were you, Bella, I shouldn't demand too much before the wedding. After that I'm sure your charms will win him round. He seems like a good catch – you don't want to mess things up.'

'You were a good catch too,' said Bella with another smile.

'But I have a great many drawbacks, as you were fond of pointing out. You always complained I was over-obsessed with my career. And then, quite apart from my ridiculous habit of going abroad, a major snag is that I don't have any money apart from my civil servant's salary, whereas from what you say Cosmo has the advantage of being both extremely rich and also very grand in social terms. He does sound a much better bargain.'

'Ye-es, but I was talking to someone in the Foreign Office at a cocktail party the other day – forgotten his name, David somebody, terribly nice. Anyway he told me you're bound to become an ambassador soon. And that did sound rather fun, and also rather grand.'

'There's nothing grand, believe me, in being posted somewhere like one of the new republics where the Ambassador has to live and work in a couple of rooms in a primitive hotel.'

She looked dismayed. 'Oh, don't get sent somewhere like that please, darling. I was thinking of Paris.'

'Bella, I should have thought that by now even you would have grasped a few basic facts about how the FO operates. I'm not senior enough to be an ambassador in any European country, let alone Paris. As I'm now in an extremely desirable posting, next time I'm bound to be sent somewhere hot and probably uncomfortable, certainly somewhere a long way from England, and not as Ambassador either, more likely as Deputy. But I don't know where yet.'

'Oh,' she said thoughtfully. 'And when will you be posted?'

'Could be next month, could be next year: one never knows.'

She gave a little sigh. 'Ah well.'

He was amused by her disappointment. Nevertheless her interest in his future prospects was unnerving. 'When are you getting married?'

he asked. 'I gather our divorce is coming through soon.'

'We haven't actually fixed a date for the wedding. Before I marry someone else and everything becomes absolute or whatever, I just wanted to make sure that it was really and truly over between you and me.' She fluttered her eyelashes again.

'Of course it is. And I should make it clear that you can't just dump yourself on me every time you have a tiff with Cosmo and want to make him jealous.'

'Why not?' She smiled a naughty little smile. 'At the moment we're still technically married. Don't you fancy me any more? Not even a teensy weenie bit?'

'Most men would find you attractive,' he said calmly, 'but now you're engaged to Cosmo. We've been leading separate lives for years and we both prefer it that way. You know we do.'

She gave him a long look. 'Well, there were certain things I used to appreciate about you. In fact, there was always one particular aspect, possibly the only part, of our marriage that used to be a sure-fire success. Come to think of it, Marky, one has rather happy memories of your biggest advantage. Not many chaps are quite as . . .'

She then began to describe to him in explicit terms exactly what she had enjoyed. In the early days this would have aroused him, but now, out of context, out of bed, it merely sounded coarse.

And Bella herself had never lived up to the erotic promise of her sexual language, always using sex as a bargaining counter, holding back, never giving herself wholeheartedly, never with any genuine joy and lust.

Suddenly he looked at his watch and stood up. 'I've got to go out. There's some food in the fridge left over from a dinner party. You can eat that. I'll arrange a hotel for you tomorrow.'

Open-mouthed Bella watched him depart.

Mark spent the evening in the cinema. It seemed easier than fending off Bella and then having a row. Or not fending her off and then being unable to get rid of her.

After the cinema, he went to a bar and sipped a slow whisky until midnight when he reckoned she would be asleep. When he arrived home he found that she was indeed asleep, in his bed, naked. He stared at the long blonde hair on the pillow and for a moment he was tempted. It had been some time since he last had sex. But the price would be far too high. He made his way to the spare room and lay thinking of Kim until finally he slept.

At eight-thirty the next morning the telephone rang. Bella answered it with a sleepy hello.

'Oh, uh, can I speak to Mark?' asked a woman's voice hesitantly.

Bella yawned and looked at the smooth empty

space beside her. 'Sorry, just woken up. I'll go and see if he's still here.' She pulled on Mark's dressing gown and padded around the apartment. 'Can you hear me? I'm on the hall phone now. Sorry, he seems to have gone. This is his wife speaking. Can I take a message?'

'Oh? No, no thanks. This is Kim Ellis. I'll ring him at work.'

Bella tossed her head and then put on her friendly chatty voice. 'Afraid you won't find him there. He's got meetings outside the office all day and then we're going away for the week-end. What a lovely place this is. I'm looking forward to spending more time here. What was your name again? I'll tell him you rang.'

'Kim Ellis. Thanks. Goodbye.'

Bella was pleased with the creativity of her own imagination so early in the morning.

Anyway it was jolly rude of Mark to decline her kind offer. But then maybe he was temporarily keen on this Kim woman, though he hadn't said a word on the subject. In the end though, he would get bored with her. He always gave up these passing girlfriends eventually and then he'd look her up and they'd make love, just like old times. Despite their differences, they were tied together by intricate bonds and long memories. In some ways this long-distance separate-lives marriage rather suited her. She could have made a mistake about Cosmo who seemed to be rather too keen on a suffocating togetherness. Perhaps she should make a few more visits to see Mark, the devil she knew, before finally committing herself to someone else.

As for the phone call from Kim Ellis, whoever she may be, Bella thought it very likely that with her bad memory she would forget to tell him about it.

CHAPTER 13

Kim had been preoccupied with the latest rumour that Richard might after all be alive. She wondered how long it would take to find out more about the man called Eves on the island in Maising. Months and months as usual, no doubt. And then nothing would come of it. She would still be in the same position – an uncertain widow. It reminded her faintly of the long-deceased Lord Lucan. For a few years after his disappearance, people sometimes claimed to have caught sight of the elusive earl, but he was eventually declared dead.

She had decided to ring Mark. Since he'd now accepted that there was to be no emotional relationship between them, there wouldn't be any harm in inviting him round to discuss the implications of what Ang had said, but, to her great surprise, his wife answered the telephone. What is more, Bella had clearly answered the phone in his bedroom, in his bed. Kim acknowledged that, having rejected him, she herself had no romantic claims – no right to feel jealous or hurt, in fact it was quite ridiculous to be so upset – but as a friend, the very least he should have done was tell her about his reconciliation with his wife. The very least.

When Mark telephoned after a few days, she managed to sound reasonably normal. She thanked him for his help and asked if he had any more news about Richard.

'Unfortunately no, but there's something else I have to tell you.'

'What?' she asked, dreading that he was about to say he was going back to Bella.

'I've suddenly been posted, sent back to England for three months to assist on a Commission on the situation in the Middle East. The chap who was supposed to have done the job has been taken ill, and as I've got experience in the area, I've been selected instead. It'll involve a lot of travelling and a lot of hard work, I imagine.'

'Oh good. Congratulations,' she said, momentarily relieved that it was nothing to do with Bella.

'You sound pleased.'

She collected herself. 'Well, I mean, I'm pleased for you – it must be good for your career, isn't it?'

'I suppose so. But it's unlikely I'll be in a position to find out anything further about Richard. I hope you don't mind, but I've given Ang your number so he can ring you direct if he hears anything.'

'I see, thank you, thank you very much. It was kind of you. Um, when are you going and when are you coming back?'

'I don't know. You see, they're going to give me another posting straight after his job. So I'm leaving Geneva permanently.'

Her heart sank. 'Oh, I'm sorry. Where will you be sent to?'

'Anywhere. I don't know, but I'll certainly try to pass through Geneva en route. So I'll look you up, if I may. Can I see you before I go?'

'Well, I . . .' Yes, said part of her. No, said her conscience.

'I've got to pack up the flat and get organised in the office, so it's all very hectic. There's an official farewell party at the WTO for me on Thursday. Could you come? Bring Henri if you want.'

'We'd love to,' said Kim, upset that he wasn't insisting on an intimate dinner for two. Which she would have had to refuse, of course.

Fortunately Henri decided he did not want to attend a dull diplomatic party, so on Thursday, in her best rather too tight black dress, she went alone to the World Trade Organisation which was housed in an imposing building beside the lake. She followed the signs to a high-ceilinged hall where Mark, tall and handsome in his inevitable grey pinstripe, was standing by the door. He greeted all his guests, including her, in the same charming manner.

Both the canapes and the champagne were delicious, but she did not enjoy the party. She knew no one among the hundred or so people, and stood making conversation to two UN women in suits while watching Mark out of the corner of her eye. She began to realise he could never leave the door: as soon as he had finished welcoming the new guests he'd have to start saying goodbye to the leavers. There would be no possibility of having a tête-à-tête about Richard or anything else. She would just have to go home.

'Goodbye then, Mark. Thank you for the party. Oh, and good luck with your new job,' she said with stilted formality holding out her hand.

He took it and drawing her towards him a little kissed her three times on the cheek, just as he had kissed many of the other women. 'Goodbye, Kim. Hope to see you again one day.' He, too, sounded unnaturally polite.

Stepping backwards, she gave an awkward little wave and then was obliged to make way for the next departing guests.

So that's that. If he was going to be home in England he'd be able to see more of Bella and that could help what appeared to be a sudden reconciliation between them. Which was just as well, what with one thing and another.

In the car park she hesitated for a moment. She could go back, suggest they have dinner together. But then he was probably busy and what could she offer him? Nothing, nothing at all. Maybe she'd go and talk to him one more time, just to say goodbye properly. She turned and walked back almost to the door of the building. Then, telling herself she was a fool, she returned alone to her car.

As she drove home through the evening traffic she felt a deep pervasive sense of loss, a feeling she was unable to shake off during the weeks that followed.

'You've been looking real down lately. Are you suffering from inappropriate body rhythms? What you might need is a polarity massage,' said BJ. 'It puts your brain in touch with your body. The energy kind of moves into you, then you feel like you're floating. Like I told Henri, it's extremely beneficial.'

'Hm,' said Kim. Shut up, BJ, she thought.

'Or maybe you should try Magnetism or Metamorphic Technique.'

'Yes, perhaps.'

'Or Reiki. Then some people have had a lot of success with Feldenkrais – it's movement techniques, a way of getting in touch with the muscles in your body. It's so important to explore your own method of moving, like I told Henri.'

'You seem very pally with him,' said Kim, suddenly paying attention.

'Yeah, such a receptive guy. It's unusual for a man of his age to be interested in alternative health. But it's you I'm worried about. Do you have a crystal?' BJ's face was earnest.

'I don't, apart from rings of course.'

'But you should wear them all the time. We already discussed this in our health guide. Don't you remember? Crystals have scientifically proven power. Each one is a solid mass of atoms, charging and recharging – that's why we can used quartz in a watch to maintain perfect time. And, like, the same vibrations of energy can maintain harmony within the body. People just don't realise that when you wear a crystal you infuse your thoughts into it, and then the crystal processes your own energy, amplifies it and focuses it back into you, and even into the universe.'

'You believe that?'

'Sure I do. It has a scientific basis, like I said. And a historical basis, people have been wearing jewellery for years. Different crystals have different properties, like amethysts are calming and . . .'

'Oh yes. I remember.'

'Don't forget, a crystal can even help you find a parking space,' said BJ.

When Kim opened the mail next day, she wondered if there was some kind of crystal to make relations disappear. She put down the letter, swearing under her breath.

James looked up. 'What did you say, Mummy?'

'I said that, oh dear, your Aunt Monica wants to come for half term. She thinks it'll be good for Damien's French as he's bottom of his class.'

'Ugh. But, Mum, that's not fair. It means we can't have any fun. Tell them not to come.'

'Monica is your father's sister. We have to be hospitable, and she's right, it may help Damien.'

'How old is he?'

'Thirteen or fourteen, I think.'

James digested that fact, then he said, 'I hope she isn't bringing stupid Tilly.'

'Of course Tilly is coming, they all are.'

James made a face, then his expression became more cheerful. 'I've got an idea. We can take them skiing.'

'We can't afford to, and anyway they don't ski.'

A picture of disgust, James stomped out of the room.

Guests from hell, thought Kim, when they were all assembled for dinner on the evening of their arrival. Even the simple concept of sitting down together around a table for a meal seemed alien to Monica's family. Only brother-in-law George responded to Kim's attempts at conversation. He had already consumed half her meagre supply of whisky and was in an expansive mood, discoursing on what was wrong with the Swiss and Switzerland, with occasional references to his bad leg. His hair had now receded to the point of non-existence and a vast beer belly was only partially concealed by a brown jumper of such devastating ugliness that it could only have been knitted by Monica.

Monica herself had discarded the jacket of her green tweed trouser suit to reveal a yellow polyester blouse and mustard-coloured sleeveless sweater, another of her own creations, no doubt. These days her hair was dyed a dark mulberry-red that did not tone particularly well with mustard. As usual, she chain-smoked, while her black eyes darted restlessly about. Looking for something to criticise, thought Kim sourly.

For dinner Kim had prepared a chicken casserole with an assortment of vegetables, a harmless choice, she reckoned. She had expected that Tilly, who was only eight, might not eat the onions or courgettes, but the child didn't appear to like rice or carrots, or even the chicken. She pushed the food about the plate, her straight mousy hair hanging around her doleful face.

Only Damien seemed to be hungry. He was wolfing down the chicken, though he, too left the vegetables untouched. Dressed entirely in black, with three gold earrings in one ear, he kept his eyes fixed on the table.

Neither child had spoken a word since their arrival.

'Would you like some bread, Tilly?' asked Kim gently.

Tilly looked suspiciously at the baguette and did not reply.

'Perhaps you'd like some butter? I'll get some,' said Kim.

Tilly buttered the hunk of baguette but then sat waiting.

'Have you got any chocolate spread?' asked

Damien suddenly. 'Like, that's what she wants. With proper bread, you know, sliced white.'

'Sorry, they don't sell English bread here. But I've got some strawberry jam. Will that do, Tilly?'

Despite the Swiss label, the jam appeared to be acceptable. Separating the pieces of strawberry from the jelly and pushing them aside, Tilly spread the bread and managed a couple of mouthfuls.

Damien spoke again. 'She'll eat chicken if there's ketchup. Don't you have decent sauces here?'

The next item to meet with disapproval was the television. 'So many channels and nearly all of them in French. But if they have German and Italian, it's amazing there's nothing in English.'

Kim explained about German and Italian being official Swiss languages but her guests were not mollified. Damien was persuaded to watch children's cartoons in French in the morning, or what was left of the morning after he'd crawled out of bed, but Kim had to spend a great deal of time and money hiring DVDs in English, much to James's delight. At least watching television was better than making conversation, or rather listening to George's monologues punctuated by Monica's smoker's cough.

All this time Kim was waiting for an opportunity to discuss Richard. It would be unnatural not to talk about him with his sister, though Monica herself had not broached the subject. It seemed best not to raise false hopes by mentioning the obscure and unlikely rumours about his survival, but there were other matters she felt it her duty to bring up.

One day when she and Monica were alone in the kitchen, Kim at last found the opportunity.

'About Richard,' she said, 'I haven't had a memorial service for him because I thought I'd wait a year. Don't know why but it seemed best.'

'No point in having one on my account,' said Monica flatly. 'He never went to church, did he?'

'No, but . . .'

'Why go to all that fuss then?'

'Well, I suppose it's the normal thing to do. Some people probably feel I should have had a service by now.'

'You're too conventional, Kim. Say a prayer for him one day if you want to, but count me out. Not my thing at all. Nor Richard's either, for that matter.'

'Right. You see, I was waiting for more information about the crash. They still haven't given me any details.'

'Look, if he'd survived he'd have shown up by now, wouldn't he?'

'Yes, I suppose so.'

Monica patted her awkwardly on the shoulder. 'So get on with your life.' This gesture, wildly demonstrative by Monica's standards, seemed to be the end of the discussion.

Later that day though, Monica suddenly asked, 'What about Richard's clothes?'

'His clothes?'

'What have you done with them?'

'Just left them in the wardrobe,' said Kim. What a question, she thought.

'When you do eventually get rid of them, could you put aside his dinner jacket for me? Damien might need one if he ever goes to a posh do.'

'OK,' said Kim, irritated and disturbed by Monica's pragmatism.

As the visit continued its patience-testing course, Kim felt obliged to organise a constant frenzy of activity. Each day she took the family on a tour of Geneva. They saw the Old Town, the Clock Museum, the Musée d'Art et d'Histoire and the National History Museum, the latter being the most popular with the children. Damien kept threatening to lock Tilly in the dead spiders' cage or feed her to the live but somnolent crocodile in the entrance hall.

They were not impressed by the art galleries. 'This museum is a waste of money,' proclaimed Tilly loudly when faced with some black and white abstract oils, but she admitted that one or two of the Picassos might have been a bit difficult to draw.

Tourist activities took up most of the day but once back at the house, her guests sat about fidgeting and squabbling with each other. Eventually, to avoid the long drive to fetch yet another DVD, Kim hit upon the idea of asking Henri if the children could watch his satellite television from time to time.

'Yes, of course. But, apart from the news channels, the only British one I receive is BBC Prime,' said Henri, 'and it's unbelievably dull and second rate. A constant stream of home improvement programmes and a soap opera about gloomy uncultured people in an obscure part of London. Then there is an appalling channel filled with pop music, American, I believe.'

'Just up their street,' said Kim.

Henri put the television in the garden room so that the children could slip in and out without disturbing him. The arrangement worked well. Yet another reason to be grateful to Henri. 'What a lovely bloke,' said Monica in a rare burst of approval.

The day before the guests were due to leave turned out clear and sunny, and Kim suggested a cable car ride up the Salève mountain so they could see the magnificent views of the city and beyond. Tilly was excited at the prospect of playing in the snow, but at the last minute Damien refused to go, saying he couldn't face another draggy boring tourist sight. Geneva wasn't a happening place and he certainly wasn't into seeing any more of it.

After a long and disagreeable argument, he was allowed to stay on his own in the house on condition that he do his holiday homework. At least there would be more room in the car without him, thought Kim. Henri had earlier promised to come with them, bringing his Range Rover to help with the transport, but then this morning he, too, had changed his mind, no doubt as sick of her guests as she was.

Thank God they've all fucked off at last, thought Damien. He turned on Kim's TV but, as usual, it showed dreary foreign people talking away. God, these stupid Frogs, he muttered. He rummaged about in the kitchen and found the ingredients for a sandwich. Leaving a trail of crumbs behind him, he went upstairs to find his CD player and his French grammar book.

Boring, boring, boring, he decided after less than quarter of an hour. He went back to the kitchen and grabbed a can of coke and a packet of chocolate biscuits. The debris from his sandwich-making was all over the table and, he noticed, the floor. He'd definitely wipe up the mess later otherwise Kim would have to do it.

She was all right, his Aunt Kim. Not bad looking for her age. Pity about Uncle Richard disappearing – not that he was much use. Even Mum more or less said so. And he'd also overhead Mum saying that anyone could see the old bloke next door fancied Kim and that she ought to get off with him, but, yuck, she could do better than that, Mr Marechal was about a hundred. Stinking rich though, and a really nice house with a great music system and a seriously massive telly.

Contemplating the pleasures of Henri's magnificent television, Damien went out into the garden.

Probably wouldn't be much on at this time of day except MTV. Good though and at least it was in English.

He wandered slowly across the lawn, through the gate and up the path towards Henri's garden room.

As he approached the house he heard rather strange sounds, like a woman imitating a steam train. He stopped and listened. The garden room blinds were down. Maybe Henri himself was watching TV. In that case, he'd stay away as he didn't feel like talking to anyone today.

'Oh, honey, honey, honey,' panted the woman, 'yes, oh yes!' It was an American accent.

Damien was unused to and shy with real girls as he attended a local boys' grammar school and, despite a deep interest in the subject, he had not yet achieved any personal experience of sex. He was, however, an avid cinema-goer and he suddenly realised that the disembodied voice in Henri's garden room sounded pretty passionate. He grinned. So old Henri was into watching blue films. He crept across the grass, stepped carefully across the stone path and peered through a gap in the blinds.

His jaw dropped. Henri's naked buttocks were pumping up and down, and underneath him on the sofa, her legs in the air, was a middle-aged woman in a white jacket and black stockings but nothing in between.

How really gross and disgusting! You expect young

people to do it, like in the movies, but old fat wrinkles like Henri and this skinny old bag – ugh. Damien retreated as quickly and quietly as he could.

'Did you have a nice day, Damien?' asked Kim when the family returned.

'Uh.'

'What does "uh" mean?'

'Bit boring. Nothing to do.' He could feel his face going red. Was he supposed to tell her or wasn't he? Should he warn her that Henri, who until today had seemed like a decent enough bloke, was in fact a dirty old man?

Perhaps she didn't want to know. She was a nice woman, Kim. He'd forgotten to clean up the kitchen and she hadn't said a word about it, or about him leaving the back door unlocked when he'd gone for a walk to get away from the horrible sight of oldies shagging.

Later that evening another thought occurred to him. Since old Henri was obviously a sex maniac, and fancied Kim, supposing he jumped on her and raped her? You read about that sort of thing in the Sun every day. Yeah, on second thoughts, he'd better warn her.

After dinner there was, for once, a film in English on the Swiss TV. While everyone sat down to watch it, Kim went to clear away the dishes.

When Damien followed her into the kitchen, she smiled at him. 'It's OK. I can manage. You watch the film.'

'Seen it already, five hundred times, boring rubbish,' he said, shoving the dirty plates in the dishwasher without rinsing them like Mum insisted on. 'Er, Kim,' he began. He took another deep breath. 'Er, if you . . . if you saw, er, something would you, would you tell someone else?'

She scrubbed round the saucepan in the sink. 'I'm not sure what you mean.'

'Well, like, grassing . . . shopping, you know.'

'Oh, you mean telling tales. Well, I suppose it depends on the seriousness of the crime. If I saw a small child stealing sweets, I probably wouldn't say anything to the shopkeeper but I'd tick off the child privately if I had a chance. But, of course, I'd report a bank robbery.' She paused and smiled. 'Why? Have you seen someone committing a crime?'

'Uh, no, not exactly.'

She looked at him, puzzled. 'What then?'

He gulped and said in a rush, 'I saw Henri having it off with a woman in his TV room.'

Kim put down the saucepan with a bang. 'I think you must have been mistaken,' she snapped, sounding really uptight and furious with him, which was a bit unfair, he thought.

'No, honestly, I saw him and . . .'

'At your age, you can't know much about these things. What did this woman look like?'

'Dunno, she was oldish.'

'Oldish?'

'Well, Mum's age or older, and she was

197

blonde . . . with thin legs and she had a white nurse's jacket.'

She paced about. 'So it could have been a nurse or physiotherapist giving some quite normal medical treatment.'

He described the scene again with a few more details until he could see that Kim was convinced he was telling the truth.

'And,' he added, 'I heard her, er, kind of, talking. She sounded like an American.'

'Did she indeed?' Aunt Kim leant against the table. Then her face went red. 'I don't want to hear another word about it. It's not our business and you're not to say a word to anyone else,' she said and rushed out of the kitchen.

He heard her go upstairs to her bedroom, slamming the door really loudly so the whole house shook. Damien waited but when she failed to reappear, he poured himself a Coca Cola, put the remaining plates in the dishwasher and went to watch television.

CHAPTER 14

Following the discovery of Henri's betrayal, Kim passed through various extremes of shock, nausea, pain and rage and, after many sleepless nights and dark introspective days, she eventually reached a sick, unhappy comprehension. Everything that had passed between them seemed spoilt and diminished; for him it was obviously just another banal affair. She had begun to believe that she was special to him and that he genuinely loved her. Now she knew it was all an illusion. She was just another in a long line of women, and a kept woman at that. She should have remembered.

She should also have remembered there was a subclause in his original proposition that other – preferably secret – lovers were permissible. She had not taken advantage of this herself. Her probably outdated middle-class scruples and sense of loyalty had prevented her from embarking on an infidelity of her own, with Mark. Though she'd wanted to. In fact if he were still here, she could take her revenge. But Mark had gone back to England and probably to his wife and that was the end of it.

All these feelings she kept to herself, soldiering on with her daily routine as if nothing had happened.

She did not confront Henri. She felt like screaming and shouting and throwing things, but she did not. If she'd learnt anything during her marriage, it was a bleak kind of compromise. To her, compromise meant a silent polite withdrawal into her shell.

After thinking the matter through she came to realise, not without a certain grim amusement, that Henri had been more loving and attentive than ever lately, so he obviously felt guilty. Which meant perhaps that he did still care for her in his fashion. And as she still cared for him – in her fashion – she decided, if she were going to stay, that the best course of action would be to find a subtle way of disrupting these cosy little aromatherapy sessions.

With BJ, too, Kim managed to maintain a more or less cool and sophisticated silence, but it was hard to be civil when they next met to work on the laborious A to Z guide to alternative health.

'What shall we have for S? Shiatsu?' asked Kim.

'Well, yeah, OK . . . but there's also Sex,' said BJ in a meditative voice.

Kim raised her eyebrows. 'But it's hardly Alternative or little known.'

'Sex is good for the aura. You know that in some

Eastern societies young girls are taught pelvic exercise. Well, most women in the West just don't have the first clue how important this is. Even regular work-outs for the thighs can benefit those inner muscles and help with sexual fulfilment,' said BJ without a flicker of a smile.

'Fascinating,' said Kim dryly. 'But I thought the teenage magazines were full of graphic sexual instructions these days – a new sexual position described in every issue, "a taste of oral sex" and all that.'

'I'm not writing for teenagers. We need to help the older woman find herself.'

'Some older women seem to have got there already,' muttered Kim.

Oblivious to the chill in her voice, Beverly-Jane rattled on blithely. 'I don't think we have to mention aphrodisiacs though. I mean, really, why? At worst they're dangerous and at best they're only placebos, kind of auto-suggestive. They don't have a place in our book. Anyway,' she added, 'the best aphrodisiac is love.'

Kim looked at her in surprise. It was hard to imagine BJ being in love with anyone except herself. Was she serious about Henri?

Then BJ grinned. 'If you can't have love, then novelty isn't a bad turn on.'

Despite her non-confrontational stance Kim was sorely tempted to pick up a pot of beansprouts and smash it down on BJ's head.

★ ★ ★

As well as the Alternative Health Guide, Kim was busy with her own work. No doubt due to his guilty conscience, Henri had recently made the effort to find her two new major editorial commissions, both of which consisted of refashioning vast chunks of the Swiss authors' tortuous English into readable prose. To do this and still keep the writer's voice was a time-consuming challenge which she enjoyed. Both the books involved were dullish histories of local events, but presumably a few people would eventually read and appreciate them, she hoped.

Her authors were certainly appreciative. 'Did I write that? It's good English,' they would say happily.

At least the extra work kept her mind off Henri, and the extra money she earned helped to make her less dependent. If she continued gradually to build up her contacts in Geneva and her reputation as an editor, she might finally earn enough to become totally self-supporting. Which would mean she could leave Henri, if she wanted to.

Then an event occurred which drove everything else out of her head. Very early one morning the telephone rang and she answered it with a bleary hello.

'Am I speaking to Mrs Ellis?'

It was an Australian accent, a voice she didn't

recognise. The hairs on the back of her neck began to prickle and she was suddenly wide awake.

'Yes?' she said quietly.

'I've got news of your husband.'

She took a deep breath, her heart pounding. 'Who are you?'

Ignoring the question, he said, 'I need to meet you in Paris.'

'Is . . . is he alive . . . or dead?'

'Oh, he's alive OK.'

Her head reeled and she sank back on the pillow. 'Is he all right?'

'Like I said, you've gotta come to Paris so we can talk.'

She managed to speak. 'Why not here? Can't we talk here?'

'Don't like Switzerland. Too quiet, nosy people at the borders. Paris is better, more space.'

'But –'

'Be there Thursday afternoon. Stay in the 16th district. And keep stumm about it. No police, no officials, no friends.'

'Is he in trouble?'

'You could say he's in a lot of trouble. So no police, like I said. Ring me when you get to Paris, right?' He gave her a telephone number which she scrabbled to write down.

'Who – what name shall I ask for?'

But the line went dead.

★　　★　　★

Henri was concerned. A few weeks ago Kim had suddenly become cold and withdrawn, and she seemed to have a great many female excuses why she could not join him in bed.

Sometimes he wondered if she'd found out about his little fling with Beverly-Jane, but surely not, they'd been the soul of discretion. Even so there had been a rather unnerving occasion when Kim had mentioned aromatherapy.

'You're smelling very fragrant today, Henri,' she'd said in a particularly unfriendly tone of voice. 'Next time BJ's giving you the treatment, I must pop round and see how she does it.'

Henri had had plenty of practice in dealing with loaded remarks from women. He'd been carefully casual. 'Good idea, my love, but you seem to be very busy at the moment.'

'Oh, but I change my teaching schedules every day, so next time I see her car turning into your drive, I'll come along.'

So he had decided it would be wise to postpone the next few aromatherapy sessions.

But today Kim seemed hyper-agitated and more distant than ever. She had announced in a most distracted manner that she was going to Paris.

'Let me come with you,' he said. 'Paris is a city for lovers.'

'No, I must go on my own.' Her voice was very odd.

He looked at her. 'But why?'

'I can't explain,' she said tersely.

He was hurt, but attempted not to show it. 'Are you going with another man?' he asked in a light joking tone.

'No, of course not. Typical of you to jump to that conclusion.'

He raised his eyebrows. 'I seem to be in the dog-house at the moment.'

'Hm,' grunted Kim.

'Is that why you're going on a Thursday so you can again cancel our rendezvous?' This question too was asked in a light bantering manner, but she obviously didn't take it as a joke.

'Oh for God's sake, Henri, the whole world doesn't revolve around sex, you know. I've got to go to Paris for a business meeting, OK?'

'What business?'

She frowned. 'I can't say.'

'Then it must be another lover.'

She sighed without returning his smile. 'Don't judge everyone by your own standards.'

'What do you mean?' he asked in a mock-hurt voice. *Merde*, maybe she did know about BJ.

'Oh, nothing. Look, it's to do with . . .' Then, suddenly emotional, she began to talk about a phone call from a strange Australian. Her words were tumbling out so fast he could hardly understand her, but eventually he realised what she was saying. Richard was still alive.

He drew in his breath. 'That's wonderful news,'

he said, shocked but more or less sincere. 'But why didn't you tell me before?'

'I haven't told anyone, not even James, in case it isn't true. It could be some kind of con trick.' She told him about the meeting in Paris.

He was horrified. 'I must definitely come with you. I agree it sounds very suspicious.'

'No, please stay at the house.' She smiled at him at last. 'James is going to Polly's, but I need you to keep an eye on everything. As I said, this may be a wild goose chase. Suppose while I'm away on this phoney trail, Richard himself arrives here. Or he could be ill, stuck in France, and just needs my help to get back. Or maybe he's in some sort of trouble with the Swiss authorities and that's why he wants me to meet him in Paris. But why didn't he ring himself? I just don't know what to believe.'

'But –'

'I've been wondering if I should contact Hoffer or Vivienne Frank. They may know something.'

'Certainly not. I don't trust anyone from that company, especially those two,' said Henri thoughtfully. 'But please change your mind. Let me come with you.'

Eventually with great reluctance, he was forced to agree she should go alone but suggested she stay with Sabine, his former love, who lived in the 16th arrondissement. Even that sensible idea was turned down. However, as a concession, he was allowed to telephone Sabine who promised to invite her to dinner.

'I should be most fascinated to meet your latest conquest, dear Henri,' said Sabine, with her deep hoarse chuckle.

Henri was far from sure that Kim was a conquest and he was not looking forward to the possible return of her husband.

CHAPTER 15

In spite of all her doubts and anxieties, Kim could not help being temporarily caught up in the heady atmosphere of Paris: the wide boulevards, the elegant cream stone of the buildings, the heroic scale of the famous monuments and the chic nervous crowds of people. Geneva seemed half-asleep in comparison.

She had arrived by train in the late afternoon and taken a battered taxi driven by a monosyllabic African to her hotel near the Bois de Boulogne. The traffic was ferocious and she was relieved when the driver found the small hotel Henri had recommended without much difficulty. The exterior was less grand than Kim expected, more like a house than a hotel, but her room was quiet and comfortable in a stiff French manner.

As soon as she had unpacked, she dialled the number given to her by the Australian but there was no reply. Distraught, she sat down on the bed. She couldn't bear it if this whole trip were yet another dead end. After half an hour she tried again but there was still no reply. Had she written down the number correctly? She must have. She couldn't have made a mistake about something as crucial as that. Pulling herself together, she decided to ring again after dinner.

Her hotel had no dining room and so she ventured out towards the nearby brasseries. Smart with their crimson awnings, pink table cloths and elaborate cane chairs, they were all empty. Seven-thirty was obviously too early for sophisticated Parisiens to dine. One should still be chatting in a pavement café, she noted.

She walked towards La Muette and finally found a place with a few customers – no doubt foreigners like herself. Unused to sitting alone in a restaurant, she felt ill at ease and, in order to pass the time until her food appeared, she drank most of the half-bottle of Chablis she'd ordered, picking at the tempting bread. When the waiter finally produced her *panaché de poisson*, it looked delicate and delicious and she began to eat it with cautious enjoyment.

But then suddenly her appetite vanished. While she was gazing blankly at the passing crowds in the street outside, she thought she saw Hoffer. Hoffer of all people, what the hell was he doing in Paris? Feeling a thump of fear, she looked down to hide her face.

After a few minutes she raised her eyes. The man had disappeared. It can't have been him, just someone who looks like Hoffer. But, much to the waiter's disapproval, she was unable to eat the rest of her fish. In order to avoid leaving the restaurant and possibly running into Hoffer, she ordered the smallest ice cream on the menu and ate it as slowly as she could.

Eventually she felt obliged to pay her bill and leave the cosy scene. She walked quickly back to the hotel without looking left or right. No one stopped her; no one accosted her. She lectured herself – what a stupid woman you are. It's perfectly safe here.

Back in her room she telephoned the Australian again. This time he answered.

'Meet me tomorrow morning in the Jardin de Ranelagh,' he said. His pronunciation was obscure and she was obliged to ask him to spell out the rendezvous. He sounded impatient. 'Ranelagh Gardens, you know, not far from the metro station at La Muette.'

'What time and whereabouts?'

'Eleven-thirty at the blue bandstand by the old merry-go-round. On your own.'

'But whereabouts is it? How will I recognise you?' she asked shakily, but he had gone.

Next morning, after an interminable night in the stuffy hotel room, she made her way to the gardens and wandered around the dusty paths until she found a blue bandstand on the far side next to a metallic hooped structure which looked as if it could have been a merry-go-round in its better days. There was no one else down this end of the park except a small dog sniffing around on the thin Paris grass. Kim consulted her watch. She was over ten minutes early. Staring around apprehensively, she sat down on one of the numerous green benches to wait.

The thought that Richard might really, actually be alive had been pounding round and round her brain ever since the phone call. But he was evidently in some sort of trouble. She shivered. She should prepare herself for the best and the worst.

'A rare thing, a punctual woman,' said an Australian voice in her ear.

She jumped, her heart thudding violently.

A young man with shoulder-length curly brown hair sat down on the bench beside her. He was tall and thin with round John Lennon glasses perched on the end of a pointed nose. In contrast to his healthy tan, his unnaturally pale eyes were small with tired red rims, as if he had recently spent a long time staring into a computer screen. He wore nondescript scruffy jeans and a frayed denim jacket.

'Mrs Ellis, I presume,' he said.

'Yes, and, er, you are?'

'Like I said, a friend of your husband's.'

She took a deep breath. 'And he's really alive?'

'Yeah, yeah, he's alive OK.'

The uncertainty was over at last. The feeling of relief that swept over her was immediately followed by dread and worry and fear. 'Where is he? Is he in Paris?'

'No, that's where you come in. We need funds to bring him here.'

'How much?' she asked carefully.

'Well, for a start there's the air fare. I'll calculate in pounds to make it easier for you. Say, one thousand each for the tickets for your husband and escort.'

'Escort?'

'He needs someone to look after him, keep an eye, you know.'

'Why? Is he ill?' Oh God, she thought.

'Not exactly.'

'What do you mean, not exactly?'

'Well, they say he's not in the greatest shape. Maybe the bloody food over there doesn't agree with him, and the climate is shit, of course.'

She drew in her breath. 'Where? The climate where?'

'Out East,' he said, waving his hand vaguely.

She hung on to the edge of the seat. 'Can I talk to him, phone him, I mean?'

'No.'

'Why not?'

'He's not on the bloody phone. No mobile coverage,' he said sardonically.

'So how do you get in touch with him? Is he in a hospital or what? Can I contact a doctor or some other official?'

The Australian laughed. 'Not a hospital, no. They don't have any doctors out there.'

'Please just tell me where he is.' She fought to

control her voice. 'I mean, is he in hiding, in trouble with the authorities? You seem to be trying to protect him, but I need to know.'

'You just don't get it, do you? Hubby is being looked after by some tribesmen who need money – see, they want independence, all that stuff – and, in exchange for returning him, to cover all their expenses, including the air fare, plus the fact that he promised them goods he didn't deliver, they want seventy-five thou.'

Kim stared at him. 'Seventy-five thousand what?'

'Pounds or rather the Swiss franc equivalent. We're going to open an account in Geneva so you can pay it in there, more convenient for you.'

White-faced she stood up. 'But I don't have any money. You've kidnapped the wrong sort of man.'

The Australian shook his head. 'Not me. I didn't kidnap him. I'm just the middle man. But I could persuade them to negotiate. What could you afford then?'

'You don't understand. I don't have any money at all. I barely earn enough to support myself.'

'What about your house? Get a mortgage. Sell it.'

'We don't own a house. The one in Geneva is rented.'

He rubbed the designer stubble on his chin. 'OK, then, maybe I could persuade them to settle for sixty thousand. It's not much. Bargain, really, but my mates are modest simple people. Like I said, your husband owes them money. They have quite a few problems, those guys, and they need a bit of cash to get sorted. Call it aid to a developing country.'

Digging her nails into the palm of her hands, she repeated 'Look, I just don't have any money at all. Absolutely none.'

He smiled at her lazily. 'Then if you want him back, you'll have to borrow it, won't you? But don't bother asking hubby's employers. I already tried them. They aren't interested. Said he could rot in hell for all they cared. Or words to that effect.'

She sat down, feeling sick. 'Who did you talk to?'

'A Mr Hoffer. Not much of a charmer, I thought.'

There was a silence. 'How do I know he's still alive?' whispered Kim eventually.

He rummaged in the pocket of his jeans and produced a crumpled photograph. Richard was sitting underneath a palm tree staring vacantly at the camera. She drew in her breath. He looked thin and gaunt to the point of emaciation.

The Australian spoke again in his slow deliberate drawl. 'By the way, during the course of your fund-raising, don't involve the police or the British Government or any local officials. And especially no bloody journos.'

'Journos?' wavered Kim.

'No newspaper guys. Like I said, my mates are not sophisticated . . . well, you know the rest.'

She fought to disguise her rising fear. At first he'd seemed almost harmless, friendly, on her side

214

even, but now she found him increasingly intimidating.

He continued, 'While we're on the subject, don't take too long about getting the cash. Looks like he'll need some sort of medical treatment fairly soon.' He stood up.

'Can I contact you tomorrow?' she asked desperately. 'Will you be at the same number?'

'No, I'll call you when you get back to Geneva,' he said, and then he strode away across the quiet park.

Kim sat on the bench, unable to move. This was all quite mad. It happened to rich families in the newspapers or characters in second-rate TV films. Not to ordinary people like Richard and herself – except of course there were all those aid-workers and people held hostage in the Middle East, killed even. So perhaps it was real after all.

Her mind darted back to the conversation she'd had in the Red Cross Museum. Ang had talked about hippies who had teamed up with an anti-government group of tribesmen. So the Australian could be one of the hippies, and Richard could have been trying to do business with the islanders, and then . . .

After a while she left the park and began to walk around the streets, desperately trying to form a plan. Wild, confused ideas rushed in and out of her head: Henri would help. As soon as she got back to Geneva tomorrow, she would talk to him – if he wasn't too taken up with BJ, that is. Or she could ask Mark for advice, but the Australian had stipulated no officials, no police. Would the British Government be willing to rescue someone like Richard who'd brought his troubles on himself? These days they could hardly send a gunboat even if they wanted to. She certainly wouldn't contact the newspapers. She could imagine the headlines 'British Gunrunner held by Freedom Fighters.' She must somehow keep the whole thing from James until his father was safely back.

And what would she do with Richard then, once he was back? Face that problem later. And it certainly would be a problem.

After some time she stopped walking and looked around. It dawned on her that she was completely lost. All the roads, all the shops looked the same. Fighting back a feeling of panic, she came across a kiosk where she bought a map of Paris, but it was late afternoon before she finally found her way back to the hotel. Wearily she climbed the stairs to her room. She tried to unlock the door but the key would not work. She turned the handle and to her relief the door opened. Then she stood still.

Hoffer was sitting on her bed. He rose to his feet. 'Good afternoon, or maybe it is already evening. Good evening, Madame Ellis.'

'What are you doing here? How did you get into my room?' She was extremely angry.

'Nice girl, the chambermaid.'

'What are you doing here?' she asked again, sinking down on the edge of the chair near the bed.

'I thought you might like to talk about your husband. I am au fait with what has happened.'

'So I gather. Do you know where Richard is? Did the Australian give you any idea? Do you know the man's name or who he represents?'

'No, but I have made some educated guesses. As I said, I am trying to help. I suggest we dine together to discuss the matter.'

Kim stared up at him. 'I'm having dinner with a friend tonight,' she said coldly.

'What friend? Another of your men? Never mind. I am staying in this hotel. Just call my room, number 17, when you get back. I don't mind how late it is,' he added with a leer.

'How did you know where I was staying?' she snapped.

'By a happy chance, I saw you in a restaurant last night and I followed you.'

Kim was furious. Horrible little man. After a pause, she said flatly, 'I was told the company wouldn't pay a ransom.'

'True, but you and I, if we worked together as a team, we could perhaps persuade them to change their mind.' He was standing looming over her.

Then he took a step closer so that his legs were touching her knees.

Wriggling round in her chair, she moved them away. 'Why? How?' Her voice was expressionless.

Hoffer paused and then he leant forward. Immediately Kim stood up and tried to push past him, but he grabbed hold of her arm.

'I think you will find I can be very helpful,' he said, whispering into her ear. His breath smelt of garlic and stale cigars.

Breaking away, she ran out on to the landing and stood there, panting with disgust. 'Get out of my room,' she said fiercely.

Hoffer shrugged his shoulders, then he walked past her. 'Very well, Madame Ellis. I will contact you later tonight when you have had time to think things through.'

She had to get out of the hotel. As soon as he had gone, she hurriedly flung her clothes into her case and ran downstairs to pay the bill. Then she rushed to the taxi rank and asked the driver to take her to Sabine's address.

She soon realised she could have walked. It was not very far away, another block of flats in another elegant street. An old woman, obviously the concierge, was dusting the marble entrance hall and, after looking her up and down, admitted her with a polite 'bonsoir, madame'. Kim took the juddering lift to the third floor and rang the bell outside an imposing double door. She breathed a sigh of relief when it was answered by a small, thin, well-preserved woman, immaculately dressed in a grey suit and a great deal of jewellery.

'Madame Delon?'

'*Oui, mais –*'

'I'm Kim Ellis. I am very sorry to be early but . . .'

Shaking hands, Sabine smiled warmly. 'Good evening. I am enchanted to meet you but indeed you are in very good time. It's lucky I am here. I was not expecting you for another two hours at least – and the suitcase? Does that mean you can stay after all? You would be most welcome.'

Kim was too nervous and upset to be embarrassed. 'I'm sorry I didn't telephone first. It was too difficult. I couldn't,' she faltered.

Sabine led her into the dark grandly furnished salon. 'Sit down, please. You look very pale. Are you ill? Henri said you had many problems with a disappearing husband. Will you perhaps take a glass of champagne or a little coffee?'

She chose champagne. Her hostess disappeared and then returned with a bottle of Taittinger. Kim gulped down her first glass.

Impassively Sabine refilled it. 'May I call you Kim?' she asked. 'I cannot help knowing we have a certain amount in common. And please call me Sabine.' She smoothed back her expensively streaked hair. Her nails were long and crimson and she wore several rings on her thin paper-white fingers.

'Thank you, you're very kind. I'm sorry to impose. It's hard to explain . . . there was someone at the hotel, a man who, well, he . . .' began Kim.

'I wish you had brought Henri with you,' said Sabine, lighting a cigarette. 'It's many years since I saw him. How is he? In good health, no problems these days?'

Kim attempted to pull herself together. 'No, he's fine, very well, much as usual.'

Sabine smiled again, drawing back her red lips. 'Yes, men like Henri never change, though his little friends are getting younger.'

Kim flushed.

'I hope I haven't offended you,' said Sabine, blowing out a cloud of smoke. 'Henri said nothing revealing, but I could tell by the way he spoke about you that he was very much in love.'

Kim shook her head. 'Hm.'

'You sound doubtful, but I assure you he is mad for you. He was most concerned by the fact that you insisted on coming to Paris on your own.'

'Well, he worries a lot.' She did not in the least want to discuss Henri: she was too preoccupied with the startling events of the day. So she stood up and asked if she might have a bath and change. At once Sabine showed her to her room, saying she must rest before they went out to dinner.

Alone in the huge bedroom with its dark wardrobes and heavy ornate chests of drawers, Kim sat down on the bed. She wondered how much Hoffer knew. No more than she did probably. She looked out of the window and gave a long shuddering sigh. It was already dark. She wasn't in a mood to go out to a restaurant but she felt too jumpy to stay alone in the apartment. Eyes closed, she lay back on the duvet, her mind racing from one thought to the next.

Eventually she heard Sabine knocking on the door saying it was time to change.

The meal in the Restaurant Flandrin passed in a daze. Sabine's other guests were a smart elderly couple and a neat white-haired old man called Max. Something about his gallant manner suggested that he was, or would like to be, Sabine's current lover. They all had a great deal to say, talking in a mixture of broken English and rapid French about politics and literature. Kim sat silent, trying to look as if she understood the conversation, but her attention was elsewhere.

The evening broke up early. The elderly couple walked away down the boulevard holding hands. She envied them their tranquillity. Max, the lover, showed signs of wishing to accompany Sabine and Kim, but he was dismissed outside the door of the restaurant.

Back at the apartment, Sabine led the way to the salon. 'Let us drink a little liqueur together,' she said, settling down on the sofa and lighting yet another cigarette. 'I should like to hear a little more about my friend Henri.'

'Oh well, he's fine, as I said. Very well indeed.'

Kim sipped the Cointreau. She'd already had

more than enough wine but she was too tired to think straight anyway. However, it added to the peculiar craziness of the day to be sitting making yet more irrelevant conversation.

Sabine, who had also drunk the best part of a bottle of wine, sounded perfectly sober. She must be about sixty, thought Kim, but in the dim light she looked some fifteen years younger.

Sabine's dark intelligent eyes searched Kim's face. 'And do you love Henri? I used to be mad for him. He is such a charming man.'

Kim blinked. 'Yes, he is. Charming to everyone. He's nice to my friends, my son, everyone.'

'Do I detect a touch of irony, that you feel he is too flirtatious with the other ladies?'

'Well, that's his nature, I suppose.'

'Yes,' said Sabine musingly. 'That is his nature. But the fact that he adores women means that one can really do no wrong He doesn't get impatient with our feminine obsessions with fashion and domestic matters. In fact, he positively enjoys female trivia. And of course he was always kind about sharing one's other interests. He used to help me with my little collection of antique perfume bottles. Not many men take such trouble. I find that all rather endearing, don't you?'

She forced herself to concentrate on what Sabine was saying. 'Yes, I do in a way. Although I don't seem to have very much time for fashion myself.'

'My dear, you are most attractive, most attractive, but it must be difficult in Geneva with the provincial fashions,' said Sabine seriously. 'I see many possibilities though. If you were to stay in Paris longer, we could go shopping together. I could help you choose your spring and summer ensembles. I am sure Henri would be happy to pay. Your hair, it is wonderful, so thick, but perhaps a new Parisian cut, something short and gamine.'

Kim smiled. 'No, it's very kind of you but I have to get back.'

'Yes, maybe you are wise not to leave Henri alone for too long.'

'He – I don't live with him. He's just, well – we aren't answerable to each other, you see.'

Waving her cigarette in the air, Sabine pursued her own train of thought. 'In effect, he is hard to quarrel with. Although some women may become unhappy if he shares his charms around too generously.'

'His wife got pretty upset, I gather,' said Kim dryly.

'Poor Heidi, what a dreary person! And the daughter, have you met her? She is tiresome too. The son is delightful but, as for Heidi and Beatrice, they are both stupid fat jealous women.'

Kim grinned. 'Yes, I met the daughter. She *is* a bit of a pain, though not fat these days.'

'His wife never understood that one must appreciate men like Henri for what they are – kind, loving, tender and affectionate, but one must also accept that they may be a little too susceptible to feminine charms.'

Kim raised her eyebrows. 'Was he unfaithful to you and did you put up with it?'

Sabine smiled. 'Yes, he was unfaithful, and I accepted it at first. But then unfortunately I changed my opinion and returned to my husband, which was a mistake since he was not nearly as nice as Henri.'

'What happened, to your husband, I mean?'

'We divorced, some years ago.'

'I'm sorry.'

Sabine shrugged her shoulders. 'I do not miss him.'

After a pause, Kim asked thoughtfully, 'Would you want Henri back?'

'Oh no. I am a Parisienne, I couldn't live in Geneva, far too dull. In any case, we no longer love each other. Henri loves you and I am content with Maximilian, though he's not as exciting. Henri's constant enthusiasm for *amour* might be a little too much at my age.'

Kim flushed and said nothing.

Staring at the ceiling, Sabine inhaled and continued, 'I believe, however, that he is at last old enough to settle down and, from what he said, you are to be the great final love of his life.'

Kim shook her head. 'He . . . I, well, I can't explain but anyway there are too many problems. Quite apart from Henri, I mean.' All evening she had been tempted to pour out the story of Richard and the extraordinary ransom demand, but she knew she must remain silent. 'I think I'd better go to bed, if you'll excuse me,' she said.

'Then *dormez bien*. But I believe I am right about you and Henri. We shall see,' said Sabine gently.

But Kim, her mind returning again and again to Richard, slept little.

CHAPTER 16

'**I**f you decide to pay, I'll lend you the ransom money,' said Henri immediately.

His generosity made life sound so easy, she thought. She couldn't be angry with him any more. 'It's far too much. I'd never be able to repay it,' she said. 'I'd have to try and borrow it from the bank.'

He put his arm round her. 'It's a small sum for me and, besides, a bank won't lend you money with no collateral.' He grinned. 'You can always repay me in kind.'

'You're impossible, Henri. This may be a matter of life and death. Don't you take anything seriously?'

'Yes, a few things.' He took her hand. 'Like you. I take you seriously. When Richard returns you can divorce him. Then you'll be free and we can spend all the time in the world together. Just think how long it would take you to pay me back in sexual favours – we could make love every day for years.' He grinned broadly again. 'What a wonderful thought!'

Smiling at him despite her reservations, she shook her head. 'I could try Richard's firm again.'

'No, not them. As I said, I don't trust them at all. They're just as likely to send someone to get rid of him as to pay to get him back.'

She stared at him. 'You really think so?'

'I do.'

She paused and then she said, 'I don't like the idea of caving in, but if Richard is really ill . . . but then I'm not sure I can trust the Australian anyway. What if we give him the money and he doesn't produce Richard?'

'We can work out a plan.' He rubbed his forehead thoughtfully. 'But we should perhaps telephone Mark and see if he knows anything.'

'He's in England.'

'So you said. Then telephone him at the Foreign Office.'

'But I don't have his number.'

'Pull yourself together, *chérie*. Phone his former secretary here, for God's sake. She will know how to get in touch with him.'

So she telephoned the Foreign Office and left a message for Mark with a grand-sounding young man. The following evening Mark rang.

'You mustn't give in to these people, whatever happens,' he said firmly when she had explained the situation. 'The Foreign Office always advises against it and the Government never pays a ransom in any circumstances.'

She sat down suddenly on the chair by the telephone. 'What d'you suggest then?'

'Go to the Consul. Tell her what you know and then the FCO here in London will get in touch with the Maising Government and put pressure on them to get Richard released.'

'But how long will that take?'

'Oh, the Foreign Office can act quickly if they need to. At the Maising end there may well be delays though.'

'The Australian said Richard was ill.'

'Probably bluffing.'

Her voice grew higher. 'What if he wasn't? And anyway he said no officials or police. That's why I'm ringing you because I though you might've heard something – unofficially, I mean.'

'Sorry, no. Not a word from Ang either, but I've been very tied up this end.'

'Oh . . . well, thank you anyway,' she said lamely. She was disappointed and confused. Some unreasonable part of her had expected Mark to solve the problem at a stroke.

'But how are you? Are you OK, Kim?'

'Oh yes, and you?'

'Busy, very busy.'

'Will you be coming to Geneva at all?'

'I don't know. This Commission may drag on. Then there'll probably be another one set up. Endless difficulties. Takes up every spare second of my time.'

'I see. Well, goodbye then,' she said, suddenly putting down the receiver. What else was there to say? He hadn't asked her how she felt about

Richard, or anything else. But then her problems were far less important than world affairs.

'Well, never mind,' said Henri. 'We can manage without him. Sometimes they are unimaginative, these civil servants. Not that I can envisage any solution other than paying the ransom. Anything else is too risky. Richard might well be killed in a military-style rescue. One cannot expect the efficiency of the SAS in that part of the world. And from what you say, even if the local police find him alive they may fling him straight into jail for arms smuggling. And, whatever your feeling about him, you wouldn't want that, nor would James.'

'No, you're right.' There was a pause and then she said, 'It'd be awful if Richard died and I'd done nothing to save him. James would never forgive me. I wouldn't want him to turn round in ten years' time and accuse me of indirectly killing his father because I was too stingy, or too apathetic to care.'

As soon as this thought entered her head, she realised there was no alternative. Henri was right. She should borrow the money from him and pay the ransom.

Later, after they had made rather distracted love and were lying in bed thinking their separate thoughts, Henri suddenly spoke. 'Supposing,' he said, 'I were to make a different type of proposition. What if I were to propose marriage?'

She stared at him in surprise.

'If you were my wife, some of these problems would be solved.'

She put her arms around him. 'Not sure how.' She kissed his cheek gently. 'But anyway I'm still married to Richard.'

'You don't love him.'

'No.'

'Then divorce him, as I said. I think it is in everyone's interests that he should return safely, then the situation between you can be regulated.'

She couldn't help asking, 'And what about BJ?'

'Who?'

'Our mutual friend, the fragrant masseuse, as you perfectly well know.'

He shrugged. 'She is nothing, a bagatelle, a pleasant woman, but unimportant.'

'I couldn't cope with bagatelles like her, even if we –'

'Then there will be no more, no more,' he said seriously.

She pushed away from him a little. 'Henri, it's impossible. It wouldn't work. You might get tempted again one of these days and I'm not the sort of sophisticated type who could turn a blind eye to the other woman.' She smiled sadly. 'But anyway we can't talk about all this now, what with Richard and everything.'

'We cannot take any action until Richard is back here, but we can talk and we can plan.'

'But . . .'

He took her face in his hands. 'Keep calm. It will be all right. I want you to remember that I love you, far more than you realise.'

'And I love you too,' said Kim. She did, it was true, in both a companionable and sexual sense, and she appreciated his generosity and understood his weaknesses. But she did not love him in the all-encompassing way he now seemed to want. Not enough to put her trust in him for ever. Perhaps she was just too old, too battle-scarred for that sort of love. After a while she said aloud, 'But even so, I can't marry you.'

'We'll talk about it another time, in due course,' said Henri comfortably.

At the same early hour as before the Australian rang again.

'I may be able to raise the money, I'm not sure,' faltered Kim. Even over the telephone he frightened her.

'You'd better be quick about it, Mrs Ellis, because your husband is a sick man.'

She took a deep breath and managed to say, 'If I get it, how will I know that you won't just take the money, without delivering him?'

'We can send him on a plane to Paris. As soon as he lands there and phones you, you pay the money into the Zuricher FDZ Bank. They have a branch in Geneva. I'll give you the account number. If the money isn't paid in, hubby is in danger of having an accident between Paris and

231

Geneva. He's quite mentally disturbed at the moment and could quite easily fall off the train.'

'Mentally disturbed?' she repeated faintly.

'In a manner of speaking.'

'What if, what if I pay thirty thousand when he arrives in Switzerland and another thirty as soon as he gets back home? I won't forget the second payment as you know where I live.'

His voice grew even more unfriendly. 'I'll have to contact my people and get back to you.'

Full of trepidation, Kim went down to the city centre to find the Zuricher FDZ Bank. It was small and discreet. Only a small brass plate showed that it was a bank rather than a private house.

Plucking up her courage, she rang the bell. The heavy door opened automatically and closed behind her, leaving her in a small hallway. A security camera surveyed her, then another door opened. The room was disconcertingly empty apart from a single heavily carved desk and a couple of leather chairs. The walls were hung with portraits of bearded men who gazed down at her sternly in the manner of Calvin or John Knox. On the far side she saw a lone female cashier behind a plate glass and mahogany-panelled partition.

'*Bonjour, madame.* Can I help you?'

She jumped. Standing beside her was a small fat Swiss looking uncannily like one of the men in the portraits. How had he managed to creep up on her?

'Oh, er, yes, monsieur. I might want to make a deposit one day.'

'You wish to open an account?' He looked her up and down with disapproval, obviously considering that she did not look rich or grand enough to become a client. She wished she had left behind her rather tatty shopping bag.

'No, no, into an account held here already. Er, how do I do that?'

He raised his eyebrows. 'You merely complete one of our paying-in slips in the normal manner. Naturally we provide them. Just ask the cashier.'

'But perhaps you could give me a pre-printed personalised one so I could fill it in beforehand, if I have the, er, payee's account number,' she said, flushing.

He regarded her suspiciously. 'And what is the account number of the payee?'

'I don't know yet. It's new, I think.'

'Well, in that case, madame, when you have the number it would be perfectly satisfactory for you to complete one of our blank forms.'

'But what if I don't have the person's name?' Her voice wavered. 'I wonder if you could give it to me if I let you know the account number, so I can fill in the form properly.'

'We do not need a name for the payee, just a number will do. And, as I am sure you are aware, we do not divulge our clients' names,' he said severely.

Feeling herself dismissed, she went out into the

street. So there would be no way of find anything out from the bank. Not that she had expected to.

She looked around. It was a sunny day. Perhaps she should walk home. It would do her good and give her time to think.

She had always driven or taken the bus before, and it took much longer to walk to Cologny than she expected. At last she found herself at the end of her own long road and began to hurry along it. Suddenly she had the uneasy feeling that something was wrong at home. Deciding it would be best to catch a bus after all, she waited impatiently by the stop. Then after about five minutes she abandoned the idea and walked quickly on, only to be overtaken by the bus hurtling past.

Eventually she arrived home, but as she opened the garden gate she was startled to see Beverly-Jane sitting on her doorstep.

BJ stood up, looking pale and peculiar. 'I'm very sorry, Kim,' she said in a rush, 'but Henri is dead.'

CHAPTER 17

'Henri is dead,' repeated Beverly-Jane. Kim stood still, white-faced and disbelieving.

'What? But he can't be.'

'It's true, I'm sorry.' BJ attempted to hug her.

Kim took her by the shoulders and pushed her away so hard that BJ half fell against the wall.

'What have you done to him?' shouted Kim, and then she ran across the lawn towards Henri's house.

Dusting herself down, BJ began to follow. 'It's too late,' she called. 'They've taken him away. An ambulance.'

Kim sank down on the garden bench and burst into tears. 'Don't come near me. Haven't you done enough?'

BJ's words came out in sharp bursts. 'I'm all shaken up too, you know. It was nothing to do with me. He was dead when I arrived. A heart attack, I guess. So I called the housekeeper. I figured she'd know what to do. She sent for the ambulance. Then she called the daughter. So I left. I thought I'd better come tell you.' She took a deep breath and then said, 'I understand you're upset, but why are you so hostile?'

Head in hands, Kim ignored the question.

'It wasn't my fault. The aromatherapy treatment couldn't have affected his heart,' said BJ.

'So that's what you call it.'

BJ paused and then she said in a wheedling little girl's voice, 'Kim, honey, if Henri told you about me and him, you won't say a word to anyone, will you? I mean, he's gone now and I wouldn't want to upset my husband unnecessarily.'

Kim turned and stared at her, 'Don't worry. I have absolutely no desire to talk about your behaviour,' she said stonily. 'Now, go away, for God's sake.'

BJ's hands were shaking. 'It was just a game. And anyway it was over. Henri broke it off. I knew he was in love with someone else but I didn't know that he . . . you . . . You should have told me. I'm sorry, I'm so sorry.'

There was a long pause and then BJ continued, 'I hope you don't think . . . Kim, I was only there today because I had to bring back the manuscript.'

'Go away,' repeated Kim in a muffled voice.

Beverly-Jane departed.

After a while Kim walked over towards Henri's house. She stopped. All the shutters were closed and there were no cars in the drive. The house was obviously uninhabited, alone, empty, already in mourning.

Then she heard a low bark. She walked around

the garden and saw Caspar sitting by the back door, his head on one side. Oh no, he'd been forgotten. She called to him and he came bounding up to her, wagging his tail.

'Oh poor Caspar, you don't understand.' She buried her face in his golden fur and held him tight. 'You'd better come home with me for now,' she said, tears pouring down again.

Two days later, Kim drove out towards the countryside west of the city. James had gone to Polly's as Kim thought him too young to attend a memorial service. He was desperately upset about Henri and only the dog seemed able to comfort him, or perhaps they comforted each other.

She learnt from his housekeeper that Henri had left instructions there should be a private funeral followed by a service in the temple in Latigny, the village where he was born.

She did not know what to expect of the temple but it turned out to be a plain unadorned Calvinistic hall. Her mind numb with grief, she could not stop shivering. It seemed a bleak, alien environment, inappropriate for Henri.

The crowds of mourners, people unknown to her, sat on wooden chairs in a semi-circle, dressed as for an every day occasion, no muted colours, no black. She recognised Beatrice at the front, flanked by two men. Kim drew in her breath. One, presumably the brother, was a younger version of Henri. The other man must be Beatrice's Italian husband, he had his arm around Eduardo whose shoulders were shaking. She gulped. Poor little Eduardo having to sit through all this. Beatrice herself seemed perfectly composed, as did the rest of the congregation, apart from Madame Dubois, the housekeeper, and Henri's secretary, who were both sobbing quietly.

Kim tried to follow the service which was performed in an ecclesiastical style of French she did not fully understand. The imposing priest, unusually tall and dressed in a plain white robe, obviously did not believe in eulogising the dead. 'Henri,' he intoned in his deep religious voice, 'was a playboy, a sinner and a disbeliever, but, despite this God would love him.'

She looked up in astonishment but the people around her remained expressionless. Even Beatrice appeared unmoved by this summary of her father.

After the service Kim followed the crowd to a large villa with a garden, a community centre of some sort, where they were offered wine and small sweet cakes.

Before she lost courage, she went to speak to Beatrice. 'I'm so sorry about your father,' she faltered.

Beatrice stared at her for a moment and then, without replying, turned her back to speak to the elderly woman standing beside her.

Confused and on the edge of breaking down, Kim retreated. She felt she should speak to poor Eduardo but he had disappeared. Or maybe she should say something to Henri's son, but she couldn't think of a good way of introducing herself.

There was no one else she wanted to talk to. She walked slowly back towards the centre of the village and stood still, looking around, trying to imagine Henri as a child playing in the street. Her heart lifted slightly at the beauty of it all, old cottages with deep protective roofs, arched doors and mullioned windows, and geraniums falling over window boxes and balconies.

Henri had brought her here about a year ago to see the small house where he was born. He still owned it, but they'd not been able to look inside because of the tenant, she remembered. She walked towards it now. It was similar to many of the other houses, a grey stone terraced cottage.

Today the shutters were closed but the small garden was bright with red and pink impatiens. A pale yellow climbing rose sprawled in profusion beside the front door. Looking around at the empty street, she rummaged around in her handbag to find her scissors. Then she cut off a rose in full bloom.

Standing there in a blank trancelike state, she realised now that Latigny must be the right place to leave Henri. It came to her that he had died when he was vigorous and happy. Henri wouldn't have liked to be old and ill. But, if only she'd been there . . .

On the way back towards the city, she took a

detour, parking the car on the left bank of the Rhone. She walked along beside the river until she found a footbridge where she stood a while. Then, leaning over, she threw the rose into the rushing water and watched until it disappeared.

CHAPTER 18

Polly put her arm around Kim who again had that falsely calm, vacant expression of a person in a state of shock. 'Are you OK? You look very pale and wan. So are you going back to England? I'll miss you so much.'

'We can't stay here any longer. We have to leave Switzerland. All decisions have been taken out of my hands,' said Kim in a small quiet voice.

'But you can't go and live with that ghastly Monica. You'd hate it, and so would James.'

'It'd only be temporary. I'll find a residential job, as a housekeeper or something. They say people always want housekeepers.'

Polly looked around. Kim's own house, not immaculate at the best of times, was now in a terrible mess. Polly was itching to take charge, but perhaps it wasn't the moment. Unable to sit still, she began to sort out a pile of newspapers and envelopes on the kitchen chair. 'Look,' she said, 'you haven't even opened these.'

'They're only bills or rubbish,' said Kim.

'Nevertheless they should be dealt with.'

'Yes, OK, later. Leave them there.'

Hearing a car, Polly looked out of the window and caught a glimpse of a yellow van. 'The postman. Shall I go and get the letters?' Without waiting for a reply, she went out to the mailbox by the gate.

'Thanks,' said Kim when she returned. Glancing through the letters, she dumped them in a pile with the others.

'But you must open them.'

'You read them if you're so interested,' said Kim, staring out of the window.

Polly selected the fattest most expensive-looking letter but it turned out to be an offer from a real estate company to view luxury apartments near the French border. She studied the next two which also appeared to be junk mail.

Then she opened a large white envelope. Her eyes widened. 'Oh, wow, Kim, read this – this is a seriously major ray of sunshine.'

Kim continued to stare out of the window. Polly shook her shoulder violently. 'Listen, it's a letter from a notary, a lawyer, whatever.'

'Telling me to vacate the house, I suppose.'

'Read it,' insisted Polly. 'Looks like the wages of sin are quite substantial,' she added with a grin.

Kim took the letter and read aloud, '"Madame, I have the honour to inform you that according to the last will and testament of the late Monsieur Henri Marechal of Cologny the dwelling in which you now reside, namely Villa la Vigne Cologny, has been bequeathed to you and your heirs in perpetuity".' She sat down. '"Furthermore",' she continued in a shaky voice, '"a sum of money namely two hundred thousand Swiss francs has also been bequeathed to you".'

'Wow,' said Polly grinning broadly. 'I always knew Henri was a good chap.'

Kim began to sound slightly hysterical. 'And I've also been given the manuscript of his novel and, listen, Pol – this is good – he's left the dog to James. Lucky that, I never got round to telling anyone we still had Caspar.' She read on and then suddenly her smile faded. 'I knew it was too good to be true,' she said faintly. 'Read the rest of it.'

Polly took the letter which went on regretfully to inform Madame Ellis that notwithstanding the above the offspring of the late Monsieur Marechal had lodged a petition to contest the will on the grounds that undue influence had been brought to bear on him during his final years.

'That's just ridiculous,' said Polly. 'Anyway he must've left her all the rest of his property. I thought he had at least ten houses.'

'Only five, I think, plus the chalet in Wengen and a couple of blocks of flats in Zurich, but maybe he's left each of his mistresses a house and nothing to his dear daughter.'

Polly laughed. 'Glad you've got some of your sense of humour back. But we can deal with old Beatrice. What you need now is a lawyer.'

'But I can't afford one.'

'Then I'll find you one who'll wait till you become an heiress.'

'Hardly an heiress.'

'Well, no, but a house in Geneva and a hundred thousand quid is better than a slap in the face with a wet fish.'

Kim found a lawyer, an ambitious young woman called Sophie-Maria Leblanc who looked about eighteen but had the reputation of being as tough and rocky as the Swiss mountains.

'Mrs Ellis, you realise this may take some time, at least a year,' said Sophie-Maria, 'but I believe we have an excellent case which we will win in the end.'

'But I need the money now. Well, I mean I would like to have it as soon as possible.'

'You can still live in Villa la Vigne until the case is settled.' Sophie-Maria put on her glasses and wrote something in a small black leather notebook.

'Yes, but I need capital both to pay you and for my husband.'

'As I told you, I will wait. But why do you need money for your husband? Please explain.'

After a moment's hesitation, Kim told her.

Sophie-Maria's beautiful features grew sharper. 'I must advise you that you should not pay a ransom to such people.'

'Nevertheless,' said Kim, 'I don't want to wait any longer than I have to.'

244

'Patience, Mrs Ellis. You are in a very strong position. But your case will not come to court for some time. As I said, they cannot turn you out until the judgement takes place.'

'Mrs Ellis.' It was the Australian again.
'Yes.' She held her breath.
'Have you got the money?'
'I can get it soon, I think.'
'Like I said, he's a sick man and getting worse so you'd better try bloody hard to get it pronto, straight away.'
'OK, but –'
'You do understand, don't you, that this money is owed by your husband to my friends for goods he didn't bloody deliver? You don't want them to start kidnapping anyone else, do you?'
'What do you mean?' asked Kim in a panic, immediately thinking of James, but the Australian had already put down the receiver.

The veiled threat to James was the last straw. In desperation Kim telephoned Madame Frank and asked if she would be kind enough to come and see her.

She arrived promptly that afternoon, well-dressed, well-coiffed and full of fragrant professional sympathy. Kim was reminded of the morning, all those months ago, when she and Hoffer had come to break the news about the air crash.

Today, as soon as they had come into the house,

Madame Frank grasped her by the hand. 'Your husband is alive, I hear.'

So Hoffer had told her. Kim took a deep breath, 'Yes, I feel the company has a responsibility to him and –'

Vivienne lowered her voice. 'I know about the ransom demand, but unfortunately I cannot help you. It is not company policy to pay a ransom. Even if Mr Ellis had not been in breach of our regulations, they would not pay. I am desperately sorry. I'm sure you love him very much. It is so terrible for you.'

Kim was speechless for a moment and then she said, 'I need to see the chairman.'

'He is in America, but it would make no difference. I have tried myself to persuade him to make an exception for Mr Ellis, but he is adamant that rules are rules.'

'What about the deputy? Can I talk to him?'

'Mr Hoffer is now acting deputy.'

Kim's heart sank. 'I see.'

'Mr Hoffer and I are most concerned, most concerned, but if you wait and hope, Mrs Ellis, there may eventually be good news.' There were tears in Vivienne's eyes.

Hypocritical cow, thought Kim savagely. 'But I can't wait,' she said.

Sophie-Maria telephoned three days later. 'I am obliged to report to you that the late Monsieur Marechal's family have made an offer, but I would most strongly advise you to refuse it.'

'What offer?' asked Kim.

'Without waiting for probate, they propose immediate payment of the two hundred thousand francs plus a small three-bedroom terraced cottage in Latigny, the original family home of Mr Marechal. In return you would give up all claim to your current house. A very poor offer indeed. Villa la Vigne is worth at least five times the cottage in Latigny. Their lawyer also said something unpleasant about publicity, but one must ignore that.'

'Publicity?'

'He mentioned that if the case came to court, you would be reported by the Press as being at best a gold-digger, at worst a . . .' she hesitated.

'You mean they would make me out to be some kind of whore?'

'Possibly, but I doubt if it would make the head-lines, just a paragraph or two, perhaps. These days adultery is not unusual, even in Calvin's city. And of course it has never been unusual for a rich old man to have a younger girlfriend.'

Kim drew in her breath sharply. Sophie-Maria had not entirely managed to prevent a censorious edge from entering her voice, or maybe it was just her choice of words.

Kim asked, 'Is the cottage freehold – would it be mine for ever? Would I get it straight away?'

'Certainly.'

Kim hesitated, then she said, 'I want you to accept the offer.'

'But why?'

'I need the money now. We've got to have somewhere settled to live as soon as possible. And I need to protect James. I don't want him to read that his mother is a tart, even in a paragraph.'

'But you are giving way to blackmail. And if you are short of money, I am sure I can arrange a loan against your expectations.'

'Please accept the offer, Maître Leblanc.'

Sophie-Maria paused. 'I advise you to consider this very carefully.'

'No, I've decided, please accept it straight away.'

'Very well,' said Sophie-Maria, her voice stiff with disapproval.

'So?' asked the Australian.

Kim spoke quietly. 'I've got the money.'

'Good on you. Your husband will soon be on his way to France. I'll call you when we can deliver him to Geneva. It may be by air, train or road. Be ready with two certified cheques. Have someone, a friend, with a mobile phone standing by near the ZFDZ bank. You know where it is?'

'Yes.'

'Right. The friend pays in half the money. We call you on your mobile to let you know where to find your husband. You collect him and call the friend who pays in the rest. Got that?'

'Yes, I think so.'

'Good. You deal straight with us and we'll deal straight with you.'

'When will – ?' began Kim, but he had gone.

Later that day the telephone rang yet again.

'Kim?'

She tightened her grip on the receiver. 'Hello?' she said cautiously.

'It's me. Mark.'

Her heart turned over in relief. 'Oh, where are you?'

'In London. Got back from Iraq today. I've only just heard about Henri's death. I'm very sorry. He was a good chap, a very nice man.'

'Yes, thank you,' she said with a catch in her voice.

'Are you all right? What are you doing? How are you managing?'

'I'm OK. But so much has happened since I last spoke to you.'

'About Richard?'

'Amongst other things.'

'So tell me.'

'Henri left me some money and I've decided to pay the ransom,' she said in a rush.

'You're mad! I told you, you must never give in to these people.'

She shook her head. 'I know, I know the theory. But in practice, I've got to get him back. He's ill. I could never live with myself if anything happened to him.'

'I see.' She could hear the concern in his voice. 'And have you paid it yet?' he asked. 'Have you worked out how you're going to fix it so they don't just take the money and disappear.'

She gave him an edited version of the details.

He did not sound reassured. 'Look, I think I can get away this weekend for a few days. Can you try and stall the Australian until then? You can't deal with these sort of people on your own. You may be in danger.'

'I think I'll be in more danger if I mess them about,' she said faintly.

'Kim, be sensible, please.'

She knew he didn't really understand why she must pay the ransom. It was *because* she didn't love Richard, *because* she didn't want him back. That was why she had to rescue him. The money was there. If she didn't use it, if she left him to die, she would, indirectly, be guilty of murder by default.

CHAPTER 19

'So you're not going to say a word to James unless Richard gets back safe and sound,' said Polly.

'No. I can't. I don't want to raise his hopes for nothing.'

'I agree. The next problem is: if I'm going to look after James as well as my own children, how can I be at the bank to pay in the money for you? I can't take hordes of kids with me – can you imagine it?'

Pacing backwards and forwards across the room, Kim rubbed her hands together nervously. 'Maybe Richard will arrive during school hours.'

'But what if he doesn't? You can't rely on anything going according to plan. You'll have to ask somebody else to bank the cheques. But who else would do it? Who can you trust? I mean, it's got to be somebody with no kids and no job, or someone who's free just to drop everything and go.'

Kim thought of Mark again, but he probably wouldn't be back in time and anyway he might well want to involve the police, if he hadn't done already. And Sophie-Maria must be kept out of it. And she didn't trust Madame Frank.

She paced about some more and then she said, 'The only other person I could try is BJ. At least she seems to have good strong nerves.'

Polly stared at her. 'Beverly-Jane? Are you crazy? You might as well take an ad in the newspaper. Can you imagine her dancing about in her cat suit, waving her essential oils and flourishing her crystal? She's bound to screw up.'

'It doesn't do to underestimate BJ. She can be discreet when she wants to be, and she sort of owes me a favour. I think I can guarantee she'll keep quiet about it all.'

'Sure I'll do it,' said BJ nonchalantly. 'If I do, does this mean we'll be friends again? The atmosphere has been kind of frosty around you. I've been receiving like waves of suppressed hostility and it's been hard to balance my inner self.'

Kim smiled tensely. 'Yes, yes, of course. I know it's a pretty major favour to ask.'

'Seriously, I mean, old Henri didn't tell me that you and he were an item. I usually steer away from guys who are involved with my friends, but I really liked him.'

'BJ, forget it. It's OK, I understand. All that's in the past. We've got to concentrate on this Richard business now. Are you sure you want to do this for me? I'll have to order the certified cheques. And give you the account number.

I hope, I hope it won't be in any way risky or difficult.'

BJ smiled. 'I kind of like risk – I've had my little
old secret affairs for years. Except I was real
scared you might tell Walt. You have to understand I love Walt, I don't want a divorce. It's just,
well, you know he's kind of quiet and sometimes
I think he likes his computer more than me. And
he travels a lot on business, and I get lonely, and
then someone's nice to me and I get tempted.
Well, it doesn't happen all the time, but if I meet
someone real cute like Henri . . . but I'm always
discreet. See, I wouldn't want to hurt Walt, like
I said.'

'BJ, I won't tell Walter about Henri whatever
happens. I'm not trying to blackmail you – and I
certainly I wouldn't want to wreck your marriage
– but will you do this big favour for me?'

'Sure I will. I think I can just about manage to
take a couple of phone calls and pay in a couple
of cheques. No problem. Should be fun. BJ, the
private eye. Maybe I should buy a new pair of
shades.'

'Are you ready?' asked the Australian.

'Yes,' whispered Kim, her heart pounding.

'We're bringing him in now by car but before
we cross the border you must pay in the money.'

'What part of the border? Where?'

'Send someone to pay in half the money and
I'll call you with the exact location.' Then he gave

the bank account number, repeated it twice and rang off.

Beverly-Jane went into overdrive. 'Yeah, Kim. I'm all ready to go. But what do you think I should wear? Something quiet, I guess. I planned on jeans and a plain black jacket. Would that be OK?'

'Wear what the hell you like, but get down to the bank, and for God's sake don't tell a soul.'

'You can count on me, Kim. I'm kind of looking forward to it. But what if I have to stand in line at the bank? What if I can't find a parking space?'

'Take a taxi,' said Kim, breathing hard. 'I'll pay you back. When you get to the bank just fill in a form. They have forms. I've already given you the account number. Then you join the queue like a normal customer, then go outside and wait till I call you before you pay in the second cheque. All right?'

'Check. Ten-four and out.'

'What?'

'I mean, OK, whatever you say.'

'BJ, this is very, very brave of you. Thank you.'

'You're welcome,' said BJ.

In the end BJ decided to wear her new black suit as it was smarter than the jeans, she reckoned. Her hand trembling, she rang for a taxi, and the guy took an age to arrive. Then she had to have him wait: the two certified cheques were already in her purse but she nearly forgot her cell phone and her crystal.

254

The bank was very grand, like Kim said. There were no other customers. BJ sighed with relief. With her elaborately curved handwriting she completed the paying-in slip and then looked around to make sure no one was about to accost her. The bank was still empty.

She approached the cashier's window. 'I want to bank this,' she said, attempting to sound casual.

The girl took the cheque and mechanically verified the slip against the payment. '*Merci, madame, et bonne fin d'après midi*,' she said in a bored tone of voice.

Like she gets mega sums of money every day of the week, thought BJ, disappointed to have caused so little reaction.

Then, losing her nerve, she rushed outside. The boulevard, too, was quiet, but there was a little dark-haired man walking towards her. BJ crossed the road and sat on a bench in the sunshine, waiting for Kim's call instructing her to make the second payment. If the long-lost husband showed up, that is. Maybe the kidnappers would just take the first payment and skip town.

It might be a long wait. BJ leant back. May as well try to get a suntan, she thought, pleased with her own bravado. Then suddenly it occurred to her they could try and jump on her while she sat there and just grab the second cheque too. A certified cheque was the same as cash, right? So she still had around forty-five thousand dollars sitting in her purse. She stood up nervously but there was no one about apart from two young mothers with their babies and a pair of fat pigeons pecking around in the gutter.

Like she'd said to Kim, she was used to risk. Adultery was risky, but not physically dangerous. Unless of course a jealous wife or girlfriend got violent. Which they never did because they never found out. At least not until she got caught with Henri. Poor old Henri, he was just a bit careless. May be it was a signal she should stop her little games. They could be more dangerous than they seemed.

BJ looked around. A young man in a leather jacket was walking down the road now. She held her breath. Maybe she should go back into the bank. She crossed the road and stood watching the young man, but he passed by without even looking in her direction. She breathed out again slowly. This was going to be a long and scary wait, she told herself, and she began to wonder why the hell she had gotten involved.

Kim picked up the telephone immediately. This time the Australian drawl was more friendly. 'Thanks. We got the first instalment. Go to the café-restaurant in the Co-op in Meyrin shopping centre. Your husband will be there by the time you reach it.'

Kim jumped in the car and turned on the engine. It failed to fire. Shaking with tension, she tried again and this time it started. She drove out of the gate and sped along the route down to the lake. The Mont-Blanc bridge was busy as usual. Meyrin? For a moment she could hardly remember the way, except that it was beyond the airport. Damn, she was in the wrong lane for rue de la Servette. The driver in the car behind jammed on his brakes and hooted indignantly as she pulled across in front of him.

Christ, she must be more careful. She stopped at a red light, impatiently drumming her fingers on the steering wheel.

Once she escaped the airport traffic, she was able to speed up and finally she reached the outskirts of Meyrin. The Centre Commercial was well sign-posted, thank God. She followed the route and there it was: a dreary shopping centre with a huge Co-op supermarket. What an unlikely spot to chose. Except that it was near one of the busiest border crossings, she suddenly realised. She drove slowly round the crowded open-air parking lot, avoiding the shoppers and their trolleys. Eventually she found a free space and drove crookedly in.

She hurried towards the restaurant at the front of the supermarket. It was a big place with red plastic tables, quite full. She stared at all the people with their coffee and their cakes and their shopping and their children.

Oh God, he wasn't here.

In desperation she ran outside again and

searched around. He wasn't in the car park either. Swaying on her feet, she felt sick. It had all been a trick after all. She was a complete fool. She hadn't saved Richard. She had lost, thrown away all that money. Just for nothing.

Unless maybe she was somehow in the wrong place.

Heart-pounding, she approached a Swiss woman and asked breathlessly, '*S'il vous plaît, madame, est-ce qu'il y a un autre supermarché Co-op ici?*'

The woman looked puzzled and then said, no, there wasn't another Co-op in Meyrin. Apart from the garden centre, she added as an afterthought.

Maybe that's what they meant.

The woman said it was some distance away, so Kim had to drive around another tangle of streets. The garden centre was one of those impossible places. She could see the tall concrete building with the huge sign saying *Co-op Brico-Jardin* but she just couldn't find the right road to reach it.

By the time she finally arrived she was trembling so much she could hardly turn the key to lock the car. She raced inside.

But there was no restaurant. Just a small empty coffee bar.

She stood stock still. Then it came to her that the only thing to do was to go back to the supermarket and wait.

Drive slowly and carefully. Concentrate. Don't panic, she repeated to herself.

The café-restaurant of the supermarket was now even more crowded. She walked slowly around checking each table one by one. Then she saw him. Sitting alone in the corner. He was gaunt, thin and hollow-eyed, but he was Richard.

CHAPTER 20

Kim took a deep breath. 'Hello, Richard, how are you?'
As soon as she saw him all the anger she had ever felt towards him gave way to pity. At close quarters he looked even thinner and more fragile, with dry flaking skin, pale yellow like a forgotten houseplant. His eyes were glazed and he stared at her as if she were a stranger.

'It's all right. Come on home with me,' she said.

He rose to his feet and picked up a small red hold-all from the floor.

'Is that all the luggage you have?'

He did not reply but held the case tightly to his chest, apparently afraid she would take it from him. Together they walked slowly to the car.

Richard said nothing as they drove through the busy city, nor did he reply to any of her questions. He was wearing a cleanish but very creased pair of beige trousers and a khaki-coloured jumper she didn't recognise. He smelt faintly of stale sweat.

Suddenly her mobile rang. 'Kim,' said BJ's urgent crackly voice. 'Did you get him yet?

Because I'm beginning to feel kind of scared out here on the front line.'

'BJ! Are you all right?'

'Yeah, sort of. Like, what gives?'

'I was just going to call you. Everything's fine. Richard is here in the car with me now.'

'So I pay in the second cheque, right?'

'Right. Yes, please. And phone back the moment you're safely home again. Thank you very, very much. You're a heroine.'

'You're darned right I am,' said BJ.

When Kim unlocked the house Caspar came bounding out to greet them, wagging his tail. Richard backed away, making small incoherent noises of fear, and so Kim pushed the dog back into the kitchen and closed the door.

Trembling slightly, Richard stood in the middle of the sitting room. When she persuaded him to sit down, he remained very still staring out into the garden. She brought him some tea which he drank quickly, but without adding any milk or sugar though he had always done so in the past.

'Would you like a biscuit?' she asked, but he did not reply. 'Well, then I'll just get you some in case you change your mind.' She found herself adopting the hearty tones of a nursery nurse.

In the kitchen she made a lightning phone call to Polly to report that Richard was safe. 'No time for details. Don't say a word to James, though. Best if I tell him myself. Everything's OK.' She didn't feel she could tell Polly about Richard's strangeness. Anyway, he'd probably be better once he'd had some food and some rest.

When she returned with the plate of ginger biscuits, she was startled to find that the door to the garden was open and that he had disappeared. She ran outside and stood still, taken aback by the sight of him relieving himself on to the juniper bush. When he had finished and zipped himself up, she came forward and took him gently by the arm. 'Sorry, I forgot to remind you, we have a lavatory downstairs.'

She led him back into the house and opened the cloakroom door. 'Look, you can pee in the loo next time, and you remember we have two bath-rooms upstairs as well. Come on now, Richard, I'll show you to your room. Let me take your bag.'

But immediately he snatched the red case from her and held it to him.

'OK, I won't touch it again,' she said, deter-mined to remain as calm as possible. 'I know it's yours. But if you've got any dirty things, you will let me wash them, won't you?'

They went upstairs. 'All your clothes are in here,' she said. 'And just here is the bathroom with a shower and a loo.'

He stared at the bathroom as if he had never seen one before.

She waved her arm. 'That's James's room, of course, but he's not here at the moment. And this door leads to the spare room where I'm sleeping.'

Then she had an inspiration and added, to frighten him, 'The dog sleeps on my bed.' She thought it unlikely Richard would want sex in his current state, but she intended to lock her bedroom door to be on the safe side.

Richard looked at her. Then he returned to his room and opened the cupboard door again. Taking out one of his grey office suits, he examined it and with very careful movements hung it back on the rail. He gave a small faint smile.

She smiled back encouragingly. 'I'm going downstairs to start cooking dinner. Did you want to have a rest? Or perhaps you'd like to see the television news after all this time out of touch?'

Richard ignored this suggestion. He went back to the cupboard and took out another suit. Then in the same careful way he hung it up again.

'Well, I'll just leave you here,' she said. 'I expect you're glad to see your things again.' As she was closing the door, he made a small distressed sound. 'Would you prefer me to leave it open? All right.'

Later she went to the bottom of the stairs and stood listening. A low sobbing noise was coming from Richard's room. She rushed up again. He was sitting on the bed holding his favourite blue shirt, tears pouring down his sallow cheeks. She moved towards him and held out her arms, but he turned away, his face half-fearful, half-angry.

Increasingly worried, she went slowly back to the kitchen. She had not known when, or even if, he would be arriving so she'd made no advance arrangements for a medical check-up for Richard. Perhaps he should see a doctor tonight, but what doctor? She did not have a regular one in Geneva. The local health centre, the Permanence Médicale, where she had once or twice taken James, would now be closed except for emergency treatment such as cut hands and bee stings. And, besides, the paramedics who manned the centre in the evenings spoke only French. She'd never be able to explain a problem like this in French.

She telephoned Polly again. After listening avidly to the story, Polly promised to contact a friend who might know a suitable doctor. She would make an appointment for Richard as soon as possible tomorrow.

Kim sat down at the kitchen table, wondering if she had made the right decision. She worried that perhaps she should take him straight to the emergency department of the Cantonal hospital, but again her heart sank at the prospect. He wasn't exactly ill, was he? Probably after a good night's sleep he'd feel able to talk.

Pulling herself together, she began to prepare dinner. She'd bought some lamb chops, Richard's favourite meal. Maybe it would restore his morale.

Taking Caspar with her she went outside to pick some mint for the sauce. She stood looking around. She would have to explain to Richard that soon they were going to leave Villa la Vigne to move to the cottage. But she wouldn't talk about the future now. He couldn't cope with any more confusion tonight. Leaving the dog to sniff around the garden, she walked back to the house.

To her surprise she found Richard sitting cross-legged on the carpet playing with her cotton reels. Totally absorbed in his game, he had arranged them in a neat row, along with her needles and scissors.

'Hello,' she said tentatively.

Startled, he looked up.

'It's OK. Well, it's – nice of you to sort out my sewing box. I expect it was a bit messy, as usual,' she said with a smile. But he quickly put everything away and stood uneasily in the middle of the room, staring at the floor.

She noticed anew how unkempt he looked. 'Would you like a bath? Come with me.'

He followed her upstairs and watched as she filled the tub with water.

'I'll leave you to it then,' said Kim. 'Now, throw your dirty clothes down over there. I'll wash them. You put clean ones on. I'll go and get your dressing gown for you.'

She collected Richard's old red paisley dressing gown and returned to find him already standing naked in the middle of the bathroom. He was using a toothmug to scoop up the bathwater and pour it over himself in the Eastern manner. She drew in her breath at the pitiful sight of his scrawny body. There were faint scratches on his arms and legs, and his ribs were clearly visible.

'Richard, you must get into the bath and sit down, remember. You mustn't throw water all over the floor. Look, the tiles are all wet and slippery.'

He stared at her blankly, unconscious of his nakedness. She knew then that she need not fear any sexual advances. Gently she took the toothmug out of his hand and helped him step into the bath. Then she put some soap on a flannel and washed his pathetically thin arms. 'Now you do the rest,' she said.

The evening passed without further incident but, alert to the slightest sound, she slept little that night. At one point, holding tight on to Caspar, she unlocked her bedroom door and crept along the landing to see that all was well. A heavy snoring came from Richard's room and she smiled in relief.

Eventually towards dawn she fell into an exhausted sleep, but at about eight o'clock she was suddenly wide awake and uneasy. She looked out of the bedroom window and saw that Richard was outside. Wearing only his pyjama trousers and a pair of sandals, he was urinating on the lawn as before. Oh well, it would be like toilet training a child.

After a hurried shower, she went downstairs.

'Richard!' she said in horror.

Back in the kitchen he had taken all her cooking knives out of the drawer and laid them in a row on the table. He looked up, an expression of anguished guilt on his face. Then he stared at one of the chair cushions which had a small neat gash in the centre.

Kim took a deep breath and, in as normal a voice as she could manage, she said, 'I think it's better if you don't touch my things actually. Please could you put them all away? Breakfast isn't ready yet, but I'll call you when it is. Why don't you go and get dressed?'

He stood there staring at her. Slowly he turned and went out of the room. Then she heard his footsteps on the stairs.

Very quietly she picked up the telephone. 'Polly, I've got to be quick. Did you manage to get me an appointment? You did. Oh, thank God.' She quickly jotted down the doctor's name and address. 'And please, Pol, could you keep James for another day or two? Can't explain now. I'll call you when I can.'

To her relief, Richard was quiet and acquiescent when she led him to the car and he behaved with the same blank docility in the surgery.

At the end of the consultation, Dr Hahn, a serious middle-aged woman, drew her aside. 'What has happened to your husband? Why won't he speak? He is certainly in need of treatment. I believe this to be a medical and psychiatric emergency.'

Kim told the story as best she could, but she knew it sounded unlikely. The doctor gave her a strange look and asked why there had been no news of this, er, hostage-taking in the newspapers.

'We tried to keep it quiet. It seemed safer,' said Kim. 'He's been away for ages, since last September, but I don't know how long he was actually a prisoner – at least three months, maybe much longer. Has he got some sort of tropical disease?'

'Malnutrition certainly and severe post-traumatic stress syndrome, with complications. Please wait here. I will telephone a colleague. I would recommend he be admitted to a private psychiatric clinic.'

'A clinic? But I can't shut him away again. Couldn't he just have some pills to calm him down or cheer him up? He'll probably feel like talking soon.'

'He will not be locked up, but I believe he must be under medical observation for two weeks, to ensure that there is no risk of suicide. It's for his own safety and that of your family.' She picked up her pen. 'I presume you have health insurance?' she asked abruptly.

'Yes, my husband's employers went on paying it while he was away. I hope psychiatric treatment is covered too. If necessary, I expect I could pay myself, privately.'

The doctor smiled grimly and pushed back her glasses. 'Are you a Rothschild? Because if that is not the case, you must allow the insurance company to pay for the clinic I have in mind.'

★ ★ ★

Kim drove out on the motorway towards Lausanne and, taking the exit at Nyon, followed the lanes through the vineyards up towards the Jura. From time to time, she glanced at Richard but he seemed to be asleep. The doctor had insisted on giving him a calming injection and he was now looking even more blank-faced than before.

She slowed down when she saw what looked like an Edwardian hotel half-hidden amongst the trees at the foot of the mountains. A small discreet sign indicated 'Clinique la Forêt'.

'Wake up, Richard. We're here.' She did not yet have the heart to explain they had arrived at a hospital.

Beside the huge double door was a bell and a sign in French and English to the effect that one should ring and enter. Holding him by the arm, she went inside. The high-ceilinged hall was extremely quiet, not a nurse, doctor or patient in sight, nor was there a receptionist. Nonplussed, she waited, chatting brightly to Richard about the elegant desk and the huge vase of lilies, though why she was making this idiotic one-sided conversation she did not know.

Eventually a young Asian woman in a blue nurse's uniform arrived. 'Good morning, madame, monsieur, I am Sister Chi. Would you be so kind as to wait here, madame, and I will take your husband to see Doctor Weinbaum.' If Richard was suspicious now, he did not show it.

Rather he could not take his eyes off the nurse, as if she were someone he recognised. They padded off together down the thick-carpeted hall.

Kim paced about uneasily. Now and then she stared out of the window. The view over a nearby golf course, the lake and then the Alps beyond was magnificent. The weather was clear enough to see Mont Blanc looming white and massive in the distance. That must be a good omen, she told herself.

At last she was admitted to Dr Weinbaum's sanctum. He was very small, with iron grey hair, bushy eyebrows and smooth olive skin. His manner was friendly and confidential, but at first he talked only about the merits of the golf course, presumably to put her at her ease.

In fact, this irrelevant conversation had the opposite effect. Rubbing her hands together nervously, she broke in. 'About my husband . . .'

'Does he play golf? What's his handicap? Maybe we can have a game,' said Dr Weinbaum.

After being distracted by many other tangential matters such as the problems of sailing on the lake with its changing winds, the doctor confirmed the diagnosis that, yes, her husband was unwell and should be admitted for rest and observation.

In the secretary's office she was obliged to fill in a long admission form and her insurance policy was checked and double-checked. Eventually, when all the formalities had been completed, she returned to ask Dr Weinbaum if she might say goodbye to Richard, who had not reappeared.

'Why don't you just slip away? He's still under-taking tests at the moment,' he said.

'But he won't trust me if I don't say goodbye.'

He smiled at her. 'If that's what you feel is best for you, then I will take you to him. You have had a shock too, my dear. We must take care of your mental state. We don't want you breaking down too.'

'I'm perfectly all right, thank you,' she said. She had subconsciously expected to be commended for the calm and sensible manner in which she had dealt with the situation, rather than accused of being unhinged herself.

271

CHAPTER 21

When she finally arrived home the telephone was ringing. She rushed to answer it.

'Kim? At last.' It was Mark's voice.

'Where are you?' she asked breathlessly.

'Here, in Geneva.'

She let out a sigh of relief. 'Oh . . . oh, that's good. When did you get here?'

'This morning. I've been phoning all day. So what's happened about Richard?'

'He, I . . . Sorry,' she muttered down the receiver. 'It's just that it was so difficult.'

'Kim, what's the matter? Are you all right?'

Her words stumbled out. 'Yes, yes, I'm fine . . . sorry. It's just all the tension and worry. Now it's over, temporarily at least, I seem to have fallen apart.'

'But what happened?'

Stifling the tears at the back of her throat, she told him about rescuing Richard and his silence, the cotton reels, the knives, the clinic.

When she had come to the end of her story,

he said, 'God, what a saga. I obviously got here too late, but you're OK, are you?'

'Sort of.'

'You don't sound as if you are. Hardly surprising. What about James, how's he coping?'

'He's still at Polly's. I tried to keep him away from it all.'

'You shouldn't be on your own.' He hesitated. 'I'd better come and see you, shall I?'

'Yes, come round, please.'

'You really want me to? You aren't too exhausted?'

'No, well, yes, but I do want to see you,' she said in a sudden rush. She was too overwrought to disguise her emotions. She just needed to talk to him, to be comforted and told she had done the best she could, and that everything would be all right in the end.

It seemed to take an age for him to arrive. She had rushed upstairs to bath and change. Caspar's brown eyes were reproachful, understandably as she had not taken him for a proper long walk for three days. She gave him an extra large dinner and shut him in the garden again, with an apologetic 'good dog'.

The house was chaotic, but why should she care after all the drama of the last forty-eight hours? She attempted a little half-hearted tidying. When at last she was ready, she stared into the mirror and saw she looked as tired and bedraggled as she felt.

Oh well. She was past worrying about her appearance. Mark probably wouldn't want to . . . or maybe he would, but she really and truly wasn't in the mood for sex. He'd understand that.

If you aren't in the mood, why are you even thinking about it and why did you bother with scent and smart underwear? asked a voice at the back of her mind.

When the bell rang, a long shiver passed through her. She walked slowly to the front door and there he was. She stood smiling uncertainly.

'Can I come in?' he asked. He was just the same, so nice, so normal. She suddenly realised how much she had missed him.

Then they were standing in the salon and her mind became blurred. Without any kind of conversation, she found herself in his arms and crying all over his shirt.

'Kim, you did it. It's over, everything is all right.' He held her close and kissed her in a comforting sort of way on her forehead. 'Tell me again, tell me all about it,' he urged.

So he poured them some wine from the bottle he'd brought and she sat down and told him about it all over again. All the while she talked he held her in his arms.

'So what are you going to do now?' he asked eventually.

'Wait and see. That's all I can do.'

'But –'

'Let's not talk any more. I'm absolutely worn out,' she said, pushing back her hair. 'I'm about to collapse, well, soon anyway.'

'Now, let's be practical, have you eaten anything today?

'No,' she said.

So he offered to take her out and she said she couldn't face a restaurant and volunteered to cook something herself.

'No, let me make dinner,' he said. As he rose to his feet she remembered that the kitchen was in a terrible mess. And anyway food was the last thing she wanted.

She slumped back, 'Please Mark. It's OK. I really couldn't eat a thing.'

He sat down beside her and took her face in his hands.

She stared back at him. 'Maybe we should just . . .'

He leant forward and kissed her gently on the lips. She kissed him back, equally gently, opening her mouth a little. Suddenly his kisses became desperate and hungry. Blindly, she responded. Her body leant towards him, acquiescent, abandoned. The responsibility was his now. She had given up taking decisions, given up worrying, given up thinking at all.

'Kim, is this what you want? I don't want to take advantage. Well, of course, I do but –'

'Mm,' she murmured.

Fingers shaking he began to undo the buttons of her shirt. It took a while. Then she helped him.

'Kim.' He touched her breasts with urgent tenderness. 'I've waited for you for so long.'

She looked up at him, her heavy eyelids half-closed. 'I know. I waited too.'

He ran his hands over her body. Shaken by the strength of her own response, she sank back on the sofa, pulling him with her.

A while later, when their breathing had returned to normal, she blinked and looked up at him with a wobbly smile. 'Wow,' she murmured, very much moved by the passion and intensity of his love-making.

He smiled back tenderly. They lay holding each other, not speaking. She felt wonderfully, deliriously happy.

Then she gently pushed him off and began to pick up her discarded clothes. 'So do you want dinner now?'

'Not yet, don't get dressed again.'

'I wasn't going to,' she said.

After he had made love to her in bed, more slowly with a careful appreciative thoroughness, she fell into a long deep exhausted sleep.

In the middle of the night, she whispered in his ear, 'I'd forgotten, I really like you.'

She thought he hadn't heard but then he muttered, 'I should bloody well hope so.'

'It's not just lust,' she insisted dreamily. 'I really do like you.'

'And I like you too.' And he began to caress her again. She thought she was too tired, that she would just accommodate him willingly but passively, and then sleep some more. But soon long shuddering waves of pleasure possessed her, time and again, ever more deep and intense, until finally he joined her.

When she woke at last with a start, she saw that the sun was shining through the gap in the curtains and Mark had disappeared. Noises were coming from the kitchen. She lay back in bed, her mind racing through everything that had happened.

She looked at the telephone. The doctor hadn't called, so presumably Richard's condition hadn't deteriorated. She picked up the receiver and telephoned the clinic to be told by a nurse that he was under sedation, that he was as 'comfortable' as could be expected and there should be no visiting this week-end.

She lay back again. Then stretching her arms, she smiled, guilty at her own surge of happiness that she could now spend the day alone with Mark. She bathed quickly and pulled on a short denim skirt and her new pink shirt. Hoping she didn't look as self-conscious as she felt, she went downstairs. Outside the kitchen door she hesitated, then composing her features into a sophisticated sort of smile, she opened the door.

'Hello,' he said in his charming way. 'I began to get breakfast ready – hope you don't mind.'

'Make yourself at home,' she said. Then she put her hand to her mouth. 'Oh, my God, how awful! We never did have any dinner last night, did we? You see, I was such a nervous wreck that –'

'Don't worry. I made myself a sandwich, a midnight feast, while you were asleep. You looked so peaceful, I didn't want to disturb you.'

'How embarrassing. Sorry.' She tumbled into his arms again.

Holding her tight he murmured, 'Would you prefer toast, madame, or sex?'

She grinned. 'Difficult decision. Probably toast first, anyway. I'm quite hungry.'

But after a while her choices seemed to be limited.

'But, Mark, I should be ringing the clinic again. I should be –'

'Stop worrying. Richard's in safe hands. Calm down, relax.'

It was some time before the conversation became more serious and even then it was spasmodic and full of disconnected thoughts.

'Where will you live?' he asked. 'I expect you'll have to move out of this house?'

She told him about Latigny.

'Henri left you a cottage too? How very generous.'

It seemed too complicated at that point to

explain about Beatrice and Villa la Vigne. 'Well, he had lots of houses.'

'I see,' he said doubtfully. 'That's good.'

'Yes, it's very good because it makes me independent for the first time in my life.'

After a pause he said, 'Could I come and see you again soon? Or maybe you can come to England and stay with me. Leave James with your friend.'

'But I have to look after Richard when he comes out of the clinic.'

'How long for? When will he be discharged?'

'I just don't know.' She looked down. 'Until you arrived, I'd had just about the worst two days of my whole stupid and complicated life and I can't decide about anything at the moment. I can't face any more discussions.' She leant forward to touch his face. 'Maybe I can cope with you, but nothing else. How long can you stay?'

He pulled her towards him again. 'All day and all night, if you want.'

'Yes, I do want. Very much.'

So he was only here for one more day. She felt another pang of conscience about James, about Richard and, belatedly, about Henri's memory. Except that Henri would probably understand and approve – he always approved of love-making – so she told her tiresome higher self to be quiet. Polly had said she'd keep James for the weekend. He'd be perfectly happy there. And Polly always said her sons behaved better when James was around to stop them from fighting each other. So, for the moment, everyone was, or should be, happy.

'But why did you pay the ransom?' asked Mark later. 'Hostages are usually released eventually. There are professionally trained teams of negotiators these days, you know.'

'Yes, but in that part of the world –'

He shook his head. 'Last year the Indonesians rescued some western students from Irian Jaya. The Maising may not be as militarily sophisticated as the Indonesians, but they would've got there in the end, I'm sure.'

'Yes, but, if you remember, some of the Asian hostages in Irian Jaya were killed. Anyway, I told you, Richard was, is ill. It was all very frightening and confusing. I had to make a decision to get him out quickly. And you said yourself he might be arrested if the Maising government was involved.'

'You're right,' he said thoughtfully. 'I can't really approve, but maybe you did the best thing in a way.'

She punched him gently in the chest. 'Sorry you don't approve, but you're not in charge of me, you know.'

Defending himself by pinning down her arms, he grinned. 'More's the pity.' After a pause he asked, 'So, tell me, has there been any come-back about Richard's alleged arms dealing?'

'No, thank God. He was probably too incompetent at it for anyone to take him seriously.' She paused. 'Why? You don't think the Maising government will come after him, do you?'

'Oh no, I'm sure they won't bother, not if you've got him out of the country. Anyway I don't think they knew – or cared – much about him. Incidentally, I wonder what his employers will make of all this.'

'Well, Vivienne Frank – she's the personnel officer, HR manager or whatever, in Richard's company – she telephoned last week sounding quite polite. She wanted to know if I'd heard anything. I said no, of course. Didn't want them interfering.'

Mark raised his eyebrows. 'Interfering?'

'They, the company, I don't trust them. Vivienne's all right, actually. I will let her know he's safe. She's quite a friendly woman in a distant Swiss sort of way. It's Hoffer, her repulsive lover, that I can't stand.'

'If he's so repulsive, why does she like him?'

'Who knows what turns her on?' Kim grinned. 'Who knows why women like men at all?'

'Who knows?' he echoed, letting go of her hands to caress her breast.

Later she said, 'Why didn't you ring me or write to me while you were away?'

'Not too many free phone lines where I was.'

She felt ashamed. 'Oh no, of course, I suppose

281

there weren't.' After a pause she asked, 'What was it like?'

He stared at the ceiling. 'Worse than you could ever imagine.'

'Worse than on the TV news?'

'Oh yes, much worse. One thinks one's inured to those sort of scenes of devastation, but it's not so. Even the military chaps felt the same. Made me realise why the World War years had such an impact on our parents and grandparents.'

'Do you have to go back there?'

'No, thank God. Look, darling,' (*darling*, she noted,) 'sorry, but I want to forget about wars for now. Let's not talk about it. When I get back to London, I just have to write up the report and then it's finished for me.' His face was serious. 'Not for the Iraqis, of course.'

'And then where will you go?'

'Depends on the FCO in London. Nothing has been decided.'

After a while she said, 'But you could have written, from Iraq or from London, I mean.'

'What was there to say? You said you weren't interested.'

She grinned. 'Maybe I lied.'

He nuzzled her ear. 'In that case, you should have written to me yourself. Why didn't you?'

'Well, quite apart from Henri and everything else, I didn't want to interfere with you and Bella – your reconciliation when you were in London,' she added carefully.

He stared at her. 'What d'you mean? Our divorce is about to come through, thank God.'

'But I thought . . . oh well, it doesn't really matter. I was jealous. I just stupidly imagined that you were in her arms every night.'

'Why on earth did you think that?'

'I phoned you in Geneva once and then I phoned your flat in London before you went to Iraq and she answered both times, sounding very much at home.'

He smiled grimly. 'She does reappear occasionally – not to see me, just to collect some of what she considers to be her possessions, stuff that belonged to us both that she wants. I don't usually argue. Life's much too short.'

'But she implied – well, her voice was all languid and sexy, as if she'd just spent all night . . .'

'Typical Bella. She always sounds like a sex pot when she talks, but it's all an illusion. Actually we haven't slept together for years. You're the only woman I want – surely you realise that.'

'You know something,' she said, 'it's nice just lying here swooning in your arms and talking. You're very easy to talk to. Surprising really. I hardly know you.'

He smiled. 'You know me in some ways.'

'Mm. And you know me, in some ways.'

'I like this part of you,' he said. 'And this . . . and this, this especially.'

Her eyes closed. 'I like all of you, but we can't

283

go on like this,' she murmured. 'We just can't spend the whole weekend in bed. Got too much to do. My life is a complete mess. Too much has happened, I can't cope.' Then she lost the thread of what she was trying to say.

Later still she returned to the rather awkward subject of Henri. Perhaps it was tactless in the circumstances, but she felt the need to explain everything – well, almost everything. 'Anyway,' she said, 'I never felt that the money I inherited from Henri was really mine. That's why I spent most of it rescuing Richard.'

'What do you mean?'

'Oh, I don't know. Maybe it was too much, more than I deserved.' She had been about to say that her inheritance had seemed to her like immoral earnings. Then she changed her mind. Perhaps it would be better not to confess that her relationship with Henri had started off as a kind of business arrangement, that it had eventually become a kind of love affair. Perhaps Mark would prefer not to know such details. Besides, she wanted him to think well of her, wanted him to remember her with approval as well as love.

He looked at her thoughtfully. 'But your scruples don't extend as far as the cottage. You're going to move there?'

'Yes, quite soon.'

'And Richard will stay there too.'

'Yes, he has to.'

'I thought you said you were going to divorce him.'

'Well, yes, but not now. I mean, not straight away. I've got to get him on his feet first. I still feel responsible for him. He's ill. I can't abandon him till he's recovered. You must see that.'

'But that may be months, years even. You can't tie yourself down again.'

She kissed him. 'I already said, I can't cope with serious decisions about anything. This is my one-day holiday from reality.'

Reality for the foreseeable future meant Richard, she knew. Mark wouldn't wait around for long, so this might be one of the last days they would ever have together. Without betraying her thoughts, she smiled sadly and said, 'Can't you just be happy with sex, gathering rosebuds and all that?'

'I am happy, very happy at this moment. But the future, I don't like the idea of Richard in your house.'

'He'll be in a different bedroom, if that's what's worrying you.'

'It's not just sexual jealousy.' His face was set. 'He won't get violent again, will he?'

'Oh no, he wasn't threatening. I think I just panicked unnecessarily when I saw him with the knives. He was probably just sorting them out. He even used to rearrange my cupboards now and then. He's always hated my untidiness.'

'What about the cushion? Sounded very odd to me.'

'But Richard has never actually been violent. Just fairly disagreeable and short-tempered, but now, quite apart from not talking, well, he seems unnaturally gentle and passive, much more so than he was before.'

Mark frowned and shook his head. 'As I am sure your psychiatrist friends would say, gentle people have their own ways of being aggressive.'

CHAPTER 22

James felt peculiar. Last night Mum fetched him from Polly's really late and on the way home she told him that Dad was alive! Alive and back in Geneva. Back in Geneva but in a hospital, a hospital which he couldn't go and visit. No children allowed yet.

He was excited and happy, of course. But what was he supposed to say to his friends? Actually I got it wrong, I have a father after all?

Then Mum said she was going to tell his teacher. And his teacher, Miss Street, made an announcement. 'James's father has come back. Isn't that good?' Everyone sort of stared at him and some people clapped and then the day went on just as if nothing had happened.

Mum said she would take him to see Dad as soon as she could, but not for a week or so. It was strange knowing he was here and not seeing him. In a way it was a relief. James knew he needed time to think about it all.

When Kim arrived at the clinic that day a new doctor was on duty, a young woman with smooth blonde hair folded into a chignon, a pale plump bun face and an even plumper bottom.

'I am Dr Anna,' she said with a professional smile. 'It was a pity that you couldn't visit your husband over the weekend. The other doctors and I have been assessing Richard and we think it most important he should have a regular time when he expects people.'

Kim flushed. 'I telephoned. I was told he was under sedation, with no visiting allowed.'

'Really? Then you were misinformed. He was only mildly sedated. Mrs Ellis, we all need to cooperate if your husband is to recover.'

For a moment Kim was too indignant to speak. Then she said, 'Of course you'll have my cooperation, but I've got several different part-time jobs and a school-age child, so I don't think I can come at a set time.'

Dr Anna said, and her voice was irritatingly patient, 'I understand and acknowledge your problems, but it would be in Richard's best interests for you to come at eleven-thirty every morning. Then you can join in the family therapy, if needed.'

Stifling a rude reply, Kim said politely that she would try but that there wasn't much point in her attending therapy sessions. 'My husband was perfectly normal before he was kidnapped and his current state has got nothing to do with me, or the family,' she added.

'Your opinion is noted though not necessarily shared by us.'

Kim stared. 'What do you mean?'

'We always reserve judgement until we get to know people better,' said Dr Anna.

'How sensible,' said Kim coldly. 'Now perhaps I had better go and see Richard, if you will excuse me.'

Shaking with anger, she began to walk down the long corridor with its thick blue carpet and soothing cream walls. Damn that bloody doctor. Without sounding self-righteous or protesting too much, it was impossible to explain to a stranger that she had been a conscientious, over-conscientious wife to Richard for eighteen years. Then she smiled suddenly and reminded herself she had just spent the weekend in bed with Mark instead of coming here, but all the same . . .

Aware of quiet footsteps close behind her, she turned and came face to face with a scrawny young woman with dead-white skin and huge protruding dark eyes.

The girl clutched her with a dry claw-like hand. 'Are you Richard's wife?' Her breath smelt odd, like oil or nail-varnish remover.

'Yes,' said Kim, drawing back.

'He's in the garden. I'll take you to him. She's a pain, isn't she?'

'Who?'

'Dr Anna. You can't trust her. Richard doesn't like her either.'

Kim stopped, startled. 'Who are you?'

'I'm Serena,' said the girl confidentially. Thin as a

famine victim, she looked to be in her early twenties. She was wearing a baggy black T-shirt with black jeans and a great deal of silver jewellery. Designer black and designer jewellery, Kim surmised. 'You're English?' she asked.

'Yes, half-English,' said Serena. 'Most people here aren't Swiss. In fact, this place is crammed with dotty foreigners.'

Assuming the girl was one of the so-called dotty foreigners rather than a member of staff, Kim spoke gently. 'And how do you know Richard doesn't like Dr Anna?'

'He told me,' said Serena with a triumphant smile.

Kim stared. 'He spoke?'

'Well, not exactly. He hasn't said a word yet, but I can tell what he feels. For instance, I know that he likes me 'cos he eats my dinner for me – but don't tell Dr Anna.'

'I don't understand. Why does he do that?' asked Kim.

Serena twisted her silver bangles round and round her narrow wrist. 'They're always trying to make me eat things, but I'm too clever for them.'

'Oh.'

She looked anxiously at Kim. 'I'm anorexic.'

'Oh, bad luck.'

'That's a nice thing to say, and you're right, it is unlucky,' said Serena more calmly. 'But most people seem to think it's my own fault I can't eat.'

Kim felt out of her depth. 'About Richard,' she said. 'I think I'd better go and find him.'

Serena looked sideways at her. 'Better be careful. There's an alcoholic who fancies him, a real old tart, at least forty-five or even fifty.'

'He seems to have made a lot of friends in a short time,' said Kim with a wary smile.

'Oh, she's a fast mover that one. They're not meant to mix with us, those alcoholics, but they do. They're meant to keep in their own groups, you see, so they can all repeat their funny mantras together.'

'Oh,' said Kim again. She wondered if this was the right place for Richard. Perhaps he should be in a more normal environment. 'Have you been here long, Serena?'

'About two months. They won't let me out until I reach a certain weight.'

'Well, then you'd better not give your food to other people.'

'Oh, no, I do eat the salad. I've gained masses already. I'm huge now, aren't I? It's only the meat and potatoes and cakes I can't eat, and the pasta, things like that. Richard and I are at the high-calorie table and they give us disgusting pork chops followed by cream pastries and revolting chocolate stuff.'

As they turned the corner, Kim heard heart-rending sobs coming from one of the bedrooms. Worried, she stopped.

'It's all right, that's the post-natal girl, she cries all the time,' said Serena casually. 'If she isn't wailing away then her baby is. What a pair!'

'But shouldn't we call a nurse? She sounds so unhappy.'

'Don't worry. She'll get over it.'

Kim raised her eyebrows. 'How do you know so much about everybody? How do you know what's wrong with them?'

Serena grinned. 'You can tell by the seating in the dining room. That post-natal girl is on the Depressed table with various other gloomy types. They've put Richard on the Eating Disorders table with me 'cos he needs fattening up. Then the alcoholics have their own corner where they're meant to talk about Twelve Steps or something. I know all about it now. It's supposed to make us feel less isolated if we hear about other people with similar problems, but frankly mental patients are a pain because they only talk about themselves all the time.' She waved her skinny hand. 'All except Richard, that is. He doesn't talk, that's why he's so popular.'

Kim smiled. 'Well, you seem to be interested in other people anyway. So there's no one really crazy here?'

'Oh no. It's a clinic for, like, temporary psychiatric problems, not a lunatic asylum – at least one hopes the problems are temporary. But anyway who's to say who's crazy and who isn't, what's normal and what isn't? It's all subjective, you know.'

They were now walking across the garden, and as they passed through a gap in the beech hedge they could see Richard sitting on a bench under an oak tree. Beside him was an ordinary-looking middle-aged woman, conventionally dressed in navy blue and beige.

Serena drew in her breath. 'D'you see that fat old bag? That's Grace. She's trying to get Richard to speak, but I know it's going to be me he talks to first. He's my friend, not hers.'

Richard smiled at them both. Some sort of progress, thought Kim. Once the two women had been persuaded to depart, she sat down beside him. He looked a little less pallid and fragile today.

'How are you?' she enquired. 'I'm sorry to have left you here, but until you speak I don't think they'll let you come home.' Why did I say 'home' she wondered. She didn't want to give him a home any more, but she obviously couldn't mention divorce at the moment.

She began to talk to him about James and what he was doing at school. Then she had another idea. 'I'll bring James to see you,' she said, 'but I can't do that unless you'll promise to speak to him. He wouldn't like it.'

As soon as she said the words, she regretted them. Her own interests, and perhaps James's, were for Richard to forget about them both. And yet she couldn't leave Richard here in this state indefinitely. Could she? As his next of kin, she was still responsible for him.

During the weekend she had tried an appeal to

his sister, but Monica had refused categorically to help, saying she wasn't any good with mental problems and stuff. She had sounded pleased about Richard's reappearance but, not effusive at the best of times, she'd said she needed to have a think about it all and rang off, leaving Kim staring at the phone. When after a few days' silence from Monica, Kim forced herself to ring again, she was unable to achieve a greater response.

Monica sniffed down the line, 'As I was saying to George, I said to him, your private clinic in Switzerland is bound to be much better than the National Health – and I don't know if Richard is entitled to the NHS. Bet he never paid any stamps. If your company insurance is covering him, he should stay in Switzerland. And even if he gets better, there's no jobs for older people here. We know loads of unemployed middle-aged blokes, even professional ones. I mean, you've got a job out there yourself, haven't you? At your age you'll never get anything here. That's what George says and I agree with him.'

'Surely it can't be as bad as that?'

'It's worse,' said Monica, coughing gloomily. 'Look, is there anything else? I'd better stop talking because there's a medical programme on the telly now and they're doing a story about a mental patient. I'll ring you back if it gives any useful information about how to deal with nutters.'

But she did not call again.

That was on Saturday. Today, talking to Richard

without any response, Kim began to wonder if he really had become what Monica called a nutter. She decided to try and find Dr Weinbaum.

She was making her way across the well-kept lawns when she met Vivienne Frank.

As large and lovely as ever, Vivienne was immaculately dressed and exuding charm. She shook hands. 'Ah, Madame Ellis, how delightful. Such good news that your husband is safe. I was so happy to receive your message this morning. And how is poor Mr Ellis? We have missed him at the office during this such very long time he has been absent.'

'How kind,' said Kim doubtfully. 'Well, he looks a little healthier, not so pale, but, the problem is, he's still not speaking.'

'Ah, the stress. One reads about it. All he needs is time and kindness, I'm sure. Do not worry yourself, Madame Ellis. Perhaps I can help. I will sit with him and talk of the old days. Something will surely inspire him to speech soon. I hope so. He does have a special contribution to make. It is his military bearing with the British manners and good looks. They used to impress our clients so much. I hope he will be well enough to come back to the office one day.'

Kim stared at her. 'But I thought he was in disgrace. Mr Hoffer said he had been sacked.'

'Monsieur Hoffer can be over-zealous,' said Vivienne airily. 'I was in any case thinking of freelance consulting work.'

'But –' How extraordinary.

'I was told that your husband is in the garden. Do not incommode yourself. I will find him.' Vivienne patted her neat blonde bob, smoothed down her skirt and teetered away down the path.

Kim grinned and wondered if she would be able to keep Serena and Grace at bay.

Suave and imposing in his gnomelike manner, Dr Weinbaum smiled vaguely at her. 'Sorry, my dear, I can only spare you a moment. I'm playing in a golf competition. One can't let one's partner down by being late.'

Plucking up her courage, Kim took a deep breath. 'About Richard, my husband, I feel very bad about this and I know he's had a difficult time but . . . I'm not sure how long you're going to keep him, but I don't, I really don't want him to come home.' She rushed on, 'Is there anywhere else he can go after he leaves here? A sort of normal hospital or something?'

'Mrs Ellis, I do not consider that there is sufficient time to discuss important questions like that. One must take each day as it comes and I'm sure that, once your husband is back to his former self, you will find that your relationship slips back into place too. Now, my dear, if you will excuse me . . .'

Kim reddened and then blurted out, 'But, Dr Weinbaum, you see, eventually, well, I want to divorce my husband. I don't want my former relationship and, I know this sounds awful, but I don't want to be responsible for him for ever.'

He shook his head sadly. 'Our patients' welfare must be our first concern. We always say it is never wise to rush into any decisions. Now make an appointment for tomorrow, or maybe next week would be better, and we can talk again. I'm sure you will feel differently when you are calmer. The shock has been difficult for you. Would you like me to prescribe a tranquilliser?'

'No, thank you, I would not,' she said, on the point of losing her temper.

Before she could speak again, he waved his hand and disappeared into the inner office. She waited a while but then she heard a car start. She looked out of the window and saw Dr Weinbaum driving away in an open Jaguar, golf clubs in the back. Somehow or other he had managed to escape by another door.

CHAPTER 23

When she returned to the house in Cologny, Kim saw with shock that the front door was open. Surely she'd locked up properly? She hesitated, her mind racing through various scary possibilities, but then she heard Beatrice's piercing voice coming from the drawing room.

'So, Mme Aubert,' Beatrice was saying, 'I think we might get a good price if we sell the two villas together.'

'Indeed, indeed, my compliments, madame la comtesse,' came the obsequious reply. 'With such desirable properties in such a very select area, one should obtain an extremely interesting sum.'

Kim walked into the room. Fortunately it was still relatively tidy. 'Good afternoon, Beatrice. I wasn't expecting visitors. Do let me know next time.'

Beatrice, smart in a beige suit, made the introductions with a perfunctory wave of her beringed fingers. 'Mme Aubert, this is the current tenant, Mrs Ellis.' She stared hard at Kim. 'Who will soon be leaving, one hopes, and moving to the cottage in Latigny.' She waved her hand again. 'Kim, this is Mme Aubert, my real estate agent. You may leave us now, Mme Aubert. Please finish measuring the properties and then write to me with your assessment.'

'Certainly, certainly, madame la comtesse,' said the pink-faced woman, backing away and almost curtseying. Having hot flushes about the huge commission she's going to make, thought Kim sourly.

Beatrice arched her eyebrows. 'I'm glad to have seen you, Kim. When are you moving? I need to send workmen to do up this place if we are to get a good price. I was particularly disappointed by the state of the garden.'

Kim took a deep breath. 'I've been rather busy lately,' she said evenly. 'Your father's gardener used to help me but he hasn't been paid since Henri died, he said. So he's stopped appearing.'

'Gardeners do not come cheap in Switzerland, you know. Nor do houses. Really, if you are staying here rent-free you might at least take some responsibility for the place.'

Kim flushed. 'My mind has been on other things. Anyway, I was waiting for your agent to confirm that the tenants have left Latigny. Believe me, I don't want to stay here any longer than necessary.' She turned. 'Just a moment, I must get Caspar out of the car.'

'Ah yes, the dog.' Beatrice frowned. 'And who said you could have my father's dog?'

'Poor Caspar was forgotten originally. So we took responsibility for him. I was going to write to you, then we discovered he'd been left to James in the will.'

'Of course, the famous will,' said Beatrice coldly. 'We shall say no more about that.' She fixed her heavily made-up eyes on Kim. 'Now, I want you to move out by the end of this month. I am sure Latigny is now vacant. It's quite unbelievable that Mme Aubert or her stupid assistant have not yet informed you of this fact. Or the lawyers, they should have organised it. Really, these people just take one's money and do nothing.' She walked out of the room and called up the stairs, 'Mme Aubert, come down immediately.'

Returning, she glared at Kim again. 'By the way, I have asked her to check the inventory. We must not forget that the major part of the furniture belongs to me.'

A few days later, Kim received the deeds and the keys of 6 chemin de la Fontaine, Latigny. She smiled in happiness as she held them in her hand. It was the first time that she would live in a house of her own and the feeling of freedom was heady and exhilarating. She thought of Henri. Her lovely wicked old guardian angel had given her a wonderful present: a new life.

Polly and Beverly-Jane accompanied her on an exploratory visit to the cottage.

'This is so cute. Must've been a farmhouse in

the old days. I just love these thick stone walls,' pronounced BJ.

'Nice little cottage but what a ghastly mess,' said Polly, gazing at the chaos left by the previous tenants.

Kim wandered around, wildly in love with everything she saw. 'Look at the beams and that wonderful huge fireplace – and even a bread oven.'

'Probably be damp and cold in winter,' said Polly.

'Swiss houses are usually too hot, not too cold. Have you seen the boiler in the cellar? It's absolutely enormous, looks as if it should be powering a ship,' said Kim.

'Think of all the oil it'll use,' sniffed Polly.

'You could grow a whole lot in that darling little garden,' said BJ. 'I'll give you some plants for indoors too. These old flagstones are wonderful: you could cover them with sea grass, and then bamboo blinds for the windows and I see old rustic furniture. We should go to the Brocante together.'

'That old stove in the kitchen looks lethal, did you see it? And absolutely filthy,' said Polly.

Kim smiled. 'But it's so pretty, and I can clean it.'

'Oh well, I'd better help you.' Polly sighed. 'Let's make a list of what we need. Now, Kim, jot this down: J-cloths, window cleaner, floor cleaner, Cif, and –'

'And we need paint, lots of white paint,' said Kim.

'I see shelves full of faience, and dried herbs and

301

gourds hanging from the ceiling,' said BJ. 'Swiss ethnic pots – I'll go pick some up tomorrow. What about drapes upstairs? I don't like drapes but you do have neighbours opposite. A girl needs a bit of privacy at times. And there's a little gallery near me where they have a set of prints that would look just right over here.'

'BJ,' said Polly firmly. 'Cleaning first, decor later.'

BJ paused and looked around thoughtfully. 'I guess if we get a crate of beer, Walt and Joe can paint this place in a couple of weekends.'

'But I couldn't ask your husbands to give up their weekends for me.'

'We don't ask them. We tell them,' said BJ. 'That's what guys are for.'

Kim grinned. 'Why have I never had that kind of control over the men in my life?'

'Been waiting for you,' said Serena, when Kim next arrived at the clinic. 'Richard is speaking now, quite normally. It was me. Like, I did it. I helped him.'

'Oh good,' said Kim, half-relieved, half-anxious. 'Well done. What happened? How did you do it?'

'Just persuaded him. Said I'd eat one or two mouthfuls of my omelette if he'd say one or two words to me. So he did. And I did. Just like that.' Serena looked sideways at her. 'You're not jealous, are you?'

'No, of course not. I'm glad you helped him. Why on earth should I be jealous?'

'Wives are often jealous of me. But I wouldn't do it, because I like you, Kim.'

'Wouldn't do what?'

'Sex. She would, though.'

Kim stared, 'Who?'

'Grace. But I made sure. I watched them, and they didn't. I never let them be alone. That Vivienne person, she's just as bad, waggling about and displaying her fat thighs in those short skirts. What a sight! You would have thought a woman of her age and shape would know better. She's after him too, you know.'

Kim laughed. 'Vivienne is a colleague, a Personnel Officer, HRO, whatever. It's her job to keep in touch.'

'Huh,' said Serena, twisting her silver bracelets round and round her skinny arm.

'Anyway,' said Kim, 'I don't think Richard is well enough at the moment.'

Serena smirked. Then she said, 'Dr Anna wants to see you. She's in the office. Shall I show you the way?'

'I think I can find my own way around this place by now,' said Kim gently.

Dr Anna, immaculate in pale blue, rose to her feet and said, 'Good morning, Mrs Ellis. Good news. With group patient-interaction mutual-help therapy, we have achieved a breakthrough with your husband. We would like to send him home at the end of the week, but I understand you feel you are not ready to look after him yourself.'

'Yes,' said Kim, feeling immensely guilty. 'I know he's had a difficult time . . .' Her voice trailed off.

'In our experience, spouses often find it hard to come to terms with mental problems. You are not alone in your feelings of self-reproach and inadequacy. We have therefore arranged, subject to your approval, of course, some temporary accommodation in a sheltered foyer for people in fragile mental states.'

'A foyer?'

'Yes, like a large family home with a supervising warden. Meals are provided but residents are expected to clean their own rooms and also share in the communal cleaning. They are free to come and go, and are assisted in finding outside employment. The foyer is designed to be a half-way house. I suggest you have him home for a meal, then for the weekend and finally for longer periods until you feel capable of shouldering the burden yourself.'

'But I want to divorce him,' Kim blurted out.

'You may well have negative feelings towards Richard at the moment. Perhaps subconsciously you blame him for his long absence.'

Kim snorted. 'I do blame him. Nothing subconscious about it. And I've had extremely negative feelings for several years now.'

Dr Anna continued calmly, 'Please think of him. When you see him, you may think that he is back to normal, but he is not. Current research suggests that it usually takes some years to recover from the stresses of a kidnapping or hostage situation.

Certainly in a year or two Richard should be more stable. But if you desert him in his present state, it will be a much slower and harder recovery. How long have you been married?'

'Nearly eighteen years.'

'Then surely you can give him at least one more year? It is not much to ask.'

'No, I suppose not,' said Kim reluctantly. She paused and then she asked, 'About the fees for this foyer?'

Dr Anna smiled. 'The state will pay, of course. Switzerland is a very caring country.'

Kim left her and walked slowly down the lawn. Suddenly she jumped. Richard was standing in front of her, tall, sandy blond and handsome, almost like his former self.

'Hello,' she said with a gentle smile. 'I'm glad you're feeling better. Good news.'

'Hello, Kim. How are you?' His voice was hoarse but he spoke in a jocular manner as if he had just come back from a long holiday in the sun. It reminded her forcibly of the way he used to act after returning from an unsuccessful business trip. It was Richard's way always to pretend that every-thing was perfectly normal until unpleasant matters became overwhelming.

Aware of being less than frank herself, she did her best to explain about the foyer, that she felt he wasn't ready to come home yet, that they had to sort out their life, that everything couldn't be as it was before, but she'd bring him home to see

James now and then, well, quite often. Oh hell, why did I say quite often? I had to, she thought.

Richard seemed to accept what she said. 'Dr Anna explained it already,' he murmured.

'Did she?' Kim was relieved.

'She said you've had your own stresses and that you had a kind of suppressed breakdown like me, but not as bad, so you need time to recover.'

She opened her mouth to contradict him. Then she shut it again. If that's what he thought then it gave her a way out.

'By the way,' he said, 'since I'm better now, next time you come, will you bring James?'

'I'll bring him on Thursday,' she promised, trying to sound happier about the idea than she felt.

Next day, stifling her guilty conscience, she drove Richard to the neat and orderly foyer run by a man in brown sandals called Maurice. Maurice spoke some English and had long blond curls and a saintly smile. Richard would be OK here.

She helped him unpack in the small bare bed-sitter with its functional whiteboard furniture and clean vinyl floors. Watching Richard arrange his socks neatly in the drawer, she said heartily, 'Not a bad room, considering. Not the luxury of Clinique la Forêt but at least it's handy for the shops. I saw a little Migros round the corner. You aren't so cut off here.'

He looked up and smiled vaguely. 'That's nice.'

'If you need more clothes, let me know. They

have a washing machine, they said, which may help. I expect Maurice can show you how to work it. And how to iron. I believe you have to help with cooking too. It's all supposed to help you become independent.' She attempted a joke. 'In fact, come to think of it, they're all training you to be a New Man. Quite useful these days.'

Looking a little confused, Richard sat down on the bed. He was still painfully thin and seemed somehow older than before, easily tired and less energetic.

He stared out of the window at the block of flats opposite. After a moment he asked, 'Will you ring Vivienne and tell her where I am?'

'Madame Frank?'

'Yes, she said she'd find some work for me.'

'Really? How kind of her.' She couldn't imagine that anyone would seriously want to employ him, but then Vivienne had good contacts in Geneva.

'Kim . . . Until I get a job, could you give me some money – for the shops, you know? Don't know what they supply here, if anything.'

Just like old times, she thought, opening her purse.

'Kim?'

'Yes?'

'Thank you. I don't know what I'd have done without you. You've saved the day yet again and I really will make it up to you. I'll find a new job and everything will be OK and back to normal, you'll see.'

She wanted to say that it never had been OK, that she didn't ever again want things to be as they were. But she merely repeated Dr Weinbaum's platitudes about taking each day one at a time.

On her way out, she passed a peculiar looking youth with ginger dreadlocks and tattoos on his arm. He was sweeping the steps in a desultory manner and smirked as she passed. Then sitting on a bench by the door were two old men in neat but frayed suits, both staring blankly. They did not return her polite '*bonjour*'.

She went to find Maurice. 'The other residents – there will be somebody for Richard to talk to, won't there?'

'Does he speak French?'

'Well, a bit.'

'Then I am sure he will find some nice companions here. We are a happy family. We share everything, our food, our work, our prayers.'

'So am I really going to see Daddy at last?' asked James, jiggling up and down in his seat with excitement.

'Yes, darling.' Her eyes on the road, Kim spoke as cheerfully as she could.

'Is he better?'

'Much better.'

'Then why is he still in hospital?'

She cleared her throat. 'It's not a hospital, more of a boarding house, with someone to look after

308

the residents, but they think it's the best place for him.'

'I hope he comes home soon,' said James wistfully.

She parked the car outside the foyer and led James inside. She knew she had no right to keep him away from Richard any longer. She could have taken him to the clinic but she'd told herself it wasn't a suitable place for a child to visit, that Richard wasn't well enough, that James would be upset, and so on. Now she had run out of excuses.

'What a funny place,' whispered James loudly, as they passed the strange old men. 'It's a bit smelly.'

'Be quiet, darling. You always say everything is smelly. It's just the cleaning stuff they use – must be some sort of disinfectant.'

As they walked down the long corridor to Richard's room, Kim found herself walking more and more slowly. With great reluctance, she knocked on his door.

For a second James looked taken aback at Richard's changed appearance, then suddenly he ran and flung himself into his father's arms. 'I've missed you, Dad.'

Richard hugged him tight and wiped the tears of pleasure from his eyes. 'Me too, me too,' he said.

Then there was a silence when everyone searched for something to say. Kim talked about the weather and about Maurice. And Richard asked James about his school.

When there was another pause, James said, 'We didn't bring Caspar because Mum said your foyer wasn't a good place for dogs. He's very nice though. Do you remember him? He used to belong to Mr Marechal. He gave him to me in his will.'

'Well, wasn't that lucky for you?' said Richard.

James face clouded over. 'It wasn't lucky that Henri died. It was very sad for me, and for Mum. He was our very best friend. He looked after us all the time you were away.'

'Yes,' said Richard hastily, 'he was a nice kind chap. And he left us a house too, I hear. Amazingly generous. Wonder why he did that?'

Kim groaned inwardly. She wasn't going to plunge into a long discussion about the cottage in front of James.

'Mr Marechal gave us a house because otherwise we wouldn't have one, you see,' explained James. 'He had plenty of them to spare and luckily his nasty daughter didn't need them all. Mum had to get a lawyer.'

'Did she indeed? And is it a nice house, like Villa la Vigne?'

'Oh yes,' said James. 'It's much smaller, and a bit far away from Geneva, but it's very pretty when you get there. That's what everyone says. Mum has been working hard to fix it up.'

'I'm looking forward to seeing it,' said Richard. 'When Mummy is feeling better.'

James looked surprised. 'Mum isn't ill. She's fine.'

'Well then, I look forward to seeing it soon. Why don't you run ahead and open the car for Mummy? I just want to talk to her a moment before she goes.'

As soon as James had left, Richard took her hand. 'When can I come home? This place, it's OK but it's not very peaceful. Dear Maurice is always rushing in and out. I sometimes think he fancies me.'

'Rubbish. You always think everyone fancies you. Maurice just likes to get people to join in, to get them going, that's his job.'

'Well, the hearty atmosphere, plus the soul-searching, it's all a bit tiresome.'

Turning away, she said, 'Yes, well, we'll have to talk about it.'

There was a knock on the door and Maurice's beaming face looked in. 'Am I disarranging you?' he asked with his angelic smile. 'But it is the turn of Richard to fix the tables now for dinner.'

'Oh no, you weren't interrupting anything,' she said gratefully. 'I was just leaving.'

James was silent for a while on the way home, then he asked, 'Shall we show Dad our new house this weekend?'

'Not this weekend,' said Kim, her eyes averted. How come she'd changed from hearth mother into a selfish cow?

'Why not?'

'Polly has kindly asked you to stay.'

311

'But I'm always going to Polly's. I do like it there, it's cool but –'

'Darling, I know it's been difficult for you, but I'm going to be very busy and I thought it'd be much more fun for you to go to Polly's. OK? She's going to take you all swimming at Divonne. And you know you're always saying how Polly makes lovely cakes and I never do.'

'Brilliant! But I wish you could come swimming too. I thought you'd nearly finished the house. What are you going to be busy with?'

'Oh, lots of things,' she said vaguely.

'I could help you.'

'You are a help, a great help, but I still need to have some time to myself.'

Damn, she thought. The mountain of guilt grew larger and larger every day but she couldn't explain that Mark would be coming to Geneva again for the weekend and she wanted to give him her undivided attention. The future was so uncertain. It might be the last time she'd see him.

CHAPTER 24

'I can't believe you're here at last,' said Kim when there was time to talk.

'You know, you're the best thing that's happened to me for years,' murmured Mark, turning over on to his side and pushing her hair away from her face. They lay close together in bed, noses almost touching.

She smiled. 'I adore all this flattery. You're so nice . . . and so sexy.'

'Mm, so are you – very, very sexy.'

She arched her back languidly. 'BJ was right – the best aphrodisiac is love.' Help, why did I say that, she thought in a panic. The word hung in the air between them.

'It's mutual,' he said.

'The lust? Yes, it is.'

He smiled happily. 'And the love . . . unless we're too sophisticated to mention it.'

Later she made dinner, which they ate with much touching of hands, and smiles and glances, anticipating that they would soon be making love again. She like the look of him sitting across the table from her, all cosy and domestic. He was wearing a blue denim shirt, slightly crumpled. She found this an endearing change from the immaculate office suit. And he looked good in blue, she thought dreamily.

'Sorry, this chicken is rather overcooked and unerotic,' she said. 'We should probably be eating oysters or lobster. My cooking isn't usually as bad as this. Well, I mean, it's normally quite tasty even if it sometimes looks a bit of a mess.'

'It's fine, it's delicious.'

'It's not at all delicious, but it's your own fault. You kept distracting me. Anyway, at least I've got strawberries and cream to follow. Can't go wrong with that.'

He leant back in his chair. 'Take your shirt off. I want to see you.'

She raised her eyebrows. 'You mean you require a topless waitress, sir?'

'Yes.'

'Um, all right.' A little flushed, she stood up. Gazing at him from under her eyelashes, she unbuttoned her shirt and let it fall slowly to the floor. She turned her back and, improvising some stripper-like shrugs and wriggles, she removed her bra and threw it nonchalantly over her shoulder. Then, shaking out her long hair, she turned towards him again with an attempt at a hot smouldering look.

Laughing, he held out his arms. 'I'm not sure if I want any more dinner,' he said huskily.

★　　★　　★

Next morning she came downstairs after her bath to find him standing by the kitchen window. She put her arm around him and they were silent for a while.

Then he said suddenly, 'Kim, I've got something to tell you. I've been posted to Singapore.'

She felt a sudden chill in the pit of her stomach and pulled away. 'Singapore? But, but how long for?'

'It's a four-year posting.'

'When will you go?'

'Almost immediately.'

She gulped. 'Oh no,' she said in a small voice.

'Well, actually I have to go back to England first to do a course, and then I'll travel to Singapore in about six weeks.'

She said nothing, not knowing what to say.

He turned to her. 'I want you to come too.'

'To England?'

'Yes, and to Singapore.' He took her in his arms. 'I think we should get married.'

She felt a flash of intense happiness, immediately followed by confusion and doubts. She buried her head in his shoulder and there was a long silence.

'Say something, Kim, please – that was a proposal.'

She raised her head at last. 'I'm very touched and honoured,' she said shakily, 'And also very surprised.'

Smiling, he drew her to him. 'Surprised? I thought you knew how I felt.'

'I thought . . . I suppose I thought you just wanted an affair. You told me you had a woman in most countries. I presumed I was your fling in Switzerland.'

'Well, I want you everywhere else too.'

She smiled. 'I'm glad. Part of me longs for you to feel that way, but the other part . . . you're so nice but . . . there's a snag or two. Quite apart from my being married already.'

'But a quick divorce is possible here, I know.'

She turned her head away. 'I can't divorce him at the moment. He needs me. The doctors, all the people in charge of him, say I have to stick around for now, and I'm rather afraid they're right. Being a prisoner all that time, it affected him badly.'

'I know, but he'll be OK in the end.' He patted her arm reassuringly. 'You can't spend the rest of your life worrying about a man like that.'

'I feel responsible for him. He hasn't got anyone else but me.'

'What about me? I need you,' he said gently.

She shook her head. 'You've got your career. You're so independent. Richard isn't, not at the moment.'

Mark frowned. 'But how long will this go on? You can't sacrifice your whole life to him. You've already supported him for years.'

'Yes, but after all he went through, I suppose I think it's my duty to support him a bit longer.'

'Until when?'

Kim stared at the floor for a moment and then she said, 'Until he gets on his feet.'

'But from what you say, he's never been on his feet for long.'

'Well, given time –'

'But I want you to come with me to Singapore. Now.'

She smiled sadly. 'I don't think I can leave Geneva. What about James?'

'I hadn't forgotten him. James must come too, of course. I was expecting him to be with us.'

'But you don't even know him.'

He smiled. 'I can soon remedy that.'

She looked up at him. 'You and I don't know each other well either.'

'No, we don't, but we get on very well. I like you and you like me. We even spoke about love in a cautious kind of manner.' He took her face tenderly in his hands. 'I don't know why you're making all these difficulties.'

'Because neither of us should rush wildly into another marriage.'

Letting go of her suddenly, he walked to the other side of the room. 'Sorry to have been slow in the uptake, but it seems you're turning me down,' he said with his back to her.

'I do love you, but, this is difficult to say. I wasn't prepared – but, quite apart from Richard, what I'm saying is I can't just drop everything. What if it doesn't work out? It's too rushed. I can't go to the other end of the world, not again. I've spent my whole life doing just that.' Hell, I've said that all wrong, she thought. She was about to begin again when he turned.

'It'd be different with me,' he said. 'After all, I do have a steady job.'

'I know, but now, you see, I've got a house of my own and work.' She waved her arm. 'And some sort of security.'

'But it's not as if you'd be abandoning a serious career. That's one of your advantages.'

Offended, she rushed wildly on, 'No, I realise it's not serious compared with yours, but I've had quite a few more commissions lately. And I'm putting down roots and making something of my life at last. And my work, I'm making something of that, because I've got contacts now. I take it seriously, however unimportant it may seem. I'm scared to give it all up when I've just found it. Maybe I would give it all up and disrupt James's life again if I was sure – but I'm not.' She was on the edge of tears. 'There's not enough time to be sure.'

He moved towards her and took her in his arms again. 'But I can give you security. And you're very adaptable and used to travel. I've thought about it and I know you'd be fine in diplomatic life.'

She stared. 'You mean I know how to use a knife and fork.'

'Well, yes, that too, but I mean that you're charming and easy-going and tolerant.'

She pushed him away and said emotionally, 'I'm nothing of the sort, I'm a mess. I'm trying to leave my husband who's had mental problems. And then there was Henri. I'm not in a fit state to go in for something as serious as marriage. Not yet. You must see that.'

'So you're still in love with the memory of Henri, is that it?' He sounded puzzled, deeply hurt.

'I didn't say that.'

'But you don't want to marry me.' He paused. 'All right, then just come with me anyway. Cohabiting, or whatever you like to call it, isn't yet the norm in diplomatic society, but I dare say it won't raise too many eyebrows these days.'

She took a deep breath. 'You don't seem to be listening. I need to stay here for a while. I do care about you very much but . . .' Her words fell away and there was a silence. She began again, 'You see –'

'You don't have to say any more,' he said roughly. 'I thought, I thought you and I –' He paced up and down the room.

'Mark, calm down, please. It's too early for either of us. We need time.'

'You keep saying that, but I haven't got time. They want me back in London next week and I want to take you with me.' He turned towards her. 'Is it yes or no?'

'You can't rush these things – we're not seventeen. And there's James and, of course, Richard. You must see I can't just drop everything.'

'So it's no.'

She put her hand on his arm. 'Well, it has to be, for now. You'll be back from Singapore eventually, I suppose. And then –'

'But anything may happen in four years. It doesn't work, living in different countries. I tried that with Bella.'

'I'm not like Bella.'

'Exactly. And I can't wait that long for you. Can't risk losing you.'

'Be reasonable, Mark.'

He pulled away from her. 'How can I be reasonable?' he shouted.

And then suddenly he stormed out.

Before she could gather her senses together, she heard him start the engine of the hired car and drive wildly off down the quiet street.

On Monday, after much hesitation, she telephoned his flat in England, but he did not acknowledge the messages she left on his answering machine. A day or two later she tried again but this time there was no reply, not even from the machine. So he had gone away somewhere, perhaps on the course he mentioned. She wrote him a letter, several letters, but she didn't send them. She had nothing to add.

If he loved her, she supposed he would return to Geneva to see her. At the very least he would stop off on his way to Singapore. But the days passed without a word from him.

So it seemed he had regretted his impulsive proposal, made in the afterglow of sex. He can't have been serious and that was the end of it, she decided in the depth of her pain. Perhaps it was just as well, as she wasn't sure of anything any more.

'Let me get this straight,' said Polly. 'You're a forty-five year old divorcee and –'

'I haven't even started divorce proceedings yet,' interrupted Kim.

'Don't bother me with details. As I said, you're a middle-aged barely solvent single mother.'

'Why don't you say fat as well?'

'You're not that fat. In fact, some might say your looks are your only tangible asset apart from the house, though looks don't last for ever.'

'What a dear friend you are, Polly.'

'It's because I'm your friend that I'm saying this. My point is that I can't believe a woman in your position would be so stupid as to turn down a proposal of marriage from a healthy, good-looking, intelligent man of your own age. A normal man who appears to have no hang-ups and who actually has a proper job, a job with status even.'

Kim smiled a little at her indignant expression.

Polly continued in full flow, 'And not only does Mark have all these qualities, but you actually like him and fancy him and, judging by the glow that reappeared on your face, all the signs were that you had a good time in bed together. So why did you turn him down? Because of some mistaken sense of duty to that appalling Richard.' She sighed. 'I despair. I've done my best but, really, I give up.'

'Yes, you've been wonderful. You've had James so often, I must owe you months of child care. When can I have your boys?'

'Don't worry. I'll get my own back in due course. Anyway you were very kind to me when I had that skiing accident. I haven't forgotten how you looked after my kids all the time then,' said Polly.

'That was ages ago. It's definitely my turn now. I'll have them any time, any weekend. Just let me know.'

'I certainly will. But, really, James is no trouble at all. If you have two small boys in the house, you might as well have three. As I'm always telling you, Toby and Matt fight much less when he's around to act as a kind of buffer zone. Now, never mind the kids. Don't change the subject. Where was I?'

'You were rubbing salt into the wounds.'

'Oh yes, so I was, but actually I can't make you out – what do you really feel about Mark?'

Kim looked away. 'Sometimes I can't seem to work out what I feel about anyone or anything at the moment. Sometimes I just feel confused. So much has happened to me this year . . . and then there was Henri. I do miss him.'

'Didn't seem to stop you have a fling with Mark,' said Polly tartly.

Kim winced. Then she said, 'It may have been cause and effect.'

'You mean, on the rebound.'

'I just don't know. I just don't know,' she said unsteadily.

Polly touched her arm. 'Sorry. I give you a hard time sometimes. I wouldn't bother, but the fact is, I thought you really liked Mark, as I said.'

'I do like him, I like him a lot.'

'Yes, but is it true love and all that?'

'Well, there's a lot of passion.'

'Nothing wrong with that. But when you first see him does your heart go pitter-patter, or is it more of a stab of lust in the loins?'

Kim grinned. 'Usually a bit of both. But I don't really trust either of those feelings – they fade, in time. I sort of felt that way about Richard, that's the scary thing, longed to hear his voice, all that.'

'But did you ever feel Richard was your best friend too?'

'No, we didn't have much in common, I suppose.'

'And Mark – can you talk to him? Are you good friends?'

Kim smiled. 'Oh yes. He can be a bit tactless and overbearing, not unlike someone else I know, but really he's very nice and *sympa*. I don't have to explain about my life to him, there's a lot he understands already. Well, apart from why I turned him down, I suppose.'

'There you are then. I knew he was right for

you.' She sat back. 'Of course with the right man, passion eventually changes to a deeper, more real sort of love.'

'Polly, how sweet! You sound like a woman's magazine. I didn't know you were a romantic at heart. Didn't know you had it in you.'

Polly looked uncharacteristically sheepish. 'Well, I'm still quite keen on old Joe, really,' she said awkwardly.

Kim paused. 'If it isn't too delicate a question, can you remember the feelings you had when you first met? Why you chose him?'

'Well, he's a very kind man. Kindness is crucial in a second husband . . . And then there was another very good reason.'

'What was that?'

'He was the only one that asked me.'

Kim laughed. 'That sounds more like the Polly we know and love.'

'It's an important point and one you should think about.'

'You're such an expert on men.'

'As you know, I'm an expert on everything. You should take my advice more often. And, regarding Mark, my advice is go for it.'

Kim sighed. 'I repeat, I'm not looking for another husband and anyway I don't think he was serious.'

'Of course he was – he's a serious man.'

'So why hasn't he rung or written?'

'It's your move. Why haven't you contacted him?'

Kim shook her head. 'I tried but I don't know if I can add anything new to what I said at the time. I didn't actually turn him down flat, just said I couldn't rush off with him at the moment. You must see I hate the idea of uprooting myself again. I can't drop everything and disappear into the sunset with Mark like a romantic teenager. It's all so much more difficult once one has a child.'

'Huh. Kids are much more adaptable than one thinks, they say.'

'But I can't go off with someone James doesn't know. Someone who's not used to children.'

'Oh for God's sake, Kim, if you ask me, anyone would make a better father than Richard.' She frowned. 'But as usual we're back to James. I told you time and time again that you can't centre your whole life around that child. You stuck with Richard too long because of him. Then you took up with Henri because you wanted stability for James.'

'But –'

'And now you say you're turning down Mark because you can't uproot your child.' Polly was sounding increasingly indignant again.

Kim shook her head. 'It's not as simple as that. It's not just because of all the upheaval. I do care for Mark but maybe it can't be true love if I won't go to the other end of the earth. But it was just bad timing, too soon after Henri, too confusing. I suppose he'll come back eventually and by then I will have managed to divorce and, well, it's in the lap of the gods.'

'Bullshit. Listen to me: when they're in a marrying mood eligible chaps like Mark don't sit on the shelf gathering dust. Someone else'll grab him, some gorgeous Oriental maiden or rich expat widow. You have to seize the day, take the tide at the flood.' Polly put her hands on her hips. 'And while we're quoting deep philosophical points, Wendy Cope is right.'

'Who? Oh yes, the poet.'

'Exactly. Well, according to her, men are like buses. And it's true. You've forgotten what it's like to be single, but I was alone for years between husbands and I remember it only too well. She's absolutely right – men arrive together all at once, like buses, or else you have a very long wait. You've had two lovers this year, far more than your fair share.'

Kim grinned suddenly. 'Quite true – since I stepped off the straight and narrow, I've had a lot more fun.'

'Yes, but it ain't necessarily so. There aren't that many suitable men around. You'll probably have to wait ages for another.'

'They aren't compulsory. One can manage without them. Lots of women do, quite happily. In fact there's statistics to prove single women are happier.'

Polly shook her head. 'Yes, but you're the quaint old-fashioned married type, all dependent, self-sacrificing, and saintly. Or at least you were until Henri shook you up a bit.'

Kim smiled. 'You're so rude and unfair, Pol. I'm perfectly independent now. A new, or newish woman: I've got some proper work. Anyway, the fact is, Richard leans on me, not vice-versa, always has, that's the problem.'

'Hm. Well, at least he's off your hands for the moment.'

'But not for much longer. Sooner or later they'll send him home. He can't stay in the foyer for ever, and he can't support himself anywhere else.'

Polly stared at her. 'What will you do?'

Kim sighed again, rubbing her hands together in an agitated manner. 'Take each day as it comes, I suppose. All that stuff. With all this pointless speculation about Mark, we seem to be forgetting the realities – Richard is my husband and I'm the person who's responsible for him.'

CHAPTER 25

With a sinking feeling Kim unlocked the door of the house in Latigny and showed Richard inside. 'Not a bad little place at all,' he said, gazing at his reflection in the hall mirror and smoothing back his hair. 'Hope there's room for all our kit.'

'It's much smaller than our last house so we had to give away some of our clothes and my old toys to Caritas. Mum took hundreds of car-loads to them,' explained James earnestly. 'And she said you should give away some of your things too.'

'She did, did she?'

'Well,' began Kim, 'you do have an awful lot of clothes and so many pairs of shoes. The third bedroom where you're sleeping has rather a small wardrobe.'

'I see,' said Richard. 'So that's how it is.'

'That's how it is,' she said firmly.

It was like having another child in the house, worse in fact, because though James could be persuaded to help with walking Caspar and other routine chores, Richard just sat at the sitting room desk all day rearranging his papers and looking pained if anyone disturbed him.

Of course it wasn't even intended to be his desk originally, but, to give him some space of his own, she'd moved her computer into her bedroom, which was now a chaotic office and general dumping ground, rather than the kind of flowery country boudoir she had once vaguely aspired to.

Breadwinning must come first, however. Though past experience had not been encouraging, she'd hoped since she was now supporting the family again that Richard might play sports with or otherwise amuse James from time to time. It was now the summer holidays and, apart from her editorial work, she still taught English to the old ladies who seemed to depend on her company as much as her tuition. The teaching was undemanding, but she was working on another new long manuscript for a Swiss writing in English and her author needed a great deal of sensitive editing.

But Richard was always too busy with his own so-called projects to have much time for James, and he always needed the car at the same time as she did, not to take his son on an outing but to visit the city on frequent mysterious errands.

'Why did you sell the other car last year? You can't have been that broke,' he kept complaining. 'Bus service here is quite appalling.'

At first, mindful that Richard was still in a

delicate mental state, she managed to remain relatively calm and tactful. In accordance with the doctors' instructions, she did not cross-examine him about what had happened. There was a great deal she would have liked to know, but in turn there were various subjects, two in particular, she wished to avoid. Not that she regretted her love affairs, quite the opposite. Henri had brought her back from the edge, transformed her life and made her whole again. And as for Mark? He had loved her and she had loved him, but nobody else could be expected to understand. Others might take a distinctly less romantic view of her conduct, people like Beatrice, people like divorce lawyers.

Indeed, Sophie-Maria had warned her to say as little as possible about Henri to avoid prejudicing the eventual divorce case in Switzerland where adultery still affected these matters. She had not even told Sophie about Mark, not that there was much to tell, sadly.

But in any event Kim had no desire to hinder Richard's recovery by discussing things he did not at the moment need to know, no desire to provoke the major battle that would inevitably ensue. For the time being, there were enough minor skirmishes to be circumvented.

The presence of James helped her to control her tongue. She always remembered her parents' endless quarrels. During the whole of her childhood, there had been a tense hostile atmosphere and Kim was trying, not always successfully, to avoid James being subjected to the same embarrassing unhappy ordeal.

Despite her efforts at peacemaking, she feared James couldn't avoid noticing that Caspar was a major source of discord between his parents. In the old days Richard, a fastidious man, used to disapprove of dogs for hygienic reasons, but now he seemed actively to dislike them. Or, she wondered, was he actually jealous of the love and attention they gave to the dog?

At first Caspar was too stupid to realise that his normal friendly advances were unwelcome as far as Richard was concerned. Eventually, however, he began to slink away, tail between legs, whenever Richard appeared.

'Were you guarded by a vicious dog, is that it, Dad?' asked James, anxious that his beloved friend was not being appreciated.

'Don't want to talk about it. Impossible for you to understand,' Richard would say in a remote voice whenever the subject of his ordeal on the island was raised.

This reticence was understandable, and she tried to make allowances for his darker moods. Eventually, however, she began to find his erratic behaviour towards James, sometimes aloof and unresponsive, sometimes over-indulgent, difficult to tolerate, and said so. Richard would merely repeat that no one knew what he had been through. She acknowledged this to be true, but often felt he was using the wounded-soldier excuse for doing exactly as he liked and the resentments that had been smouldering throughout her marriage gradually built up.

Richard did not bring out the best in her, she knew. When he was around, the self-control and patience she had acquired over the years began to desert her, along with her sense of humour. Even a small unimportant matter would infuriate her, such as the day he took it into his head to rearrange the contents of the kitchen cupboards when she was out teaching.

'Only trying to help. You had it arranged in a very illogical fashion. Much better like this,' he said with a complacent smile.

'Why don't you ever do something useful like the shopping or unstacking the dishwasher? Instead you totally change my kitchen when I've got it the way I wanted,' she shouted, boiling over.

'Why should we always do everything your way?' he shouted in return 'I live here too and I need a quiet organised home. Weinbaum said so.'

Feeling that he was partially right, she took another deep breath and, ashamed of her own intolerance, resolved not to lose her temper in future, or at least for the rest of the day.

Richard drank several glasses of whisky that night. 'How about a nice little fuck?' he suggested as she stood in the kitchen. He moved forward and patted her on the bottom.

'No thanks,' she said in a neutral voice. Caspar,

who had been lurking around hoping to help with the cleaning-up after dinner, moved closer as if to protect her.

'Going through one of your chilly phases, are you? What about my conjugal rights?' said Richard.

In an attempt to disguise her repugnance at the idea of the said conjugal rights, she turned away to give the dog a scrap of meat from the roasting pan. 'Richard, you know you shouldn't drink with those pills you're taking.'

'Or is it women's problems?'

'Yes, something of that nature,' she said, aware that that would instantly cool his ardour. 'Look, I must take Caspar out for his evening walk.'

He stomped out of the room muttering that she seemed to have much more time for the bloody dog than she did for him.

Later she peered into the sitting room to see Richard snoring in front of the television. She was careful to lock her bedroom door, but he did not make any further approaches.

Again she suffered a temporary pang of guilt. He was still her husband but she felt remote from him in every sense.

That night, more than ever she lay longing for Mark, the feel of his hand on the small of her back, the way he looked at her after they had made love. He was often in her thoughts, especially, as now, before she went to sleep. But her fantasies gave her little comfort.

★   ★   ★

'So what's it worth, this old cottage?' asked Richard one day, sounding more like his former over-confident boyish self.

'I don't know,' she said.

'You see, I need some money to set up a new business, thought we could get a mortgage on the house.'

Furious Kim stood up. 'No, you damn well can't. It's my house, in my name. The first and only real home I've ever owned. Henri left it to *me*, not you, and I have no intention of mortgaging it. No way.'

'Your house, eh? But we promised to share all our worldly goods all those years ago. At our wedding – you remember it, I'm sure.'

She glared at him. 'Every time I share anything with you, it just disappears into thin air. For instance, what happened to all that money in the savings account?'

'Ah yes. That was an investment that went wrong. Happens sometimes. Financial markets, commodities, they go up and down. You wouldn't understand.'

'I understand only too well that we're not rich enough to take risks.'

'Nothing ventured, nothing gained, they say.'

Kim clenched her fists. 'Knew I was mad to pay a ransom for you. That really was a dud investment.'

'And just how much did you spend?' he asked with an irritating smile.

334

She paused. 'Sixty thousand pounds.'

'Sixty thousand? Bloody hell. Must've been out of your tiny mind. How did you get hold of it? We've never ever had our hands on that sort of money. What a bloody waste! You should have got the Government to rescue me.'

Her voice rose. 'I was told you were ill. I didn't know how much longer you'd have lasted. I did what I thought was best at the time. It was my money, from Henri's will, and I chose to spend it that way, odd though it may seem.'

Richard smiled placatingly. 'Well, yes, in that case I suppose it was decent of you. You could've just left me there to fester. I am very, very grateful, really I am.'

She sat silent, breathing hard.

Then he said, 'Please, Kim. I only need about forty thousand.'

'No.'

'Bit less, maybe?'

'No, I will never, ever give you money for any more of your wild schemes.' Her voice was fierce. 'If you think I'm going to finance your gun-running activities then you're very much mistaken. I suppose *that* was the so-called investment that went wrong. How could you get involved in that sort of thing? How could you?'

Richard looked at her and then he said easily, 'If one doesn't supply these people with what they want, then someone else will.'

'You wouldn't sell drugs, would you?'

'No, too dodgy, but –'

'But what?'

He gave a confident wave of his hand and then spoke slowly and clearly as if to a child. 'The arms trade is legal, not like drugs. Selling weapons is just like any other export business. The British Government does it, lots of other countries too, and –'

'Oh bullshit,' said Kim hotly. 'You know perfectly well it's not the same as exporting wheat or whatever. And anyway those arms sales are between governments, carefully controlled, or meant to be, not like you and unsophisticated little tribesmen on an island.'

'On the contrary, people like the CIA are fond of giving weapons to freedom fighters they approve of, regardless of the official government. And you see there are some countries that don't have a proper police force or much security. So we just help them out. Private enterprise,' he said. His smug expression showed he felt he had won the argument.

'But you weren't helping out any government, were you?'

He looked shifty. 'My little tribesmen, as you call them, had a legitimate grievance.'

'Richard, I don't believe you. I don't believe you knew the first thing about whatever grievances they had. Anyway, whatever the hows and whys, it's wrong, a dirty business. What you were doing was not only immoral, it was dangerous and silly.

I was told you could've been stuck in some Far Eastern jail for years on end. That's another reason why I didn't just sit back and let the local police try to find you. I thought that even if they managed to rescue you alive, they'd immediately lock you up again.' She glared at him. 'Not such a bad idea, come to think of it.'

'But –'

'I refuse to say another word on the subject,' she said. She went out into the garden and sat by the flower bed violently pulling up weeds until she felt calmer.

Later on that day he suddenly asked, 'So why did Henri leave you the house and the money anyway?'

She was sorely tempted to tell him the truth, but it wasn't the right moment. Not that there ever would be a right moment. She shrugged her shoulders and said, 'He felt sorry for me and James. We were destitute, remember.'

'Bully for Henri,' he said with an unpleasant smirk.

'He was going to lend me the ransom money, but then he died, so I used what he left me instead. So that's your share.'

He looked at her thoughtfully. 'We'll talk about it another time. Perhaps you'll change your mind about the mortgage. For a different kind of deal, not weapons, if you don't approve. There's something else I have in mind. A small commercial aircraft company. Good little business. If we get in on the ground – good pun that, eh? – we could make a mint. Secure our future.' He smiled again. 'Got to think of James.'

'I think of him all the time and that's why I will never put this house at risk, never ever mortgage it,' she said angrily and left the room.

Matters came to a head when, one sunny afternoon, she returned home to the cottage. As soon as she opened the front door, James flung himself on her and burst into tears.

She hugged him as he shuddered and shook in her arms. 'What's wrong, darling?'

'Caspar,' he mumbled once his sobs had subsided a little. 'Daddy, he –'

'He what?'

'Gave him away.'

She stared. 'Daddy gave him away. What do you mean? Who to?'

He began to cry again. 'That lady, Beatrice, she came and said he was her dog and so Dad gave him to her.'

'Beatrice? What on earth was she doing here?'

'She just came. He made her tea.'

White with rage, Kim asked, 'And where is Daddy now?'

'Upstairs.'

She stormed up to find Richard sitting on his bed. 'What the hell's going on?' she asked fiercely. 'You had absolutely no right to give Caspar away, he's James's dog, not Beatrice's. Henri left him to

James in the will. I'm going to see her straight away, she's got to give him back.'

Richard's eyes glittered. 'Not possible. Said she was leaving for Italy this afternoon. Wanted her child to have a dog to play with on his summer holiday, keep him amused and all that.'

'How could you do this to James? Don't you know how much he loves Caspar? And I do too, you know that.'

'Always wondered why you were so keen on that bloody animal. Now I know. Taking care of your lover's dog, were you? In remembrance. I had a very long chat with la Contessa Beatrice. What an interesting woman. She told me some fascinating things about you. Seems you didn't waste any time once my back was turned. You and old Henri, never thought you were that sort of girl. Still, one's got to hand it to you – your efforts weren't in vain. You managed to screw quite a lot of money out of him. Must've put on a better performance than you usually did with me. Faked it, did you?'

She flushed. 'Didn't need to, not with Henri.'

He rose to his feet. She thought he was going to hit her but instead he reached up to the top of the wardrobe for his suitcase and began to pack.

As she watched her words tumbled out. 'Lucky for you Henri was so generous. God knows why I spent the money he left me rescuing *you*.'

'Give me the car keys,' he said.

'No.'

'Give me the bloody keys.'

She glared at him. 'If you remember, I paid for this car out of my savings when we first came to Geneva.'

'God, you're a mercenary bitch,' he said.

'I need the car to work. I need to work to feed James. If that makes me a mercenary bitch, so be it.' She drew in her breath. 'Anyway where are you going?'

'I phoned Maurice. Told him I didn't want to stay here and he said he'd take me back.'

'Then I'll drive you there with the greatest of pleasure,' she said coldly.

James refused to come with them and Kim did not insist. Neither she nor Richard said a word during the drive into Geneva. It had all been said many times before.

When they arrived at the foyer, Maurice took her aside. 'You must make allowances for him. He is still a sick man.'

She shook her head. 'I've run out of allowances,' she muttered.

'But he's had a difficult time. Who knows how long the ill effects of imprisonment will last? I understand there was a problem about a dog.'

She exploded again. 'He had absolutely no right to give the dog away.'

Maurice touched her arm. 'I know, I know, but you and I, we have no right to judge people, especially those who have suffered,' he said with a gentle smile.

On her way back she went to look for Beatrice's house down by the lake. In her anxiety, she took several wrong turns, but eventually she found the grand villa behind a high wall. Though she rang repeatedly on the bell beside the solid green gate, no one came to the door. She tried to walk around the house in case she could see into the garden from the lake, but walls of other large villas blocked her way.

Returning to the main road, she took out her mobile and dialled Beatrice's number, but though she hung on for several minutes there was no reply.

Fearing that Richard must have been telling the truth about the trip to Italy, she drove back to the city to see Sophie-Maria who immediately telephoned Beatrice's lawyer.

Sophie-Maria put down the phone. 'It seems,' she said, with just a trace of embarrassment, 'that the Countess and her lawyers considered that when you agreed to accept the cottage and the money, you gave up all rights to everything else in the will.'

'But the dog was left to James, not to me,' protested Kim sharply.

'Unfortunately, there is not much I can do until the Countess returns to Switzerland,' said Sophie-Maria. 'Let us hope that she does not leave the dog in Italy, because then it would be very expensive to retrieve. And one Labrador dog is much like another. Would it be an alternative, perhaps, if we were to find an appealing new puppy for your son?'

'No, we want Caspar,' said Kim emotionally. She was furious at the hopelessness of the situation, the powerlessness of the law when it really mattered and, most particularly, Richard's spiteful, ungrateful, typical bloody awful behaviour. Good thing he'd gone back to the foyer as she couldn't bear to spend another moment in his vile company.

James was waiting for her, as she knew he would be. 'So you didn't get Caspar back?'

She held him tight. 'No, not yet, darling. It may be some time before we find him. I'm sure we will do in the end though.' She'd been rehearsing this speech all the way home, dreading his reaction.

'I never want to see Daddy again,' he said, bursting into tears.

She was still furious with Richard but she forced herself to say, 'Well, maybe it wasn't his fault. Beatrice is very grand and bossy. She probably overwhelmed him.'

'I hate her and I hate Daddy. He knew Caspar was mine,' sobbed James.

She stroked his hair. With an effort she murmured, 'Maurice said we have to make allowances for

342

Daddy. We keep forgetting what he's been through. And the doctors at the clinic –'

'I don't care, I don't care. He's cruel to Caspar and I hate him,' he repeated fiercely and rushed upstairs to his room.

CHAPTER 26

A few days later the telephone rang. Kim rushed towards it, hoping that it would be news of Caspar, but a young female voice announced, 'Don't suppose you care, but I've got Richard. How could you leave him in that weird dump?'

'Who's speaking?'

'It's Serena, from the clinic. You remember me, don't you?'

'Of course I do.'

'Well, they've let me out now, so I went and collected him from that downmarket foyer place. I thought you, like, loved your husband, but, I mean, if you don't want him, then I do.'

'So where is he?' asked Kim in shocked amusement.

'Not telling you.'

Kim raised her eyebrows. 'But your parents? What do they say?'

Serena's voice grew shrill. 'I'm twenty-two, an adult, in case you hadn't noticed. Daddy promised me anything I wanted if I started eating, and so he can't go back on his word.'

'Serena, I'm a bit worried about –'

'That's typical. You're just jealous because you're fat and forty. Richard loves me. He says he likes thin people.'

Drawing in her breath, Kim reminded herself that the girl was still an invalid. 'I know he seems normal enough,' she began patiently, 'but you must understand that he's not stable, he's –'

'I'm not normal or stable either and so Richard understands me. We understand each other. He doesn't mind what I do or say. He's the only person who's never tried to force me to eat. He absolutely sympathises and know what it's like to be different.'

'But, Serena –'

'Don't try to talk me out of it. I know what I want. You're just a dog in the manger. A bitch in the manger, I should say.'

Flushed with excitement at her own rudeness, Serena slammed down the telephone and went back toward the swimming pool in the pink marble courtyard. Richard was lying on a sunbed beside the pool. His eyes were closed.

Her heart gave a strange little jump. He was now tanned and healthy-looking, but still lean, hungry and seriously handsome, she thought. Like a Greek god with that fair wavy hair and long nose. Sometime soon she'd take him off to London to buy him a hip new wardrobe, designer gear but kind of distinguished and classic.

Serena slipped off her bikini top displaying her flat little bosom and sidled over towards him. She ran her fingers through the sparse blond hair on his chest and began to tug at his bathing shorts.

He opened his eyes and smiled up at her. 'What will the servants think?'

'Like, who cares?'

'Let's go up to your room,' he said more urgently.

'No, here. Or nothing.'

He drew her down towards him. 'All right, we'll play some games, very nice games, but no fucking, not here. There's got to be some rules. Bad manners to embarrass the servants.'

'But I can do anything I want. You said so. You absolutely promised.'

But when it came to the point, Serena slipped away from him and disappeared. It seemed to Richard that her appetite for sex was not much greater than her appetite for food. Rather like shagging a coat-rack – reminded him of that skinny kid he'd had on the island when he'd first arrived there.

The island. He still felt strange about how they'd turned on him, those natives and their hippie friends, but people were often like that. Nice one minute, bloody nasty the next. Just because of a delay in supplies. How was he to know the supplier was bent? Paid the money, but no weapons delivered. They didn't believe him, the natives, or the hippies, when he explained.

Not his fault. No reason to lock him up. In the dirt, alone. Couldn't stand the dirt, never could stand dirt. So hot. Wouldn't let him wash or even swim, not often anyway. No clean clothes, not often anyway. Latrines, just ditches. No bog roll, just leaves.

Food went straight through you, such as it was. Dysentery. Arse never got properly clean. Inflamed, sore as hell, shit and agony.

Lost count of time. Days all the same, so hot. Hippies disappeared leaving the halfwit guard, who never said a word. No one said a word. All of 'em stopped talking to him. Tried to explain it wasn't his fault about the supplies but no one listened. When no one listens, you stop talking. No point in talking if no one listens.

Then there was the fever. Head went funny. Hard to remember but there was the fever. Then more days alone. More weeks, months alone. So hot.

Hard to remember anything. Something happened to the coat-rack kid. She tried to bring him extra food. They beat her, or something. Did they? Thought they'd beat him next. Or kill him. Hazy in the fever, in the heat, in the dirt. Better to forget.

Better not to think about it, better to forget. Put it behind you. Think about the future.

Think about now, today, with Serena. Better to think about Serena. Be practical. Think about the future, not the past. Serena isn't sexy but she's

347

young and rich. Rich more important than sexy. You've only got to look around to see her advantages, Serena. So what does it matter if she's not the best lay in the world? Doesn't matter a damn.

And if things didn't work out he could always go back home. Always depend on Kim being there. Trouble is, now he couldn't trust her to be faithful, he wasn't sure if he still loved her.

Even if she rescued him. Sort of.

Impossible to forgive her for that Henri business. The whole point about Kim was that she was the faithful reliable type. And he had been faithful to her – mostly. Well, he'd had other woman occasionally but it hadn't meant anything. In fact, he hadn't strayed nearly as often as most blokes. Because he loved Kim. He really did. She meant the world to him. Or used to. But now, now she'd changed, spoilt everything, it just wasn't the same any more. Not the same at all.

And anyone could see that he just needed a decent sum of money to start a new life but she wouldn't cough up. She never had enough faith in him. Ever.

Reason why he got involved in the bloody private arms deal in the first place was for her, the family. Seemed like the answer when the guy approached him. Put everything he had into it, plus he borrowed some from Vivienne. Generous of her. He was surprised really at the time. Mind you, they'd always got on. Might have fancied her if she'd been ten years younger. Course he didn't tell Viv what he wanted the money for exactly.

Promised to pay her interest though. Pay her back soon. Always paid his debts.

Kim didn't understand he only wanted to get the family finances on a permanent even keel. Wouldn't have taken the risk otherwise. But she never appreciated what he did for her. She never had enough faith.

Little Serena had faith in him though, which was good. Just what he needed. So she was the answer. Until he got on his feet.

Accept the past but stay with the present, Weinbaum said. Or was it Maurice? Or Doctor Anna? They all say the same sort of thing in their smug, knowing way. But they have a point, these shrinks. Except Maurice had some very strange ideas. At least he'd escaped from that bloody foyer and bloody holy Maurice.

A distraught Maurice rang Kim and she had to engage in a half-hour telephone conversation in broken English and broken French to reassure him that it wasn't his fault Serena had stolen Richard away. Maurice kept repeating that he liked him but Richard kept himself apart, remote, wasn't a joiner, tended to sit in his room, wouldn't even come to meals sometimes, but that eventually, with prayer . . . if only he had stayed . . . Kim said of course she knew Maurice had done his best and she realised his residents were free to make their own decisions, but she agreed that, in this case, no good would come of it.

It couldn't last. Two egoists like Richard and Serena would be at each other's throats within six months, or possibly six days, thought Kim. Then what?

The next person to telephone was Serena's father, who announced that his name was Mr Smith. He was almost incoherent with rage and insisted she come immediately to take Richard home, or back to the foyer, or anywhere.

'My little girl Serena, well, she's just a baby,' he kept repeating in a strange accent that mixed Manchester and New York.

Kim made an effort to be polite. 'But what if he won't leave? I can't force him.'

'If you want money, my lass, I'll let you have it. Take him away from Switzerland and I'll pay your fares. Anywhere in the world.'

She bristled. 'I have no intention of leaving Geneva.'

'Name your price. I don't want my little girl's life ruined by a no-hoper.'

'Listen, Mr Smith, I am not open to bribery. I'm sorry for Serena – I sympathise with her eating problems. But I've tried telling her that Richard is unsuitable. She's just not in the mood to listen. And as for Richard, he's always been a law unto himself. Why don't you just wait until they get tired of each other? Introduce Serena to some nice young men.'

'She's never liked younger lads. In fact, your

Richard seems to be the first fellow she's ever really fancied. That's what's worrying me.'

He sounded on the point of breaking down and Kim suddenly felt some sympathy for him. He had rescued his daughter from the jaws of death and now she'd taken up with the most unsuitable man she could find.

'I understand,' she said reluctantly. 'Look, I'll try to send someone to talk to him, but I don't think it'll do any good. Far better to give them time to –'

'No, no, I don't want to give them time. They might get up to all sorts. What if he gets her in the family way?'

'Richard may be irresponsible but he's not that stupid. Anyway I'd have thought your little girl was a bit too thin to be fertile,' said Kim tartly.

'Aye, but now she's eating better . . . well, you never know. I'll give you the address. You will come and see him, won't you?'

'That'd be pointless. I think it would be better if I sent someone else,' repeated Kim. 'Someone he'll listen to. I'll try the man who runs the foyer.'

Cursing herself for getting involved, Kim put down the telephone. Immediately it rang again. This time it was Vivienne Frank enquiring after Richard. Kim told her the story and then had the brilliant idea of persuading her to go and talk some sense into him. Apart from her inexplicable attachment to Hoffer, Vivienne was a sensible woman and, as a Personnel Officer, already trained in matters like counselling and general advice-giving. And, of course, she was an expert on Swiss healthcare and might be able to find Richard some different, less institutional accommodation.

Vivienne – they were on first-name terms now – agreed. 'You are right, Kim. Time spent with that fragile Serena girl would be full of tension and uncertainty. Far better he should quickly return home, try to stand on his own feet in a more normal environment. I shall speak with him and try to show him where his best interests lie.'

'No, don't try to persuade him to come back here. He should go back to the foyer or some other place like that.' Kim took a deep breath. 'This is strictly confidential, Vivienne, but I must explain that I've decided to divorce him as soon as he's well enough to cope. I'm sure you understand, people must tell you their problems all the time.'

There was a slight pause. 'Thank you for confiding in me.' She sounded a little taken aback.

Kim rushed on guiltily. 'Of course, I'll delay matters until he's settled. I mean, I still feel responsible for him after all these years.'

'Are you divorcing him because of Serena? Because if so –'

'Oh no, that's unimportant, relatively anyway. I admit my pride is slightly dented that he's gone off with a girl half my age, but I've got no reason to suppose it'll last. I mean, he could be serious about her but it's more likely he just wanted to pay me back and he wanted to get away from the foyer. You see he felt uncomfortable there. I think Maurice was keen on togetherness and group therapy – tried to make him face facts about himself, about why his life went wrong. The sort of thing that nobody likes, I suppose.'

'Oh,' said Vivienne.

'Anyway, as I said, Serena may be the catalyst but I've wanted a divorce for a long time. But obviously I must break it to him myself. I don't think he'll mind too much, but you won't say a word about it, to him or to anyone else, will you? I'm only telling you now in your professional capacity, so you understand why I don't want him to come back here.'

Vivienne put down the telephone. How sensible. How interesting. Even a traditional woman like Kim Ellis had managed to make a decision to regroup and reorganise herself.

One should never be afraid of change. Her own life, too, was in need of reassessment. She was contemplating her fiftieth birthday next week.

Thus far her career had been satisfactory. But she had become aware of the glass ceiling that so many Swiss women complained of. Personnel/Human Resources work had its limits. She was tired of it. Recently she had allowed her emotions to surface from time to time. This was not such a good idea. Emotion was not admired in a Swiss company. And now she was older her well-preserved good looks seemed to be a liability rather than an asset. The chairman had refused to promote her to be director of the subsidiary in Lausanne. He did not actually say that big-breasted blondes cannot run companies, but those were his views, she suspected. And Hoffer had not helped her career the way she imagined he would. He did not take her seriously enough. Lovers never did.

No, on reflection, there had been men who had taken her seriously but they soon became frightened and jealous of the professional competence that lay under her femininity and did not stay.

Perhaps, if one needed a man at all, which was doubtful, one should aim for a different type.

It was time to establish some new clear targets. Hard decisions must be made.

CHAPTER 27

Prompted by James's mournful face and her own anxiety, Kim rang the lawyer most days about Caspar, but unfortunately there was no progress to report. They both missed him dreadfully. Kim tried to organise extra amusements for James, trips on the lake, outings with Polly's children, but the gap left by the dog's absence was impossible to fill. She put his bowl away in the cupboard but James took it out again and filled it with fresh water each day. Then he gave up and the empty bowl sat by the door in constant reproach.

If he asked about Caspar, Kim would say heartily that she was sure he was all right, that he would be having a nice time by the sea in Italy, a kind of holiday, but eventually the lawyers would get him back, safe and sound. They must do. *Please, please*, she said silently.

As if by common consent, neither of them spoke about Richard.

Kim had no further news of him and Serena. This long silence made her curious. It seemed too good to last. She considered calling Mr Smith or Vivienne, but eventually decided that discretion was the best policy.

Then one day she returned home from a supermarket trip to find an unpleasant surprise. Hoffer was standing on her doorstep. She shuddered, remembering his repellent advances in Paris.

'What are you doing here?' she asked coldly, avoiding standing too close to him.

'May I please come in, madame?' he asked in an uncharacteristically humble voice. Today his fierce terrier eyes were dull and his face pale. Normally dapper, he wore a crumpled suit and smelt of stale cigars.

Kim frowned. 'Can't we talk out here?'

'It is most delicate.'

Reluctantly she opened the door and, propping it open with her grocery bags, stood waiting in the hall. She was damned if she was going to show him into the sitting room, or even the kitchen.

'It is about Vivienne,' he said, resting one hand on the banister as if to support himself. 'Do you know where they've gone?'

'I asked her to go and see my husband, if that's what you mean. But it's a confidential matter which I can't discuss.'

'You do not understand. This man, Monsieur Smeeth, has bribed them to leave the country.'

'Bribed who?'

'Vivienne and your husband. They, she . . .' His

voice broke off and he looked as if he were about to burst into tears.

Kim gaped at him open-mouthed. 'Vivienne and Richard? But . . .' And then she began to laugh. 'I didn't know that they . . . how funny, oh dear!'

Hoffer stared angrily at her. 'I did not expect you to find the matter amusing. It seemed they must have had a long-term liaison. Your husband is not a trustworthy man, but Vivienne – I am extremely disappointed. I did not imagine . . . you see, she and I –'

Kim interrupted his sad confession, 'But what about Serena?'

'Who?'

'Mr Smith's daughter.'

'I know nothing of her except that her father wanted to be rid of Richard.' He wrung his plump scaly hands together. 'But, please, Madame Ellis, what information do you have?'

'Absolutely none.'

Hoffer looked more downcast than ever. 'The chairman is anxious. He fears that they, Vivienne and Richard, will set up their own business and take clients away from the company. He's very angry and is even threatening to dismiss me – most unfair since I was not in the least responsible.'

So there's some justice in the world, thought Kim in malicious satisfaction.

'Madame Ellis, I really must insist on looking at his files to check what addresses he has taken.

It's rumoured they have gone to Eastern Europe and . . .'

She glared at him. 'Richard's been too ill to do any work at all since he got back. I'm sorry, but I must insist you leave.'

'So you do know something.'

'No, I don't. Now please go. Don't open that door or the dog will probably attack you. He's very aggressive with strangers.'

Of course there was no dog, but fortunately Hoffer was ignorant of that fact. He backed away immediately, thrusting a business card into her hand. 'Please call me, Madame Ellis, if you hear where they are. Meanwhile I will do my best to trace them for you.'

'Don't try too hard,' said Kim under her breath.

She watched from the window to make sure that he had gone and then she began to put away her groceries, chuckling to herself from time to time about Richard and Vivienne. Of course she felt indignant if it was true he'd deceived her over a long period, indeed she used to see fidelity as his only virtue.

On the other hand, maybe Hoffer was wrong. Maybe it was a new affair: Vivienne's heart could have grown fonder during Richard's absence and then she'd taken one look at the disarmingly frail and vulnerable patient in the clinic and immediately recognised her love for him, while birds sang and violins played all around her. What a vision! Poor woman, she had *such* bad taste in men.

Or maybe there was method in Vivienne's madness, an ulterior motive. Maybe with a British partner she could more easily set up a new business in the European Union. She could just be using Richard for the time being. Maybe she would send him back again one day.

Oh dear.

She was stacking the wine rack when she noticed the bottle of champagne she had been saving for Mark's return. Her smile faded. Despite her worries, she'd still been thinking about him a great deal. He would now be in Singapore, she reckoned, but there had been no detour to visit her en route, no letter, no phone call, nothing. A curious, sad, unfinished affair. It was clear that he wasn't coming back. The timing had been all wrong but perhaps, as Polly said, she should have had the courage to seize the day. She had the feeling she had lost something valuable, something important she might never find again.

She wondered if it was too late to write and say that she was free now, more or less. It wouldn't be hard to find his address, just 'British High Commission, Singapore' should do. Yes, maybe she would write some time, but not to announce she was about to rush out and join him, just an exploratory letter to say hello and to keep in touch. Wouldn't be any harm in that. Unless – a jealous stab – he was already in the arms of the predicted seductive Oriental maiden. Or a glamorous young expatriate businesswoman, or a female diplomatic colleague, an efficient Scandinavian blonde perhaps. Yes, he'd be surrounded by all things bright and beautiful. She'd missed the bus as far as Mark was concerned. Polly was undoubtedly right.

Henri, Mark and now Richard were all part of the past. She would start a new life.

But there was always the danger that, even if Vivienne loved Richard, she would soon get tired of him if she had to live with him on a day to day basis. So now that he had provided every excuse, the best thing would be to take action, just to make sure that he remained in the past.

Taking a deep breath, Kim picked up the telephone and called Sophie-Maria. 'Maître Leblanc, about the divorce, I'd like you to go ahead with it now, please.'

In as much as an ice-maiden lawyer can purr, Sophie-Maria did so. At the end of the conversation Kim put the phone down and danced about, punching the air. She felt wonderfully elated and free. Why the hell did it take you so long, she asked herself. For the rest of the day, she couldn't stop smiling.

Sophie-Maria made steady progress in regard to the divorce but she made no headway at all in finding Caspar. At the end of the summer holidays, an exasperated Kim decided to take matters into her own hands again. The day James went back to school she picked up the telephone and called Beatrice's house to see if she had returned from Italy.

'*Allo*?' said a child's voice.

'Eduardo! Hello, it's Kim. Do you remember me from the ski holiday in Wengen?'

'Who?'

'Your grandfather's friend, Kim.'

'Oh, yes, I remember. The one that Maman doesn't like. But I like you,' he added hastily.

Kim smiled. 'Is Mummy there please? When did you get back?'

'Yesterday, but Maman has gone straight off to America leaving me all on my own with Carmen and Pedro. Even Nanny isn't here until tomorrow. It's not fair. I'm so bored.'

'Well –'

'I know, can you come and see me?'

'Yes, actually, I think I probably can. Um, Eduardo, have you got Caspar with you?'

'Caspar? Yes, he's in his kennel in the garden. Maman doesn't like him indoors 'cos of his dirty paws, too big and bouncy, she says.'

Kim changed into her only chic yummy mummy outfit then dashed round her house collecting copies of local newspapers and magazines. Then she made a few telephone calls and, full of excitement, drove into the city.

When she arrived at Beatrice's mansion, the heavy gates were open and little Eduardo was

361

dancing about on the front door step, attended by a timid-looking Filipina. He gave Kim a hug and imperiously ordered the woman to produce tea and lemonade. Meekly she did as she was told.

'What shall we play?' he asked, dragging Kim inside. His shiny black hair had been cut short and he was dressed, as usual, like a miniature male fashion model. 'Come and see my room. I've got a new computer with lots of games. It keeps me quiet, Maman says. I'm going to a new school next week. Would you like to see my cars – I've got a hundred. Did you bring a present?' His bright smile reminded her of Henri.

She stared around at Beatrice's immaculate house which was decorated to an icy perfection, with pale blue carpets, white sofas and delicate Italian glass. 'Actually, Eduardo, yes, I *was* thinking of buying you a present.'

His black eyes shone. 'Cool. What?'

'A puppy.'

'Wow! Amazing!'

'We have to go and fetch it, OK? But it's not exactly a present, more of a swap.'

'A swap?'

'Yes, I buy you a puppy and you give me back Caspar.'

His face fell. 'But I like Caspar.'

'But a puppy would be much more fun, wouldn't it? I rang up a lady who's selling them. We could go now, this morning, any time, she said. You can choose the one you want.'

'What will its name be?'

'Oh, you can choose that too, whatever you like.'

The idea of naming his own puppy seemed to clinch the deal. Eduardo agreed immediately. He led Kim out into the garden towards a large metal cage where poor Caspar was sitting on his haunches, a picture of gloomy watchfulness. As soon as he saw them, he yelped and began to jump up and down, wagging his tail furiously. Kim ran to open the gate and he flung himself on her, nearly knocking her over.

Tears in her eyes, she bent down to hug him, 'Sorry, I've been so long,' she whispered. 'And James'll be so happy. Can't wait to see his face.'

She examined Caspar carefully, not easy because he kept wriggling and licking her face. He seemed perfectly healthy but a little thinner which was no bad thing, she thought. 'Darling, darling Caspar,' she kept saying as she led him to the car, stopping now and then to pat him and rub his ears.

Ensconced on the back seat, Caspar accompanied them on their drive to buy the puppy. Hardly believing that he was actually safe and sound, she kept turning round to look at him. He was panting cheerfully, perfectly relaxed, as if he'd never been away. At least dogs don't seem to suffer from post-traumatic stress syndrome, she thought.

Eduardo's excitement mounted as they arrived at a small house in a village not far from Latigny. A thin harassed-looking Englishwoman showed them into a garden shed where a yellow Labrador bitch, smaller than Caspar but even fatter, was lying surrounded by a heap of wriggling puppies.

'Oh aren't they sweet, look at their dear little ears!' said Kim.

Eduardo was speechless with joy as he looked at them all.

'Frightfully sorry they're not pure bred,' said the owner in her loud breathy voice. 'Such a naughty dog, Judy escaped last time she was on heat and fell in love. We're not sure who or what the father is. Maybe the farmer's Alsatian, down the road. They've had all their injections, by the way. All ready to leave us but I'm afraid they're not very house-trained yet.'

So much the better, thought Kim. 'They're a heavenly mixture, all tawny and woolly and gorgeous,' she said aloud. 'Call them, Eduardo.'

It took a while for Eduardo to choose, and eventually Kim found herself agreeing to buy not one but two plump little puppies.

'Then they'll always have each other. It's lonely if you don't have a friend,' said Eduardo.

She drove him back home and deposited him and the puppies, along with food and a heap of instructions for the Filipinos and Nanny, who knew all about dogs, according to Eduardo.

'Nanny has her own dog in Scotland. She'll be very pleased with these two. Ouch!' he said as one of the puppies nipped his hand with its sharp teeth. He put it on the floor and it disappeared under the sofa. 'I'm going to call the girl-dog Jelly 'cos her legs are all wobbly. And the boy is going to be Spot.'

Kim smiled. 'But he isn't spotted.'

'I know but that's what the dog in my reading book is called. It's a nice name. They can sleep in my room, so they won't miss their mummy,' said Eduardo.

'Oh dear, look, Spot is peeing on the carpet – and Jelly is doing something terrible with that tapestry cushion. Oops. She seems to have chewed off half the cover. I hope they won't do too much damage,' she added insincerely.

CHAPTER 28

Having sorted out her life at last, Kim kept reassuring herself and everybody else that she and James were perfectly happy in their newfound independence. It was true, certainly as far as James was concerned. Overjoyed to have the dog back, he was preoccupied with Caspar, and with the new school term and the football team. He said little about his father. Kim was amazed by his resilience. It seemed he had survived all the dramas relatively unscathed, or apparently so. She was afraid he might be suppressing unknown fears and worries that would eventually surface in his teenage years. For now, though, he continued to behave like a busy, carefree schoolboy.

Kim was busy too. Her reputation as a reliable and sensitive editor had spread and she was involved in several writing projects as well as Beverly-Jane's *Fundamental Food Book*, which they'd begun as soon as *A to Zee, New Health for You'n'Me* was safely at the publishers. As BJ's enthusiastic approach involved endless research, there was little time left to be lonely. Except perhaps at night.

She would still think about Mark every night just before she went to sleep. She would have imaginary conversations with him to explain herself and he would understand. And then, so her fantasy went, they would make love again and again, just as they had those weekends a long time ago.

Finally she wrote to him. For a woman used to working with words, it took her a long time and a great many drafts were thrown into the waste paper basket. In the end it was rather a dull effort. She asked him how he was, and for news of his life in Singapore. She wrote that her work was going well, that Polly was as bossy as ever and BJ as zany. Then she said the good news was that Richard had recovered and the even better news was that he'd left the country with Vivienne, permanently she hoped. That she had started divorce proceedings but it would take a while.

The envelope sat on the hall table for two days and eventually she took it to the post office, but not before she had opened and re-written the letter, leaving out the sentence about divorce. It now sounded better, more light-hearted and non-committal, she thought.

She reckoned she must allow several days for mail to reach Singapore and perhaps he might not have time to reply straight away. But some weeks passed and she didn't hear from him. She began to mind about this a great deal.

Then one day she received a letter with hand-writing that made her catch her breath, but it had a Geneva postmark. She tore it open and found a card on which was printed: 'Mark Fitzpatrick requests the pleasure of the company of Kim Ellis at Restaurant la Perle du Lac, Geneva, on Tuesday, October 1st, at eight o'clock.'

Sinking into a chair, she read the words again and again. There was no telephone number to call in reply, nothing else but the printed invitation. Immediately she rang Mark's former secretary only to discover that she, too, had been posted away from Switzerland.

'Do you have a contact number for Mr Fitzpatrick?' she asked the receptionist.

'Oh no,' said the girl vaguely. 'He left the office here months ago, you know. But you could try sending him a letter via the FCO in London.'

Kim then rang his London flat but there was no reply, not even an answering machine. After some thought, she wondered if the invitation was just some kind of joke perpetrated by Polly but, when approached, she denied all knowledge of it.

'You'd better go anyway. And I'll look after James for the night. Just in case,' said Polly, her eyes alive with interest.

'Actually, I agreed to go out with BJ that evening, to see some weird art gallery.'

'Ring her up and cancel, for God's sake.'

'You know something, Pol? I think I will.'

Kim telephoned BJ who said cheerfully, 'Sure, Kim honey, I *absolutely* understand. Lurve is more important than some old art show. A girl's got to do what a girl's got to do, I always say.'

After an elaborate bath and a protracted session in front of the mirror, including a great many unnecessary changes of garment, followed by a nervous journey through the heavy evening traffic thinking she was going to be late, Kim arrived at the Perle du Lac at exactly eight o'clock on Tuesday evening. She hesitated outside the door of the restaurant. She was too punctual. He, if indeed it was Mark, might not be there yet.

Pulling herself together, she went in. The maître d'hôtel greeted her politely and, weaving through the elegant dining room, led her to a table over-looking the lake.

She stood still, her heart thumping wildly. There was Mark, just sitting there waiting for her. As she moved towards him, he stood up, smiling his familiar smile, and she knew instantly that nothing had changed between them.

'Hello,' she said, with great happiness.

'Kim, how lovely to see you.' He kissed her three times on the cheek and hugged her for a moment, and then, face flushed, eyes bright, she sat down opposite him.

The hovering waiter handed them each a menu in a huge leather folder. '*Bonsoir, madame, monsieur.* Will you take an aperitif?'

'What would you like? Some champagne?' asked Mark, settling back calmly, as if they had seen each other yesterday.

'Thank you, wine, yes, lovely, anything. It's so nice to see you. I couldn't believe it when I got the card. Thought it was a hoax. Why didn't you phone?'

'I wanted to give you a surprise,' he said. He had an endearing way of crinkling up his eyes when he smiled. She'd forgotten that.

'Did you get my letter?' she asked.

'No?'

'I wrote to you in Singapore.'

'Saying what?'

'Saying that Richard's gone. For good, it seems.'

He smiled. 'I know. Best news I've heard for years.'

'If you didn't get my letter, how did you know?'

'Tell you in a moment. So exactly what happened with Richard?'

'It's a long story. Tell you in a moment,' she echoed. 'But what are you doing here?'

He leant back. 'Perhaps we should order first, get rid of that worried waiter lurking behind you.'

Anxious to talk, she hardly knew what she

chose from the elaborate menu. 'So?' she said when the waiter had finally departed, 'how long are you here for? Are you on your way to Singapore? I thought you were there already, but I see you're not.'

'No, as you say, I'm not. I didn't go in the end. It wasn't popular but I refused the posting. I've been in London, negotiating a new job here.'

'You mean you're coming back? How long for?'

'Oh, two years or so. More, if I want.'

Flushing with pleasure, Kim stared at him in amazement. 'But they, the UK Mission . . . I mean, the receptionist didn't know anything about you.'

'No, I've left the Foreign Office, or rather taken a couple of years' leave of absence, *en disponibilité*, as they call it. I'm about to begin working for the Red Cross/Red Crescent Federation.'

'Here in Geneva?' she asked again, unable to take in what he was saying.

'Yes.'

'That's . . . that's wonderful. And the Red Cross, how noble.'

'Oh, not especially. I'm just going to be an administrator here, not a delegate. They do all the noble, heroic stuff at the sharp end. Saw them in Iraq. Made me think, actually.'

'So what will your job be?'

'Just pushing paper about. Involving disaster relief. Like all large international organisations, the Federation needs people to run things, but one might as well push paper about for a good cause, I suppose.'

'But don't they, the Foreign Office, mind you taking off?'

He shrugged his shoulders. 'Admittedly they weren't pleased by my last-minute refusal to go to Singapore and I dare say they consider I'm opting out, making a sideways move, rather than striving ruthlessly ever upwards, as one should, in their view. But, as you say, on the surface it seems a worthy thing to do. My motives weren't entirely altruistic and humanitarian, though. In fact they were highly personal, to be honest.'

'So you made this great move because . . .' she hesitated.

He leant forward. 'Because of you. You were right, we didn't have enough time. This way we can get to know each other.' He grinned. 'Though there's always the danger that when you know me better, you'll go off me again. For instance, I don't think I was very diplomatic when we last met. I'm sorry, Kim.'

'About what?'

'Oh various things. I was a bit patronising. And impatient.'

'I don't remember. But anyway, it was me – you, well, you asked me to marry you, and I was hope-lessly tactless and insensitive –'

'No, I didn't make allowances. I didn't appreciate how ill Richard was and how responsible you felt, what a conscientious person you are. That's what BJ said.'

'BJ! What's she got to do with it?'

'Just before I was about to leave for the Far East I phoned her to see if you were all right. Thought it was more discreet than ringing you direct in case it upset your husband. Anyway, BJ asked me what in the heck I was doing going off to the other end of the world. Like, what was important in life anyway. I quote. She told me Richard had gone and that I should darn well get back here because you needed me, she reckoned. So I asked her what made her think you needed me and she said, "Trust me, honey, I am empathetic to Kim and she just misses you like crazy." So I chose to believe her.'

'Good old BJ.' A thought struck her. 'She set me up, didn't she? Inviting me out this evening so I'd be free to cancel and come here instead.'

'Yes,' he said. 'I didn't want you to make a date with someone else tonight, a date you couldn't break. All a bit Machiavellian, sorry.'

'Oh, I forgive her, and you.' She paused. 'And it's true what she said – I did miss you like crazy.'

For a while they just sat smiling at each other.

Then she said slowly, 'You've done all this, changed your life, your career, partly because of me?'

'All because of you, actually. See what a good influence you are.'

Kim paused again, then she said seriously, 'I'm

honoured, really. No one has ever . . . I mean, I feel very responsible.'

'Good. That means you'll have to be extremely nice to me.'

'I think I can manage that,' she said with a happy smile.